P9-DDQ-026

"How about you?" Tom asked as he caught up with her. *"What's your passion?"*

You. The answer popped into Andrea's mind uncensored, but she had enough good sense to keep the word from slipping from her lips. "Teaching. Reading. I sew a bit."

"You didn't mention traveling. As a passion, I mean."

"Well, that one goes without saying." Yet, in that moment, the thought of moving on when Jessie's school year ended tightened a knot in the pit of her stomach.

"What do you like about traveling?" Tom asked.

She groped for a response, but all the usual reasons rang false. "It's fun to meet new people, see new places. Every day's an adventure." She winced at the trite cliché.

"But what about the people you leave behind?"

The softly spoken question hung there while the answer clutched at her insides. She'd always convinced herself she felt no regret in severing ties when she'd moved on, but when she thought of leaving Tom and Jessie, the sense of loss threatened to overwhelm her.

Dear Reader,

As you take a break from raking those autumn leaves, you'll want to check out our latest Silhouette Special Edition novels! This month, we're thrilled to feature Stella Bagwell's *Should Have Been Her Child* (#1570), the first book in her new miniseries, MEN OF THE WEST. Stella writes that this series is full of "rough, tough cowboys, the strong bond of sibling love and the wide-open skies of the west. Mix those elements with a dash of intrigue, mayhem and a whole lot of romance and you get the Ketchum family!" And we can't wait to read their stories!

Next, Christine Rimmer brings us *The Marriage Medallion* (#1567), the third book in her VIKING BRIDES series, which is all about matrimonial destiny and solving secrets of the past. In Jodi O'Donnell's *The Rancher's Daughter* (#1568), part of popular series MONTANA MAVERICKS: THE KINGSLEYS, two unlikely soul mates are trapped in a cave…and find a way to stay warm. *Practice Makes Pregnant* (#1569) by Lois Faye Dyer, the fourth book in the MANHATTAN MULTIPLES series, tells the story of a night of passion and a very unexpected development between a handsome attorney and a bashful assistant. Will their marriage of convenience turn to everlasting love?

Patricia Kay will hook readers into an intricate family dynamic and heart-thumping romance in *Secrets of a Small Town* (#1571). And Karen Sandler's *Counting on a Cowboy* (#1572) is an engaging tale about a good-hearted teacher who finds love with a rancher and his young daughter. You won't want to miss this touching story!

Stay warm in this crisp weather with six complex and satisfying romances. And be sure to return next month for more emotional storytelling from Silhouette Special Edition!

Happy reading!

Gail Chasan
Senior Editor

Please address questions and book requests to:
Silhouette Reader Service
U.S.: 3010 Walden Ave., P.O. Box 1325, Buffalo, NY 14269
Canadian: P.O. Box 609, Fort Erie, Ont. L2A 5X3

Counting on a Cowboy

KAREN SANDLER

SPECIAL EDITION™

Published by Silhouette Books

America's Publisher of Contemporary Romance

If you purchased this book without a cover you should be aware
that this book is stolen property. It was reported as "unsold and
destroyed" to the publisher, and neither the author nor the
publisher has received any payment for this "stripped book."

To Gary,
the hero of my real-life romance.

 SILHOUETTE BOOKS

ISBN 0-373-24572-6

COUNTING ON A COWBOY

Copyright © 2003 by Karen Sandler

All rights reserved. Except for use in any review, the reproduction
or utilization of this work in whole or in part in any form by any
electronic, mechanical or other means, now known or hereafter
invented, including xerography, photocopying and recording, or in
any information storage or retrieval system, is forbidden without
the written permission of the editorial office, Silhouette Books,
233 Broadway, New York, NY 10279 U.S.A.

All characters in this book have no existence outside the imagination of
the author and have no relation whatsoever to anyone bearing the same
name or names. They are not even distantly inspired by any individual
known or unknown to the author, and all incidents are pure invention.

This edition published by arrangement with Harlequin Books S.A.

® and TM are trademarks of Harlequin Books S.A., used under license.
Trademarks indicated with ® are registered in the United States Patent
and Trademark Office, the Canadian Trade Marks Office and in other
countries.

Visit Silhouette at www.eHarlequin.com

Printed in U.S.A.

Books by Karen Sandler

Silhouette Special Edition

The Boss's Baby Bargain #1488
Counting on a Cowboy #1572

KAREN SANDLER

first caught the writing bug at age nine when, as a horse-crazy fourth grader, she wrote a poem about a pony named Tony. Many years of hard work later, she sold her first book (and she got that pony—although his name is Ben). She enjoys writing novels, short stories and screenplays and has produced two short films. She lives in Northern California with her husband of twenty-one years and two sons who are busy eating her out of house and home.

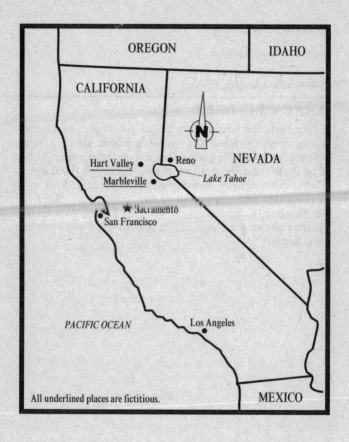

OREGON

IDAHO

CALIFORNIA

NEVADA

Hart Valley ● ● Reno

Marbleville ● —*Lake Tahoe*

★ Sacramento

San Francisco

PACIFIC OCEAN Los Angeles ●

All underlined places are fictitious. MEXICO

Chapter One

Tom Jarret pulled onto Hart Valley's Main Street, his entire focus on reaching the elementary school at the other end of town. He didn't see the pretty young woman on Hart Valley's only crosswalk until she'd nearly crossed into his path. He slammed on the brakes, stopping just behind the crosswalk's white line.

Startled, the young woman jumped back, her long brown braid swaying with the motion. A thick hardback book clutched in her hands, her chocolate-brown eyes locked with his. Without conscious will, his gaze strayed down the slender lines of her body. Her royal blue tank top left her creamy shoulders bare and delineated the curves of her small breasts. Her jeans fit neatly at her narrow waist, shaped her rounded hips, hinted at long, tempting legs.

To his utter surprise, desire curled low in his body, for an instant burning away his urgency to get to the school. The young, dark-haired woman stared at him, for one heartbeat, two, then with a slow curve of her lips, she smiled.

If her eyes sent fantasies dancing through his brain, her smile completely addled him. Without conscious thought, he shifted the truck into Park, reached for the door, ready to jump from the truck and ask her name. She was a complete stranger in a town where no one remained a stranger for long. How could he have missed her?

Then, with a shy dip of her head, she continued on across the street, hurrying along the sidewalk back the way he'd come. He watched her in the side view mirror, saw her step inside the Hart Valley Inn. One of his sister Beth's guests then. Easy enough to find out her identity.

He shook his head, angry with himself. He had no time for women, pretty or not. He had to keep his mind on his daughter. Shoving his truck into gear, he gunned away from the crosswalk. The roar of the pickup's engine caught the attention of Mort Gibbons and his wife over at the Pump 'n' Go. Tom lightened his lead foot, gave Mort and Arlene an apologetic wave.

He turned left just past the Pump 'n' Go, saw Hart Valley Elementary School where the road dead-ended. Anger warred with worry inside him as he pulled into the school parking lot. Worry over his daughter, Jessie, was too painful to bear, so as he shut off the engine with a savage turn of the key, he let anger win.

Take a breath, he told himself as he resisted the urge to break something. Calm down.

He closed his eyes, dragging air into his lungs. He imagined the wide pastures of the Double J ranch, his herd of quarter horses grazing the sweet spring grass.

He saw Jessie there, smiling up at him, and a sense of tranquility washed over him.

Pushing open the door, he climbed from the truck. Beyond the parking lot, a group of students chased each other across the ball field. Boys and girls raced pell-mell from one side of the grassy field to the other, completely carefree.

Did Jessie still possess the joy of childhood he saw in those schoolkids? If she did, he'd seen few traces of it in the years since her accident. The child she'd been at age five might have dashed across that field with the same abandon. The somber nine-year-old she was now...

He shook the bad memories loose. He'd better head for the principal's office, get this over with. Shutting the truck door, Tom hurried across the parking lot. He slowed as he got close enough to see through the office window, stopped entirely when he saw his daughter's dark blond head just visible through the glass. Even from this distance, he could sense the tension in her body, a tension that never seemed to release.

He caught a glimpse of the principal as she approached Jessie, saw his daughter's head tip up. Tom could imagine Jessie's face—the familiar fixing-for-a-fight expression. The same stubborn set of jaw he saw in the mirror, softened by her mother's deep brown eyes.

Taking a breath, Tom pulled open the office door and stepped inside. Both Jessie's and the principal's heads swiveled toward him, irritation in Mrs. Beeber's eyes, relief in Jessie's. For an instant, Tom could see the old hero worship Jessie once felt for him and his heart melted. Then his daughter's gaze shuttered and she looked away.

Battleaxe Beeber took a step toward him, her black eyes narrowed in distaste. "Good of you to finally show up, Mr. Jarret."

Tom's hackles rose at the principal's self-righteous tone. "*Finally* show up? I came as soon as I got your call. I was out fixing fence in my back pasture."

Mrs. Beeber flung out her hand dismissively. "So the notes home…my previous calls…they weren't persuasive enough?"

"What notes?" Tom turned his gaze on Jessie, saw her head dip down as if she'd suddenly found her toes fascinating. "What calls?" he asked in a dangerously quiet tone. "Jessie?"

A quick sidelong glance from Jessie, then she returned to studying her sneakers. "I hid a few notes."

"I've sent home at least a dozen," Mrs. Beeber stated imperiously.

Jessie gave the stout woman a dirty look. "Nine. There were nine notes."

"And I called—"

"How many phone calls?" Tom cut in before the principal could embellish the truth. "Jessie?"

"Three times." Jessie cradled her right arm with her left, as if to further hide the burn scars her long sleeved T-shirt covered. "I let the answering machine pick up, then I erased the messages."

It wasn't right what she'd done, hiding the notes and erasing the calls. He had every right to be angry. But as she hunched there, seeming so fragile and alone, Tom's ire washed away. He lost the heart to scold her, especially in front of the woman they'd privately nicknamed the Battleaxe.

He tore his gaze from Jessie, turned to the principal. "You said she was in a fight."

"In the cafeteria." Mrs. Beeber squared her shoulders, jaw set like stone. "She caused an injury to one of the children."

Jessie surged to her feet. "Is Sabrina okay?"

"She has a concussion." The principal glared at Jessie. "Sabrina tried to stop the fight and your daughter knocked her into a table."

"It was an accident!" Jessie declared, taking a step toward Mrs. Beeber. Jessie's arms hung at her sides, the right one crooked at the elbow, never quite as straight as the left.

Distaste clear in her face, Mrs. Beeber flicked a glance at Jessie's right arm. "Nevertheless—"

"Did she start the fight?" Tom asked, struggling to hold back the anger that threatened to rise up again.

Jessie shook her head vehemently. "I didn't, Dad."

Mrs. Beeber sniffed. "So she says."

Jessie tugged at his hand. "Stephanie called me a name. I told her to shut up, but she said it again. Then I…" Remorse flashed across Jessie's face. "I didn't mean to hit Sabrina."

Jessie swiped a tear from her face with her left hand. Rebellious and angry one minute, sweet and sad the next. Tom wished he could wrap his daughter in a protective bubble, guard her from every hurt.

Guard her from officious, insensitive women like Battleaxe Beeber. Tom swallowed his pride and turned to the principal. "I'll take care of Sabrina's medical expenses. And Jessie will apologize."

"No," Mrs. Beeber said, her tone cold and brittle. "Your daughter's caused one fight too many."

"But I didn't—" Jessie began.

Mrs. Beeber's dark look quelled Jessie's protest.

"Hart Valley isn't equipped to provide for a child like Jessie."

Tom's fists clenched. "A child like Jessie—what the hell do you mean by that?"

Color rose in Mrs. Beeber's cheeks. "A...disabled child. She'll have to transfer to the special day school."

Jessie gasped. "I can't! My best friend is here."

"I'm sorry," Mrs. Beeber said without a trace of regret. "I'm expelling your daughter from Hart Valley Elementary."

Tom looked out the ranch house kitchen window and scanned the gravel road that emptied out into his yard. It was more than twenty-four hours since Mrs. Beeber expelled Jessie, and Tom still wanted to throttle the old Battleaxe. How could the Hart Valley school board have hired such a mean-spirited woman as principal? Obviously, the board didn't consider kindness toward children a requirement for the job.

Tom let his gaze travel up the gravel road as far as the hilltop where the road dipped back down again. Staring at the strip of dirt and rock wouldn't make a car appear any quicker, but he couldn't seem to help himself. He wanted Andrea Larson here, now. He wanted to get the interview over with, to see if Ms. Larson could corral the nest of snakes Mrs. Beeber let loose yesterday when she kicked Jessie out of Hart Valley Elementary.

But she was late.

Another quick glance. No sign of a car. Not even the cloud of dust that always announced a visitor once the last of the spring rains ended. His sister, Beth, had assured him Ms. Larson would arrive by noon for the interview and now it was nearly one.

Behind him, Jessie still dawdled over her peanut butter and jelly sandwich, the comic book spread out before her forgotten. Yesterday, when he'd brought her home from school, he'd been so mad he could've spit nails and Jessie was smart enough to keep quiet. Today, she'd been nothing but surly, finding new ways to rile him and test his endurance.

Finally, he sent her to her room and spent the rest of the afternoon on the phone, first unloading his problems on Beth, then calling the private school in nearby Marbleville. The tuition at Marbleville Academy took his breath away, but he would have found a way to pay it. But when the secretary discovered the circumstances of Jessie's departure from public school, she suggested politely that perhaps the Academy might not be an appropriate place for his daughter.

Then Beth had called him back after supper and handed him a miracle. She'd found a credentialed teacher right under her nose—one of the guests at the inn. Beth had explained Jessie's predicament and the woman had agreed to talk to Tom about the possibility of her teaching Jessie at home.

But now she was late and Tom vacillated between worry that she'd changed her mind and irritation that the woman was such a flake she couldn't be bothered to arrive on time. He'd called the California Commission on Teacher Credentialing to confirm Andrea Larson's credential, so he knew she was the genuine article. She'd agreed to bring references and samples of curriculum to the interview. But he hadn't even spoken to her yet, had so far dealt with her through Beth. What if she was an ogre like Mrs. Beeber? What if she took one look at Jessie's burn-scarred arm and couldn't hide her disgust?

The motherly type, Beth had said. A good, honest person who seemed to genuinely love children. But could she deal with Jessie on a bad day? Could she look past his daughter's surly, self-defensive barriers to the sweet child beneath?

Gripping the cool tile surrounding the kitchen sink, Tom peered out the window again, searching for that telltale cloud of dust. Nothing but green rolling hills and bright blue sky.

Her stomach knotted with tension, Andrea Larson drove slowly along a dusty gravel road, searching for the turn to Tom Jarrot's ranch. She was sure she'd taken every back road and dirt track in the county, had found every dead end and weed-choked deer trail within a twenty-mile radius of Hart Valley. Beth Henley's convoluted directions, accompanied with a blithe, "Don't worry, it's easy to find," proved to be a monumental fib.

It didn't help that she still wrestled with misgivings about extending her stay in Hart Valley. Yesterday morning at breakfast, Andrea had resolved to spend one more night at the Hart Valley Inn, then get an early start in the morning. By yesterday afternoon, she'd packed her things and returned the last of the books she'd borrowed from the inn's library. During supper at Nina's Café, she'd flipped through her map book and worked out where she'd travel next.

Then less than an hour later, she'd committed herself to a job interview—for a teaching position homeschooling a nine-year-old girl.

The Toyota hit a pothole and bounced so hard, Andrea whacked an elbow on the car door. She slithered to a stop and rubbed her stinging funny bone. Continue on? Or turn around and see if she'd somehow missed the turn? She sighed and leaned on the steering wheel. How did she get herself into this?

Blame it on the cowboy she'd seen yesterday morning. Broad shoulders a woman could lean on, light-brown Stetson shading his rough-hewn face. Eyes an intense blue that shot straight to her heart. During those few moments when her gaze locked with his, she'd imagined riding off into the sunset with him on a spirited horse.

That fanciful image had revisited her off and on throughout the day yesterday. It had still danced in her mind's eye when she stepped inside the Hart Valley Inn after supper and spotted the innkeeper, Beth Henley, at her desk, worrying a pencil with her teeth. If Andrea's thought processes hadn't been so garbled by the cowboy in the pickup truck, she would have just hurried through the lobby and up to her cozy room. Instead she'd hesitated long enough to see the distress on Beth's face, the concern in her eyes. Andrea couldn't just pass her by, felt obligated to ask Beth what was wrong.

Wearily, Andrea brushed back the hair that had escaped from her braid and peered through the dust at the massive blue oak up ahead. The tree jutted partway into the roadway, thick branches shading the road. Was that a sign nailed to the tree? The letters had nearly faded to illegibility, but as she pulled up to the oak, she could just make out the words Double J Ranch. An arrow, more faint than the letters, pointed to the left, toward a rutted dirt and gravel road.

This was it. The house was a little more than a half mile down that road. Now that she was nearly there, doubt returned ten-fold. She could make the turn, do the interview as promised. Answer as many of Tom Jarret's questions as she could, skate around the ones she couldn't, try to be honest while hiding a piece of her past.

Or she could go back the way she came. Avoid resurrecting the disastrous mistakes of two years ago. Pass on the opportunity to do the one thing in her vagabond life that had always brought her joy—teaching. Hope that in a month, in a year, she'd find the courage to lay the past to rest and step into a classroom again.

The choice seemed to shimmer in the dust. Stay or go. Before now, it had always been such an easy decision.

Unbidden, the image of the cowboy drifted into her mind again. Those steady blue eyes, the workman's hands gripping the wheel of his truck. If she got the job as Jessie Jarret's teacher, stayed on in Hart Valley, she might see the cowboy again, might have a chance to meet him.

Andrea shook her head. Meeting a man would be the worst reason to stay. She'd made that kind of choice two years ago, with tragic results. If she and the good-looking cowboy crossed paths again, she'd just look the other way.

Determined to follow through with the interview, Andrea turned the wheel and pulled onto the road leading to Tom Jarret's house. Based on Beth Henley's description of her brother, Tom wasn't anything like the fantasy she'd spun around the man in the pickup truck. Older than Beth by several years, the gruff rancher kept mostly to himself since his wife left him and seemed completely befuddled by the antics of his young daughter.

Andrea winced as her Toyota moaned and groaned up the slight grade between gnarled oaks and spear-straight pines. The grass on either side of the road wore the vivid green of spring, the verdant rolling hills dotted with lazy cattle. It was a breathtaking sight, almost too fresh and intense to be real.

Her car's temperature gauge alarmingly close to the danger zone, she finally topped the rise. With a gasp of surprise, she stopped the automobile to take in the view. Set like an opal in a field of emeralds, a rambling white ranch house dominated the gentle valley below. A sunbeaten red barn sat to one side, a corral beside it. Several outbuildings, obviously newer, were scattered here and there around the house and barn. Horses, sleek and well fed, grazed in the pastures that stretched as far as the eye could see.

As her ill-tuned engine threatened to stall and die, Andrea put the car in gear and continued on down into the bowl of the valley. Beth had said her brother had been relieved when she'd suggested Andrea could homeschool Jessie. It had seemed like a win-win situation for all involved.

As long as she didn't have to tell him what had happened two years ago.

Excitement building inside her at the prospect of a new teaching assignment, Andrea realized she dearly wanted the chance to teach Jessie Jarret. Beth had told Andrea little about her niece except her age, her sharp intelligence, the bad attitude that cropped up from time to time. Andrea didn't expect a sweet, even-tempered little girl. Even still, she relished the challenge.

Turning into the circular drive in front of the house, she stopped the car and shut off the engine. For a moment she remained in the car, her gaze taking in the welcoming wraparound porch, the rose bushes around the house just starting to bud. A curtain flicked aside in one of the second-story windows and Andrea caught a glimpse of a small face framed by dark blond hair.

Ready or not, here I come. Andrea opened her car door and climbed out. She headed for the porch, climbed the steps and strode across the porch to the front door. Opening the screen, she rapped on the front door, then stepped back to wait for someone to answer.

The door swung open, and a tall, broad-shouldered man filled the doorway. Andrea lifted her gaze from the white T-shirt stretched enticingly across a well-muscled chest, to the strong column of suntanned throat, to the rough-hewn face tipped down to greet her. Blue eyes burned into hers.

Her heart slammed into overdrive. My God, she realized. It's my cowboy.

As Andrea stared up at him, his brilliant blue gaze ran the length of her body, from head to toe, pausing for an instant on her mouth. There was nothing lecherous in the quick scan; it seemed as if he wanted to be sure she was real.

Andrea could understand the impulse. She'd thought she'd overembellished their encounter on Main Street, that she'd drawn the cowboy taller, his shoulders broader in her mind's eye. But that bit of fantasy she'd enjoyed since yesterday paled in comparison to the reality of the man before her. If anything, he seemed taller, broader than the fantasy, a blatant billboard for maleness in his T-shirt and worn blue jeans.

"You're late." He blurted the words out.

Andrea shifted on the doormat, clutching the handles of her soft-sided briefcase more tightly. "Sorry. I'm afraid I got lost."

He nodded. "Roads aren't well marked."

He continued to stare at her. Maybe he wasn't Tom

Jarret. Maybe Beth's brother truly was the crotchety old cowpoke the innkeeper had described. The real Tom could be busy somewhere, riding out on the range or chasing cattle or fixing fences—whatever ranchers did. The brawny man with the intense blue eyes could be Tom's foreman sent here to greet her.

"Andrea?" he asked.

His tentative question seemed to confirm her theory. Her cowboy was just a ranch hand filling in for the boss. Assured, she smiled up at him. "Andrea Larson. And you're…?"

He glanced down at her mouth, then locked his gaze with hers again. When was he going to stop staring at her? As long as those blue eyes were on her, she couldn't seem to think straight.

She swallowed, her mouth bone-dry. "You haven't told me your name yet."

"Beth didn't give you my name?" He blinked, his expression puzzled. "I'm Tom Jarret."

Oh, Lord. He *was* the cowboy. Or the cowboy was him. Andrea shook her head, trying to sort out her jumbled thoughts. She smiled gamely. "Good to meet you." She thrust her hand out.

He took her hand and shook it, the heat of his palm against hers stealing softly up her arm. The moment seemed to stretch as the warmth in her arm curled up to heat her face.

The straps of her briefcase cut into her fingers and brought her back to earth. She tugged her right hand, but for a moment, he resisted the pull. Then he let go so quickly, he banged his elbow on the doorjamb.

"Sorry," he muttered as he stepped aside and motioned her inside. "Come in."

Get a grip, Andrea. Her cowboy fantasies were mess-ing with her mind, and it was time she abandoned them. Tom Jarret was a potential employer, not Mr. April from some "ranch studs" calendar.

As she stepped into the living room, she couldn't suppress a smile as she scanned the comfortable space. This was what home looked like, she realized. The well-lived-in room looked like something out of a storybook, with its deep-cushioned sofas and chairs, rag rugs on the polished oak floor, east-facing windows letting in the midday light. A stack of schoolbooks lay strewn across the coffee table, but other than a bit of dust, it was neater than she might have expected.

She turned back to him. "You have a lovely home."

"Thank you." He shoved his hands in his jeans pockets. "I thought you might be older."

That makes two of us, she thought. "Is that a problem?"

He shook his head. "But as young as you are…"

She tipped her chin up to him. "As young as I am…?"

"You can't have been teaching very long."

"I'm twenty-six, Mr. Jarret." She took a breath, closed her fingers tighter around the briefcase handle. "I received my credential five years ago." What she'd left unsaid seemed to scream louder than the spoken words. Andrea was sure he'd hear it.

But he nodded, as if her answer had satisfied him. "Five years. That's good."

A sick feeling settled in the pit of Andrea's stomach at the way she'd misled him. But she'd only told him the truth about when she'd been awarded her credential. "What else would you like to know?"

"I wrote down some questions." He dug in the front pockets of his jeans, then searched the back pockets, finally retrieving a crumpled sheet of paper. He read off the first one. ''How many years have you taught?'' He smiled up at her. ''I guess we've already answered that.''

She nodded, the sick feeling intensifying. She tried to tell herself the exact truth didn't matter, that she could do this job and do it well. But her conscience was having none of that, and she knew she had to take a chance and admit at least part of the truth.

Chapter Two

"Actually, I've only taught for three years." Andrea's bright smile dragged Tom's gaze to her mouth again. He forced himself to focus on her eyes. "The last two years I took the opportunity to travel."

Jessie's teacher at the school, brand-new this term, hadn't even a year's experience. Andrea's three years were an improvement. "But you want to start teaching again?"

"Absolutely."

"Have you taught kids Jessie's age?"

"Some older, some younger."

He checked the sheet of paper again. "Do you have a criminal record?"

Her smile broadened. "Do I look like someone on the lam?"

He'd never been so damn fixated on a woman's mouth before. What was it about Andrea Larson's?

He took a step back from her, bent his head back down to his list of questions. "I don't suppose you do."

"But I bet you looked into that already."

He shrugged, feeling a bit guilty that he'd probed her background, even though he had every right. "I did."

"Good. That means you care about your daughter." She shifted her briefcase to her other hand, the motion drawing his gaze to her slender arms. At least he wasn't staring at her mouth. "What else?" she prompted.

He read over the paper again. "Do you have references from your last couple of jobs?"

When he looked up at her, she seemed startled. Then her face relaxed. "I didn't stay long enough at my last job to use it as a reference. I have names and numbers for the two before that."

She zipped open her briefcase, pulled out a sheet of paper. Several names with accompanying addresses and phone numbers were typed neatly on the paper. "They're all principals at elementary schools where I've taught. The two most recent are at the top of the list. You should still be able to reach them there."

Tom took the sheet of paper from Andrea, then gestured at the books piled on the coffee table. "The Battleaxe…Mrs. Beeber," he corrected himself, "sent those home. Look them over while I make these calls."

He headed for the kitchen, glad to have some time away from her. Grabbing the portable phone from the counter, he looked down at Andrea's list, his thumb ready to dial. But the neatly printed names blurred and his imagination took over, until all he could see, all he could think about, was Andrea Larson and her shapely body.

Tom slapped the sheet of paper to the counter, banishing the image. He was as red-blooded as any man,

but he usually had a little more self-control around
women. When he'd seen her on Main Street, she was a
stranger, and he'd felt free to fantasize. Last night as he
lay in bed, his gut still in knots over how he would get
Jessie through the school year, he'd let his mind run
wild over his mystery woman, knowing he'd probably
never see her again.

But now…now she stood large as life in his living
room. Now he had to behave himself because the sexy
object of his raunchy dreams might become his daughter's teacher.

Picking up the paper again, Tom dialed the first one
on the list. Once he reached the principal of the Southern California elementary school, Tom peppered the
man with questions, perversely searching for an excuse
to eliminate Andrea from consideration. Although he
had no backup plan if Andrea didn't work out, he
wanted to make damn sure she was the right teacher for
his daughter. And since he wasn't as clearheaded as he
ought to be around her, he needed as much information
as possible to make his decision.

But if he hoped Andrea's last two employers would
give him good reason to say no, he was disappointed.
Both remembered her clearly and fondly, both would
have gladly employed her again. In fact the principal at
Clearview Elementary in San Diego asked Tom to pass
along a request that Andrea return; there would be an
opening for her in the fall.

So he returned to the living room with no ammunition
to send Andrea on her way. But as he paused in the
doorway and caught sight of her, he knew he was in
big trouble. She sat on the edge of the coffee table,
textbook open on her lap, her heart-shaped face tipped
down as she read. Her long braid had swung forward

and now its end curled against her wrist. In that moment, she took his breath away.

Saying yes to Andrea Larson would be a damned sight more difficult than saying no. Because yes meant she would be staying a while. Yes meant he would have to guard his every impulse.

As he stepped into the living room, she looked up at him and smiled in greeting. Something zinged in the pit of his stomach, then kicked his heart into overdrive.

He wanted to just stand there and stare at her, but he forced himself to speak. "Any problems with the books?"

She rose, held out the math book she'd had in her lap. "I've studied algebra, trigonometry and calculus. I think I can handle fourth grade math."

"I called your references. One said you could walk on water. The other wants to hire you back."

She looked away, as if the praise embarrassed her. Putting aside the math book, she picked up the literature reader. "This has some good excerpts in it. But if I was teaching her, I'd want her to pick some of her own reading material."

"That would be fine." He found himself wishing she'd look up again, so he could see those chocolate-brown eyes. Suddenly they held as much fascination for him as her mouth.

She set down the reader, lifted the California history book. "We could do field trips out to some of the old gold mines. Or over to the state capitol."

"She'd like that," he said, although there was no telling what his mercurial daughter would like. Some days she hated everything.

Andrea glanced at him sidelong, rewarding him with

a glimpse of her eyes. Then she straightened and swung her braid back behind her.

She held the science book in her hands. "I'm afraid I'm a bit of a science geek. I've memorized the periodic table of the elements, can quote you Newton's laws chapter and verse...." Clutching the science book close to her chest, she looked up at him. "I don't suppose you know the names of Jupiter's sixteen moons?"

A flush had risen in her cheeks, a few tendrils of silky brown hair had escaped from her braid. He wanted to curl his fingers around her nape, pull her closer...

Her breath seemed to catch. "Do you?" The soft question sounded like an invitation.

Did he what? Want to pull her into his arms and press her against him? Hell, yes!

His heart thundering in his chest, he struggled to get a grip on his good sense. Somehow, despite his best intentions, Andrea's interview had taken a U-turn into dangerous territory. His mind seemed to have gone on vacation while his body clamored for something more up close and personal.

He tried to focus on the question she'd asked. Something about Jupiter's moons? He played it safe, told her, "No."

She just stared, no help at all when her lips parted that way and her eyes whispered unintentional invitations. The V-neck T-shirt she wore exposed a tantalizing bit of her collarbone, tempting him.

"Io." The small high voice from the foot of the stairs dispersed Tom's errant thoughts in an instant. He backed away from Andrea just as his daughter Jessie stepped into the room.

Her right arm cradled against her body, she planted herself in front of Andrea. "Europa, Ganymede, Callisto, Metis, Adrastea, Amalthea.'' She took a breath. ''Thebe, Leda, Himalia, Lysithea, Elara, Ananke, Carme, Sinope.''

A pause, then Andrea said, ''You forgot Pasiphae.''

''No,'' Jessie said, thrusting out her small, stubborn chin. ''I just wanted to see if you knew it.''

At the admiration in Andrea's brown eyes, Tom's chest swelled with pride. Jessie was challenging on a good day and downright heartbreaking on a bad one. But damned if she wasn't smart as a whip.

Andrea set aside the science book. ''I'm Andrea Larson.'' She put her hand out to Jessie.

Jessie ignored Andrea's hand, looked up at him. ''What's *she* doing here?''

God, that little girl could rile him so easily. Tom took a breath. ''We're talking over whether she should be your new teacher.''

''I don't need a teacher.'' Jessie cut him off as neatly as she cut a cow from the herd. ''I can teach myself.''

''No way,'' Tom said.

Jessie's expression turned mulish. ''Why not?''

Tom struggled for patience. ''First of all, I don't want you here by yourself.''

''I'm nine years old, Dad. I'm home alone lots of times when you're working.''

''Second, you need a teacher to tell you what to do.''

''Hah!'' Jessie barked out a laugh. ''You know what I did in class half the time? I read a book or played on the computer. 'Cause I got bored when the teacher went on and on about stuff I'd already learned.''

Hell, it was true; the teacher had told him as much. He racked his brain, searching for a suitable response.

Jessie knew she had him buffaloed. She grinned, planted her hands on her hips. The cuffs of her long-sleeved T-shirt hiked up a bit with the motion, uncovering her wrists.

Andrea's sharp intake of breath was so faint, Tom knew only he had heard it. But Jessie, preternaturally observant, saw the brief flicker of reaction in Andrea's face to that inch-wide swath of angry red scarring.

Jessie's brown gaze shuttered in reflexive defense. "You got a problem?" she asked Andrea pugnaciously.

Without even an instant's hesitation, Andrea smiled, pulled Jessie's right arm toward her. Andrea ran a finger over the colorful bit of woven string that circled Jessie's right wrist. "I like your friendship bracelet."

Jessie's gaze narrowed in suspicion. Besides her pediatrician, only two adults in Jessie's life were comfortable enough with her burned arm to touch it—Tom and his sister, Beth. It was as if people feared Jessie's scars involved some communicable disease they risked catching if they touched her.

But Andrea didn't flinch, didn't even comment as she tugged Jessie's sleeve up further so she could examine the friendship bracelet more closely. A warmth fountained up inside Tom at Andrea's kindness, her easy acceptance of Jessie. He wanted to let the gratitude that welled inside him spill out.

But he barely knew this woman, certainly had no right to react this way to her. Tom turned away, tamped down the unwelcome feelings.

Oblivious, Andrea continued to admire Jessie's bracelet. "Did you make it?" Andrea's hand rested against Jessie's right arm as she studied the bracelet's weave.

"Sabrina made it," Jessie said, a cautious note in her voice. "She's got the one I made for her."

Andrea lifted her gaze to Jessie. "Could you teach me how to make one?"

Jessie eyed Andrea with suspicion. "I guess."

Andrea straightened. "Do you like math word problems?"

Andrea's sudden change of subject seemed to catch Jessie off guard. "No. I hate 'em."

"So do I," Andrea said. "But I know some tricks to make them easier. How about a trade? You show me how to make a friendship bracelet, I'll teach you about word problems."

Tom hid a smile as he watched his daughter weigh Andrea's offer. Jessie was no dummy—she knew Tom couldn't allow her to stay home without a teacher. Andrea had cleverly offered a way for Jessie to accept the inevitable while still saving face.

"I guess," Jessie said nonchalantly. "But friendship bracelets aren't easy, at least the ones Sabrina and I make. I'll do my best to show you, but…" Jessie shrugged.

"I'm pretty good with my hands," Andrea said. "Maybe not as good as you, but I can probably figure it out."

Jessie beamed at Andrea's offhand compliment and a warmth lit inside Tom again. Times like these, when Jessie could forget the horror of the fire four years ago, were so rare, so fleeting. Tom wished he could collect them all up, distill them for the bad times.

But he could never forget what had happened, no more than Jessie could. He'd been gone at the time, up in Redding, and that made the memories ten times worse. He could only imagine Jessie's terrible fear when the candle flame had caught her sleeve, the pain as she ran from the house screaming for her mother. And Lori—

No. He wouldn't think of her. His ex-wife was long gone and the past with her. It was Jessie who mattered now.

Pride still shone in her face at Andrea's compliment as Jessie headed for the stairs. "I'll go get the string, then."

"Wait a minute," Tom called after her. "What about your schoolwork?"

Jessie looked up at him, then at Andrea. "Is she gonna be my teacher?"

Tom glanced over at Andrea. "How about we give her a trial run, for a week or two?"

Jessie's gaze narrowed on him. "What if I say no?"

If he'd thought he could trick her into thinking she had a say in the decision, his daughter had proved him wrong again. "I make the final choice, Jessie. And I'd like to give her a try."

He could see the storm clouds in his daughter's face give way to acceptance. "Okay." Then the annoyance in Jessie's dark brown eyes softened to a plea. "But can't we skip school for one day?"

Despite Jessie's surrender, he shouldn't let it slide. He had to set an example, instill in his daughter the importance of education. But he was a sucker for Jessie's sweet smile.

Andrea saved the day. "Tell you what...we'll get started on a bracelet, then do a page of math. That ought to keep your father happy."

Jessie turned her hopeful gaze on Tom. He nodded and she gave out a whoop before racing up the stairs. Tom had to laugh.

"You're a miracle worker," Tom told Andrea. "She's never this agreeable."

"It won't last," Andrea said. "By tomorrow she'll probably hate me again. Kind of a girl thing."

"I have to admit the female mind completely baffles me."

Andrea smiled up at him, her brown eyes alight with mischief. "It's a pact we all have, keeping men confused."

Why did she have to be so damned appealing? It was all he could do to resist moving closer to her, touching her.

Suddenly, she stepped away from him. "There is something we have to discuss, though."

Could she read his mind? "What do you mean?"

"Me living here."

"Living where?"

"At the house."

His brain must be more scrambled than he thought. "What house?"

She gave him a peculiar look. "Your house. Didn't Beth tell you? While homeschooling Jessie I would stay here at the house. With Jessie. With you."

At his dumbfounded look, Andrea's answer was clear—Beth hadn't said a word about her staying there at the ranch. She would have laughed if she weren't so unsettled at finding the crotchety old cowpoke she'd been expecting was actually a far younger and far too sexy hunk.

He stared down at her. "You can't stay here."

Of course she couldn't. Living under the same roof as Tom Jarret would be a maddening distraction. But his instant rejection of the notion inexplicably riled her.

She dug in, intent on arguing the point with him. "Why not?"

"Because." He held her gaze a moment more, then an edgy energy seemed to take hold of him. He paced away from her, then back. "Because you're... And I'm..."

"Afraid you won't be able to resist my charms?" She asked the question lightly, intending it as a joke, but now her insides churned as she waited for the answer.

"Absolutely not." He seemed almost horrified at the notion.

Heat rose in Andrea's cheeks at his emphatic tone. Of course he wasn't interested in her. But did he have to state it so baldly? "Then I don't see the problem."

"It wouldn't look right." He paced off again. "You'll have to stay in town. Drive in every day."

"I can't afford to stay at the inn that long."

He turned toward her. "Then somewhere else. The Willits sisters—"

"That won't work."

He took another step closer. "Why not?"

Her financial situation had never embarrassed her before and she hated having to justify herself now. "I stayed at your sister's place longer than I should have." She lifted her chin. "I haven't got the resources to rent a room elsewhere."

He pinned her with his brilliant gaze. She could imagine the judgments running through his mind, that she was a deadbeat, that she couldn't manage her money. But there was no shame in asking for room and board in conjunction with a job—she'd done it before. Why should this be any different?

Because this wasn't that little old couple with the room over their garage or the forty-something widow with the camper out back. This was Tom Jarret, six-foot-plus, broad shoulders, blue eyes to die for. This was her fantasy cowboy.

Andrea folded her arms across her chest, feeling edgy and defensive as she gave her usual pitch. "If I stay here at the ranch, my salary won't need to be much beyond room and board." She took a breath. "But if you'd prefer to find someone else to teach your daughter…"

Andrea waited for Tom to call her bluff, to tell her he'd have to look elsewhere for a teacher. Yet even as she acknowledged the folly of sharing Tom's home, she prayed for the chance to stay.

Because suddenly she wanted this job desperately. Beyond the fact that she could use the money, Andrea longed to find a way to ease the haunted look in Jessie's eyes. Certainly for Jessie's sake, Andrea could put aside the unwelcome attraction she felt for the girl's father.

Tom, as if he could hear Andrea's thoughts, stared at her another long moment. "Maybe I'd better find someone else."

Jessie must have been listening just out of sight. She appeared in the doorway, her arms full of cardboard boxes. "Andrea has to teach me. I don't want anybody else."

Jessie's sudden fealty cheered Andrea. "And I want to teach you."

Tom put a hand on his daughter's shoulder. "But it isn't going to work, Jess."

Jessie shook off her father's hand. "Why not?"

Tom turned to Andrea, no doubt expecting help. But Andrea didn't feel inclined to give it to him.

Tom turned back to his daughter. "Because she needs a live-in position and that's not what I'm offering."

Jessie crossed to the coffee table, set down the boxes filled with string and beads. "Why can't she stay here?"

"It's a grown-up thing," Tom told his daughter in a no-nonsense tone meant to close the subject.

But Jessie persisted. "What do you mean, grown-up?"

Tom looked over at Andrea again. This time, Andrea took pity on him. "Because your dad and I…we're a grown-up man and a grown-up woman. And to stay in the same house…"

Jessie's brow furrowed, then her eyes widened. "Oh. Right." She looked thoughtful a moment, then she smiled. "You can stay with me in my room. Then it would be okay."

Andrea went down on one knee, bringing herself to eye level with the little girl. "I would love to share your room, Jessie. But that still won't work."

"You won't ever have to see my arm," Jessie said, her expression earnest. "I'll keep it covered, I promise."

Jessie's fervent vow shocked Andrea, shook her so deeply she couldn't even speak for a moment. She looked up at Tom, and the stoic pain in his gaze wrenched her heart.

Her urge to needle Tom seemed so petty in the face of the profound hurts he and Jessie had suffered. She felt a bit ashamed of herself.

"Jessie," Andrea said as she gently raised the sleeve on the little girl's arm. She placed her hand lightly against the tight, shiny skin of Jessie's scar. "This problem has nothing…*nothing* to do with your arm."

Jessie wouldn't look at her, her small face shuttered.

Andrea could only guess at the pain behind those innocent brown eyes.

"Jessie," Andrea tried again. "If there was any way—"

"You can stay in the foreman's apartment," Tom blurted out.

Hope fluttered in Jessie's face. "Can she, Daddy?"

Andrea straightened. "What about the foreman?"

"We don't have one," Jessie said. "Not since Mommy—" Jessie's hand flew up to cover her mouth. "Never mind."

Did Tom forbid Jessie to talk about her mother? Andrea looked over at him, tried to interpret the emotions behind his stony expression. Was it Tom who demanded Jessie's mother leave? When Andrea asked, Beth had said her brother's ex-wife was "out of the picture." Because of Tom's doing?

Tom turned away, pulled open a drawer in a side table. "It's above the equipment shed." He dug through the drawer, produced a set of keys. "It's not fancy, but there's a bathroom and a small kitchenette."

Even as she felt relief at the solution, Andrea wondered at the past that lay behind this man and his daughter. "It sounds perfect."

"Fine, then." Tom shoved the keys in his jeans pocket. "I'll go open it up for you."

Jessie sighed and let slip a tiny smile, but Andrea could see the little girl had already rebuilt her walls around her. Andrea wanted to give Jessie a hug, to try to wash a bit of that reserve away. But she sensed the child would reject her show of affection.

So instead, Andrea rose and took the top two boxes from Jessie's stack. "Now that we've settled where I'm staying, let's get to work on that bracelet. Can I pick any color I want?''

As they settled down at the coffee table with the string and beads, Jessie launched into a dissertation on which colors went with which and the importance of the proper choice of beads. Before long, the contents of the cardboard boxes were strewn across the table and Andrea had sneaked a word problem into the mix using the colorful string and beads.

Andrea was aware of Tom watching them. At first, she wondered if he was monitoring her, making certain she was a competent teacher. But when she looked up at him and locked her gaze with his, the emotions swimming in his face surprised her—sorrow and regret, the pain of lost dreams.

But then he smiled and said two words that struck Andrea to the core. ''Thank you.''

Tom cut the string on a bale of straw and pulled out a generous armful. Usually, he finished mucking out the barn's ten stalls in an hour-and-a-half. Today he'd dawdled over the task for nearly twice that long.

The pile of straw for Sonuvagun's stall would finish the task, but he was still loath to go back into the house. The attraction he felt for Jessie's new teacher was enough of a bother, sending his thoughts in entirely inappropriate directions. But even more, having a woman in the house again, the light sounds of Andrea's voice in counterpoint to Jessie's set off an ache inside him he didn't welcome and didn't care to acknowledge.

How long had it been since anyone but Beth had been at the ranch? For a good year after Lori left, he'd been too angry and bitter, not to mention exhausted dealing with Jessie's surgeries, to even think about women.

Once the divorce was final, he'd let Beth set him up every once in a while, mostly women from Sacramento who'd come up to Hart Valley for the weekend. Knowing they'd be heading back home Sunday night, that they would pass out of his life as quickly as they'd come in, he'd been loath to bring them home. Maybe it was time he got back into circulation and started thinking about making a commitment again. Not that his daughter's teacher would be that woman.

But she *would* be staying a while, at least until mid-June when the school year ended. A little over eight weeks. And then, he supposed she'd move on, to whatever waited for her down the road.

Sonuvagun nudged him, sniffing Tom's pocket in search of a carrot. Tom rubbed the gelding's ears, then stepped out of the stall into the barn aisle. Brushing bits of straw from his T-shirt, Tom latched Sonuvagun's stall door, then made one last check of his pregnant mares. Satisfied all five expectant mamas were in good condition, Tom headed out of the barn.

With the late afternoon sun in his eyes, he couldn't quite see through the living room's big bay window. Were they still inside, working? Had they gone into the kitchen for a snack? The image of Andrea serving Jessie milk and chocolate chip cookies, then sitting to enjoy a cookie herself stirred a long-forgotten memory. Not of Lori, who rarely set foot in the kitchen if she could avoid it, but of his own mother.

Lord, he'd only been seven when she died. How could he remember anything about her? Yet stubbornly the image remained in his mind's eye—the warmth of the kitchen, the taste of the cookie in his mouth, his mother's smile.

Tom shook himself, unwilling to entertain for even a

moment longer what was probably just a fantasy. He ought to get up to the foreman's apartment and double check to make sure Andrea had sheets and what-not. Maybe even make up the bed for her.

Or maybe not. Just the thought of handling the linen and blankets that would warm Andrea's body sent his imagination soaring off in entirely the wrong direction. He'd make sure she had everything she needed, then leave it to her to handle it all.

One last look at the bay window, then Tom headed across the yard toward the small two-story outbuilding painted the same brick red as the barn. On the first floor, he stored the small tractor he used to move feed and grade the arenas, along with odds and ends he always needed close at hand—hoof trimmers, leather punches, sundry veterinary supplies. Stairs to the left of the storage shed led up to the foreman's apartment on the second floor.

When he reached the top of the stairs and tried to open the door, he was surprised to find it locked. He was sure he hadn't left it that way. Pulling the keys from his pocket, he unlocked the door and pushed it open.

Hearing a soft gasp, Tom froze, the door open just far enough to set one foot inside. He couldn't help himself—he looked. Then all at once wished he hadn't and was glad he had.

There in the bathroom doorway, wearing nothing but a pale-blue towel, stood his daughter's brand-new teacher.

Chapter Three

Tom stared at Andrea for what seemed an eternity before his good sense finally returned and he dragged his eyes away. He stepped back outside, pulling the door nearly shut, his heart hammering in his chest.

As he sucked in a lungful of air, he tried to figure out what to do next. Leave, to give Andrea time to get over the awkwardness? Call out to her to apologize?

Go back inside and tug that pale-blue towel from her body, explore the long silky length of her thigh, the smoothness of her bare shoulders…?

No, that he should definitely not do. He ought to go, find a horse trough to stick his head into. Then pour a bucket of cold water over his hyperheated flesh.

Andrea saved him the decision. She'd apparently come to the door; he heard her just on the other side. "Give me a second. I'll get dressed."

Her voice barely shook as she said the words. If she

felt as mortified as he did, she didn't show it. But she must; he'd seen the shock in her face when he'd taken that fatal step inside the apartment.

Shock...or anticipation? Embarrassment...or excitement? Was it his own wishful thinking that colored his memory of that instant of surprise?

He shook his head, trying to clear it. Leaning back against the railing of the small landing outside the foreman's apartment, Tom rubbed his hands over his face. Obviously it had been too long since he'd been with a woman. That one brief glance at Andrea kept replaying itself in his imagination, embellished with erotic details straight from his libido.

He heard her footsteps coming closer and he shoved his hands into the pockets of his jeans. She opened the door without hesitation, looked up at him boldly as if the humiliating moment a few minutes earlier had never happened. She wore a light-green T-shirt and khaki slacks, on which the only feminine feature was the tiny, belted waist.

But the flutter of her heartbeat in her throat and the faint wash of color on her cheeks gave a different message. She was rattled, but apparently she was determined not to show it.

His respect for her clicked up a notch. He cleared his throat, kept his voice even. "I'm sorry. I thought you were still down at the house."

"Jessie's working on the last of her math. I decided to run up for a shower."

He nodded, not sure what else to say. Discussing his daughter seemed safe. "How's she doing?"

"Fine, for the first day." She shifted her feet, hooked the right one behind the left.

Tom's gaze fell to her feet, saw her feet peeking out

from the cuffs of the khaki slacks. An image burst into his mind of his tongue tracing a path along those delicate toes, then up the instep of her foot to her ankle to—

"Was there something you wanted?" She switched feet, bringing her left one behind her right.

Her question, the sudden movement intruded on his fantasy, brought his errant thoughts to an abrupt halt. "What? No." Other than to get another look at those shapely toes. Good God, what was wrong with him? He forced himself back to reality and his gaze back on her face. "I wanted to make sure you had everything you need—towels, sheets, blankets."

She settled a strand of damp brown hair behind her ear. "Jessie told me where to find them. I've got the bed made up. There's even some coffee in the kitchenette."

"Good, then…" He stepped back, turned toward the stairs.

"Which reminds me…" She smiled up at him. "We didn't discuss salary."

He'd been so relieved at how well she and Jessie got along, it hadn't crossed his mind. Then the vision of Andrea wrapped in a towel had completely scrambled his thoughts. Tom rubbed at the tension growing between his eyes. "What are you usually paid?"

"Depends on the school district. Los Angeles pays more than a smaller county like Marbleville." Her cheek dimpled as she smiled. "Maybe you should give me what you paid the foreman."

The joke fell flat for Tom; he still couldn't think of the man without anger gnawing at his insides. Forcing a smile, he asked, "What do you think is fair?"

"Since room and board are included...two-fifty a week?" Her brow furrowed. "Or is that too much?"

"Not enough." He quickly calculated how much he could pull out of savings. "Make it four hundred."

She seemed almost appalled. "That's too much."

"Not for an experienced credentialed teacher."

Doubt flashed in her soft brown eyes. "Then I'll do the cooking."

He shook his head. "No. You're teaching my daughter. You're not a maid."

"But I love to cook. And we can make it part of Jessie's lessons." She rested her hand lightly on his wrist. "Please."

Her fingers warmed his skin, tempted him to take her hand in his. The soft flowery scent of her shampoo drifted toward him, and in that moment, he probably would have deeded the Double J to her if she'd asked.

He pulled a deep breath into his lungs. The aroma of the stable still clinging to him stung his nostrils. He felt suddenly as awkward as a boy. "That sounds fine," he said, pulling away. He grabbed for the railing and started down the stairs, still looking back at her over his shoulder.

She stepped out onto the landing. "Roast chicken okay? I found one in the freezer."

A long ago memory of his mother's cooking teased him—a kid-sized plate with a savory chicken leg, a pile of mashed potatoes swimming in gravy. He had a pretty good grasp of the basics in the kitchen and had kept himself and Jessie well fed. But somehow having a woman cooking for him again seemed more right.

He paused halfway down the stairs. "Roast chicken sounds great."

He continued down the steps, across the yard and

toward the barn. He didn't want to look back again, afraid she was watching him, afraid she would see the emotions tumbling inside him in the lines of his face. In the few hours she'd been here, she'd dragged up far more of his past than he cared to revisit.

Sonuvagun could use some work. Running a few reining patterns in the big arena would take his mind off Andrea, the sight of her, the scent of her. The big bay gelding was still recovering from last year's suspensory injury and a slow workout would be a good way to get the horse back in condition.

But as he hauled Sonuvagun's saddle and headstall from the tack room to where he'd cross-tied the gelding in the barn aisle, he wondered if he was only fooling himself. Somehow, in the space of those few hours, the sweet-faced young woman with the soft brown eyes had gotten under his skin. All the reining patterns in the world might not work her loose.

But he damn well had to try. Andrea Larson was his daughter's teacher, nothing more, nothing less. He had no right to think of her any other way.

With a new determination, Tom swung the saddle on Sonuvagun's back and snugged up the cinch. Switching halter for bridle, he led the gelding from the barn and headed for the big arena. Resisting the urge to look back at the foreman's apartment, he chased Andrea from his mind with the first few steps of reining pattern number one.

Andrea looked up from the pot of mashed potatoes as Tom entered the kitchen, his light-brown hair wet and slicked back. He'd changed into a clean T-shirt and jeans, and the knit and denim seemed sculpted to his rangy body. The spice of aftershave had replaced the aromas of alfalfa and horse. She didn't know what was more tantalizing—a cowboy who smelled like his work or the cleaned-up version.

She still couldn't quite banish the memory of Tom in the doorway of the foreman's apartment. The hunger in his eyes as his gaze raked her body, the tension in his hand gripping the door. She'd never had a man look at her that way, see her as desirable, want her as much as he seemed to in that moment.

That he was a near stranger to her, that he was her employer and therefore off limits, only seemed to add to the flashpoint of desire that had burst inside her. Then embarrassment took over and Tom had stepped back outside the room, leaving her chilled and mortified.

Now as he strode to the cupboard for a glass and filled it from the tap, Andrea felt an aftershock of that heat pool within her. Unwilling to let the feelings overwhelm her again, she returned her focus to finishing the potatoes. She bent to retrieve a serving bowl from the cupboard below, then piled fluffy mashed potatoes into it.

Tom swallowed the last of the water and set the glass on the counter. "Dinner smells great."

Andrea felt extraordinarily pleased by the simple compliment. "Thanks," she said, lifting the filled bowl from the counter.

As she turned toward him, Tom took the bowl from her. His fingers brushed hers in the process, setting off another tingle.

Tom set the potatoes on the table, then tugged open the refrigerator door. "Where's Jessie?" If he'd reacted to touching her, there wasn't a trace of it in his voice.

"She's washing up." Andrea kept her tone as even

as his as she moved to the large ranch stove to give the gravy a final stir.

Milk jug in his hand, Tom shoved the refrigerator door shut with his hip. "I'm impressed. Clean hands at meals is low on Jessie's priority list."

"It took thirty minutes of begging." Andrea transferred the gravy from saucepan to gravy boat. "As it is, I had to agree soap was optional."

Tom poured milk into the tall glass at Jessie's place, then returned the jug to the refrigerator. Andrea had just gotten her heartbeat under control, had begun to hope the incident in the apartment would be forgotten when he turned to her and fixed her gaze with his. "Andrea—"

"If it's about what happened earlier..." She held up a hand to forestall him as heat rose in her cheeks. "I know it was terribly awkward, but please..." She prayed awkwardness was all he'd seen in her face, that he hadn't caught the desire. "We don't need to bring it up again." She said the last in little more than a whisper.

He kept his sharp blue gaze steady on her, his expression giving nothing away. It hit Andrea suddenly— it might not have been hunger she'd seen in his eyes. Perhaps it had only been embarrassment at seeing her too skinny body, her hair wet and tangled around her shoulders. Not exactly a vision of sensuality.

Finally, he spoke. "I agree. We don't need to mention it again." Then he turned away and shouted up the stairs. "Jessie! Dinner, now!"

With trembling hands, Andrea opened the oven door and pulled out the roast chicken. The already carved bird smelled heavenly, but with the cartwheels her stomach was doing, Andrea doubted she could eat a bite. She set the hot platter on a trivet beside the mashed potatoes, then added a basket of sliced bread and a bowl of green beans with bacon she'd kept warm on the stove.

Tom pulled out her chair for her and waited until she'd seated herself before he headed for the other end of the table. Andrea couldn't remember ever having a man pull out a chair for her.

Tom seated himself just as Jessie announced her arrival with the pounding of footsteps down the stairs. The little girl's hair was damp around her face where she must have splashed it with water. She'd pushed up the sleeves of her long-sleeved T-shirt to wash her hands and they were still up above her elbows.

A barely audible intake of breath brought Andrea's gaze over to Tom. He stared at his daughter's right arm, the scarring exposed by the pushed up sleeve. "She never…"

Andrea could barely hear Tom's soft-spoken words over the noisy scrape of chair legs on hardwood floor as Jessie sat herself at the table between Tom and Andrea. Then Jessie grabbed for a chicken leg and Andrea shifted her focus from father to daughter. Andrea put out a hand to stop Jessie's grab, fingers on the back of the little girl's scarred wrist.

The chicken leg just out of reach, Jessie glared up at Andrea. "What?"

Andrea tugged Jessie's hand away from the platter. "No fingers, please." She held the serving tongs out to Jessie.

Jessie gave her a mulish look. "Dad lets me use my fingers."

Andrea flicked a glance over at Tom. He raised one

brow, obviously leaving it up to her. Andrea returned her attention to Jessie. "Dad shouldn't. Use these."

Ignoring the tongs, Jessie crossed her arms over her chest. Andrea gently pulled the little girl's hand free and laid the tongs into it. Jessie cocked back her arm, ready to throw the serving tool across the kitchen.

Then she stopped, her gaze fixed on her arm. For the first time, she seemed to realize she'd forgotten to pull her sleeves back down after washing. The metal tongs clattered to the table. Color filled Jessie's cheeks as she quickly jerked down her sleeves.

Matter-of-factly, Andrea picked up the tongs and replaced them in Jessie's right hand. Jessie sat frozen a moment, then she looked sidelong up at Andrea. Whatever she was searching for in Andrea's face—disgust, discomfort, uneasiness—Andrea was determined Jessie wouldn't see it.

"Oh, all right," Jessie said finally as she reached out with the tongs. She snagged two chicken legs and plopped them on her plate before leaning the tongs against the platter. Then she scooped up a massive pile of mashed potatoes and a respectable spoonful of green beans.

She filled her mouth with chicken before speaking again. "Word problems are easy, Daddy," she said around a huge bite. "Andrea showed me how."

The rule about not speaking with your mouth full would have to wait for another meal. Jessie's attitude adjustment meant the world to Andrea and she had no intention of chiding the girl further. Instead, she served her own dinner, helping herself to some white meat, potatoes and gravy.

Taking her first bite, Andrea looked across the table

at Tom. He still sat with his plate empty, a quiet joy in his face as he gazed at his daughter.

He glanced over at Andrea and smiled. Pleasure flooded her at his obvious appreciation. Wanting to say something, but unsure of the words, she just smiled back, then bent her head to her food. For the rest of the meal, she felt Tom's gaze on her often, but she didn't dare meet it again.

Tom threw a flake of grass hay into Sonuvagun's stall, then dropped a scoop of grain into the gelding's feed bucket. He'd fed the horses a bit later than usual after insisting on washing the supper dishes, despite Andrea's protests. She'd made dinner, he would clean up. When Andrea had offered to dry and put away, Jessie had been delighted; that was usually her chore. But Jessie's delight was short-lived. Before Andrea could so much as dry a dish, he'd taken the dish towel from her hands and given it to his daughter instead.

So Andrea had sat at the table while he and Jessie cleaned up, going over the day's schoolwork, listening to Jessie's endless chatter—about her quarter pony mare, Trixie, about her best friend, Sabrina. Somehow Andrea managed to focus on both Jessie's arithmetic and the bits and pieces of the nine-year-old's life.

He latched the feed room door, then headed for the barn doors. About to close the barn up for the night, he heard the sound of the front door opening and footsteps on the porch. The sun had just about set, washing the sky with oranges and pinks so bright it made his heart ache. Jessie came racing across the yard, Andrea behind her at a more sedate pace.

"Don't close the barn yet, Dad," Jessie called out as

she reached his side. "Andrea wants to see Trixie." Jessie ducked inside the barn.

As Andrea walked along the gravel path that led from the house to the barn, her face was in shadow, her expression a mystery. She smiled as she got closer, and the loneliness the pretty sunset had started up in him eased.

She chuckled softly. "I told her I could wait until tomorrow, but later doesn't seem to be in Jessie's vocabulary."

"Unless it has to do with taking baths or picking up her toys," Tom said.

Jessie reappeared, dragging Trixie by her lead rope. The pony tried to snag a piece of hay caught on her halter, none too happy being taken from her evening feed. "Andrea's never ridden a horse, Dad. Can you believe that?"

Tom winked at Andrea. "Hard to believe."

Jessie towed her sorrel pony up beside Andrea. "But she says I can teach her how to ride. We're gonna do it tomorrow."

Andrea put out a tentative hand to Trixie. Ears tipped forward, the mare sniffed her fingers.

"She's looking for treats," Tom said as he reached in a back pocket for a sugar cube. "Lay your hand flat."

Andrea did and he set the lump of sugar in her palm. But when he let go of the sugar, his fingers lingered of their own accord. They stroked lightly across her palm and the texture and warmth mesmerized him.

He might have taken her hand just then, even brought it to his lips for a kiss, but the impatient mare saved him from that lunacy. Eager for her treat, Trixie shoved his hand out of the way with her nose and delicately took the sugar cube from Andrea.

Tom took a step back, shoved his hands in his front pockets. What the hell had gotten into him? His father had taught him better than to touch a woman without invitation or permission. But her nearness seemed to turn him inside out and upside down until he didn't know what he was doing.

Andrea locked her hands behind her back. Her laugh sounded weak and forced. "I thought we'd include horseback riding in her curriculum." She backed away a few steps. "I'd better get back inside. I want to prep for tomorrow's lessons."

She turned on her heel and headed for the house. Guilt lanced through Tom as he watched her go. He'd made a mess of things with her, and he'd be lucky if she stayed on as Jessie's teacher.

"Put your pony away," he told Jessie. "She wants her dinner."

Jessie led the mare back to her stall, then skipped across the yard toward the house. She turned when she reached the porch. "Come on, Daddy."

"In a minute," he called out to her. He tried to think what to do to delay going inside, at least until Andrea headed up to her apartment. He'd cleaned tack a week ago, but he supposed he could give it all another once over.

As he rubbed saddle soap into a pair of split reins, he heard the front door open, then the sound of footsteps on the gravel path. He thought they hesitated a moment before continuing on toward the foreman's apartment. He held his breath, praying she wouldn't come into the barn, wishing she would. To his relief and regret, the light footsteps continued.

It was dark by the time he crossed the yard toward the house, and his shoulders ached with tension and work. He'd have liked to say he didn't give the foreman's apartment so much as a glance, but he'd be lying. He'd more than glanced; he'd stood on the front porch, hidden in the shadows, and stared a good long time at the warm glow from the windows.

Then calling himself a host of names he would never speak in his daughter's presence, let alone Andrea's, he stomped inside the house and to his room. He shut the blinds on the side of his bedroom that overlooked Andrea's quarters first thing. He didn't intend to open them again.

A stripe of moonlight cut across the minuscule bedroom of the foreman's apartment, lending barely enough illumination for Andrea to make out the drab beige walls of the room. She glanced over at the red glowing numbers of the small clock radio on the nightstand—nearly 1:00 a.m. She felt as wide awake and restless as she had at midnight when she'd finally turned off the bedroom light.

She could still feel his touch on her hand. It seemed imprinted there, as if his fingertips had redrawn the lines on her palm, changing the course of her life. The notion terrified and thrilled her all at once.

A part of her screamed caution, urged her to pack up her things and leave the Double J before she got herself in any deeper. Yet in her one day here, she'd lost her heart to Tom Jarret's prickly nine-year-old daughter. Jessie was like an intriguing puzzle Andrea yearned to decipher, one that locked itself up tight as often as it yielded its secrets.

And Jessie's father…straightforward and plain-speaking on the surface, beneath a tangled weave of bright and dark. As enigmatic as his daughter, Tom Jarret offered a glimpse into a new world Andrea had been certain she didn't want—one of permanency, family, shared experiences.

It didn't matter. She'd only be here the few weeks until Jessie finished school. Then the restlessness would overtake her, sever any links she might have formed, send her back on her wandering path. She would be glad to leave, grateful to escape the humdrum of life spent in only one place.

She always had before. Leaving was one thing she did extremely well. She would be glad to drive away from the Pueblo J for the last time.

Of course she would.

Chapter Four

Three days after Andrea had arrived, Tom decided Jessie's teacher just might work. Crouched in the stall of one of his brood mares, rewrapping a bandage around the mare's injured right hind leg, Tom thought he'd handled things pretty well where Andrea was concerned.

Of course, he saw little of her during the day. He rose before she and Jessie did, grabbing a quick breakfast before heading out to work the horses or fix fence or any of the dozens of daily tasks that never seemed to end. Lunchtime he put off until Andrea and Jessie finished in the kitchen, then he'd slap together a sandwich or reheat leftovers from last night's dinner.

That left suppertime to get through, to endure Andrea's company without an inadvertent touch or a look that would burn right through him. He tended to rush through his meal—almost a sin considering the way Andrea could cook—then get the dishes done with Jessie's help, keeping his back to Andrea while she corrected Jessie's schoolwork at the kitchen table. After dinner, he holed up in his office until Andrea left for her own small quarters. And often just sat there, aching and alone, wishing he could have extended the dinner hour rather than cutting it short.

The familiar knot of longing lodged in his stomach as he gathered up the vet supplies he'd used on the mare. He thrust the feeling aside, reminding himself Andrea was here for Jessie, not as a cure for his loneliness. No denying the sweetness of Andrea's company, the gratifying way she drew Jessie out. She'd get his daughter laughing at the silliest jokes. He hadn't smiled so much in years, felt so much contentment.

But he knew damn well it wouldn't last.

A few short weeks and Andrea would be gone. Depending on Andrea's presence when she was only a temporary part of their lives would be a mistake.

Tom returned the vet supplies to the storage box in the barn aisle, then dumped the bucket of medicated water he'd used to clean the mare's leg. He took a quick look at his watch—one o'clock, safe enough to go in the house. Andrea and Jessie would be working in the living room and he could have that brief moment to say hello to Andrea before heading for the kitchen.

He shook his head. His mind was on the wrong track again, looking forward to seeing Andrea, eager for her smile. Irritated with himself, Tom slammed the stainless steel bucket on the vet box. The noise spooked one of his expectant mamas and brought Sonuvagun's head out of his stall. As the mare laid her ears back flat, Sonuvagun gave him a look that seemed to say, Don't mess with the females, Tom.

Which was only good horse sense, Tom realized as he stepped from the shade of the barn into the bright spring sunshine. He'd keep his eyes to himself when he went inside the house.

But the living room was empty when he got inside. Jessie's books were scattered across the coffee table. Wadded up paper littered the living room floor. A plate with a half-eaten brownie sat beside a nearly full glass of milk on an end table.

Were they outside? They'd taken a walk yesterday out in the pasture—looking for wildflowers, Jessie had said.

Tom continued on to the kitchen, head tipped down. He didn't see Andrea standing in the corner by the refrigerator until he'd nearly bumped into her.

He jumped back, whacking his hand on the edge of the kitchen table. "Sorry."

"No problem." Andrea gripped a glass of water in her hand and her arms were crossed tightly over her chest. "Can I make you some lunch?"

He didn't like the tension in Andrea's face. "Where's Jessie?"

She pursed her lips, the motion riveting. "In her room."

He dragged his gaze back up to her eyes. "She's working up there?"

"Things didn't go smoothly this morning." She set aside the glass of water. "So how about lunch?"

He ought to just throw together a sandwich and grab some fruit and go eat in the barn. But now that he was with Andrea, his resolve seemed to scatter like grass seeds in a breeze.

"Lunch would be great." He stepped to the sink and turned on the faucet. "Is there a problem with Jessie?"

He glanced at her sidelong, watched her pull out condiments and cold cuts, then reach for the loaf of bread in the bread basket. She hesitated with her hand on the plastic bread bag, as if she was considering what she wanted to say. Then she opened the twist tie on the bread and pulled a plate from the cupboard above.

"We're having our ups and downs. Just getting used to each other."

Tom finished washing up and shut off the faucet. He reached for a paper towel just as she did, their fingers tangling briefly.

She pulled her hand back and waited as he tore off a sheet. Color rising in her cheeks, she wouldn't meet his eyes.

He felt like an idiot as he stood there drying his hands. The simplest things seemed charged with a sensual energy where Andrea was concerned. It wasn't fair to her or to his daughter that he couldn't seem to keep his errant thoughts in check.

Rounding the table, he pulled out his chair and took his place. She worked quickly and efficiently, yet when she turned and handed him the plate, he could see she'd arranged the sandwich, red flame grapes and chips with care. His stomach roiled with hunger and he took a big bite of the sandwich.

She pulled out a chair opposite him and sat. "There's something I want to talk over with you."

Her expression was so serious, alarm tickled up his spine. Had she guessed at his attraction toward her? He'd tried so hard to keep himself under control, but now it seemed every look, every narrowly avoided touch screamed out, obvious and inappropriate.

He opened his mouth, ready to apologize. But then

she continued. "I'd like to take that field trip to the state capitol next week."

He gulped in a breath, then took another mouthful of sandwich. Busy chewing, he gestured with the sandwich to encourage her to go on.

"Hart Valley Elementary has a teacher training day next Thursday, so Jessie's friend Sabrina is out of school. Jessie wants her to come along."

He swallowed, took a drink from the glass of milk Andrea had poured him. "Sounds like a great idea."

She nodded. "But I don't really trust my car to get us there and back. So I thought we could drive over to Marbleville and catch the bus into Sacramento."

"I don't know." The thought of Andrea and the two girls by themselves in Sacramento made him a little uneasy.

"The bus fare isn't much. And you'd really only have to pay for Jessie. I'm sure Sabrina's parents will send some money with her. And I can pay my own way."

"I'm not worried about the fare. It's an awfully long trip by bus, though."

An idea popped into his head, one he was a fool to even consider. Setting down his sandwich, he took a napkin from the holder and wiped his mouth. He mentally listed all the reasons his idea was a bad one.

Then he looked up at Andrea, and her gaze locked with his. The brief visual contact sent a jolt through his body.

Settle down! he told himself, feeling like a randy teenager. And keep your suggestion to yourself.

He meant to, he really did. But the prospect of spending the day alone at the ranch while Andrea and the girls explored Sacramento set off the loneliness again. And he couldn't seem to help himself.

"I've got a better idea," he said. "I'll drive you and the girls. We'll all go together."

Tom's offer hung in the air between them like an unexpected gift and there was no way Andrea could have refused it. An hour's drive to and from downtown Sacramento with Tom beside her on the bench seat of his truck would be more temptation than she ought to face. Even with the girls behind them in the fold-up seats of the extended cab, Andrea would struggle to resist touching him. But Tom's driving would make the planned field trip that much easier, with the added treasure of a few precious hours of his time.

For Jessie, of course. Because although Tom obviously loved his daughter, his preoccupation with the work of the ranch meant he spent very little time with her. Here was a chance for some quality one-on-one between Tom and Jessie.

Her own desires and wishes were beside the point.

"That would be great, Tom. Jessie would love having you with us."

He stared at her a moment, his gaze dropping to her mouth and fixing there with a disconcerting intensity. An edgy heat burst inside her and drove her to her feet. Her chair squealed against the hardwood kitchen floor as she pushed it back.

She moved to the counter to put away the fixings for Tom's lunch. Suddenly, preparing a simple meal for him seemed a terribly intimate act. Everything she'd touched, he was touching now. Her hands felt unsteady as they replaced the lettuce in its plastic bag and put the lids back on the condiment jars.

She held off as long as she could, then looked back at him over her shoulder. As she watched, he lifted the grapes from the plate, then plucked one from its stem.

He raised the grape to his lips, slipped it inside. She could almost taste the sweet-tart flavor as he bit down.

She nearly lost her grip on the mustard jar. As it was, it clattered against the counter and Tom's head swung up. She froze at the unexpected light in his blue eyes, her mind emptied of thought.

With an effort she tore her gaze from his, said the first thing that popped into her brain as she set the mustard in the cupboard. "So, any plans for the weekend?"

As soon as the words were out, she cringed. It sounded like she was about to ask him for a date. She snatched up the glass of water she'd poured after her confrontation with Jessie and brought it to her mouth. She nearly choked on the water she gulped down.

"Are you okay?" he asked as she coughed to clear her throat.

She nodded, setting aside the water, sloshing a bit of it on her hand. "I hadn't planned any lessons for Jessie for the weekend. I could just make myself scarce and leave you two to do whatever you usually do."

He ate the last of the grapes, then set the stem on his plate. "Weekends aren't much different than weekdays around here. There are still horses to feed, stalls to muck. Jessie and I usually just go our separate ways."

"She's by herself all day?" The thought of Jessie moping around the house, bored and lonely, plucked at Andrea's heart.

His jaw worked as he dropped his crumpled napkin on his plate. "We keep in touch with walkie-talkies. And sometimes she'll go over to Sabrina's."

"But when do you spend time with her?"

He pushed his chair back, picked up his plate. Emotions flickered across his face—irritation, the beginnings of anger and more than a trace of guilt.

He headed for the sink, keeping the table between them. "Jessie doesn't need me with her twenty-four hours a day." He pulled open the cupboard beneath the sink and tossed the remains of his lunch in the trash bag there.

"No. But she needs more than the hour you see her at dinner."

He jerked open the dishwasher door and shoved in the plate. "You've been here three days. You think you know more than me how to raise my daughter?"

He slammed the dishwasher door shut and looked ready to stomp out of the kitchen. She saw Jessie's face in the stubborn set of Tom's jaw, that same urge to walk away when she probed a little too deep into sensitive areas. At least now she knew Jessie came by her bull-headedness honestly.

"I wouldn't dream of telling you how to parent your daughter," Andrea said carefully. "I just thought—" She bit back the lecture, changed course. "What are you planning for the weekend? What needs to get done? Besides feeding and mucking."

His gaze narrowed, as if he suspected a trick. "The tack room needs to be cleared out and reorganized. I have to replace a tie post the colt broke. And the stall fronts in the barn need painting."

"Then we'll help you."

He stared at her as if she'd grown a second head. "Help me? You and Jessie?"

She nodded, warming to the plan. "I know it might take you a little longer if Jessie's giving you a hand.

But I can supervise her so you can still get everything done. And she'll love it.''

He laughed. ''Are we talking about the same person? Jessie has never met a chore she didn't hate.''

''It won't be the chores she'll love.''

Andrea held her breath, waiting for Tom's response. His dubious expression, the tension in his jaw told her he wanted to say no. She put up a hand to stop him although he hadn't said a word.

''Wait,'' she said, then moved to the kitchen door. She shouted up the stairs, ''Jessie! Come down a minute.''

After the blow-up between them earlier, Andrea wondered if the nine-year-old would deign to answer her summons. But after a few moment's silence, she heard Jessie's door open and cautious footsteps on the stairs.

Andrea stepped back, gesturing Jessie into the kitchen. Jessie looked from Andrea to her father, worry creasing her brow. No doubt she figured Andrea had told Tom about the trouble they'd had earlier and thought she was about to be punished.

''Yeah?'' Jessie scowled. ''What do you want?''

''Your dad's got quite a few chores to do around here this weekend,'' Andrea told her.

Jessie crossed her arms over her middle. ''So, what else is new?''

''So, he could use a little help,'' Andrea said as casually as she could. ''I thought I might give him a hand and wondered if you wanted to join us.''

A smile flashed on Jessie's face for a heartbeat, then she squelched it. ''Maybe,'' she said, sounding almost bored. ''If the chores aren't too stupid.''

Andrea glanced over at Tom. He seemed torn between bemusement and amazement that his daughter would voluntarily consider doing chores. Andrea winked at him and she could see him hold back laughter.

Andrea quickly listed the work that had to be done. Jessie nodded, still cool and aloof. "I could probably do that. Yeah, I'll help."

Andrea felt like pumping a fist in triumph. "What time do you think we should start?"

Jessie made a face. "Early, I guess. Trixie gets mad if she doesn't get her breakfast right on time."

"Then I'll make sure I start our breakfast early. Pancakes okay?"

Jessie struggled against another smile. The three days they'd homeschooled, Jessie had dragged herself out of bed so late, there was only time for cold cereal before they started their lessons. "I guess pancakes would be all right." She backed a step toward the door. "Is that all?"

"Just one thing," Andrea said and Jessie's gaze shot toward her father again. "We won't have to take the bus to Sacramento next week. Your dad will drive us."

Jessie's smile lit her face with the brilliance of the rising sun. "Great! That's good. I mean, the bus would've been fun, but Dad's truck…" She turned to her father and said breathlessly, "Thanks," before she ran from the kitchen and up the stairs.

Tom just stared for a moment, then he turned to Andrea. "How did you do that?"

"It's not what I did. It was you giving her a chance to be with you."

"I never thought…" He looked away, then back at her. "Thanks."

With his intense gaze on her, Andrea felt his gratitude clear to her toes.

* * *

Saturday morning dawned almost too beautiful to be real. From the moment Tom opened the blinds in his bedroom to the soft light of spring, he could feel a specialness to the day. The world seemed to hold its breath as sunrise revealed it—the shimmering green of the pasture grass, the brilliant white of snow still capping the Sierras, the pale-blue sky growing more vivid as the sun edged up.

Then as he'd headed for the barn to feed the horses, he'd caught his first sight of Andrea as she descended the stairs from her apartment. She'd seemed less real than the day, with her long dark hair still damp from her shower and her sweet smile filling him with a warm pleasure.

When he'd gone back inside for breakfast—jaggedy shaped pancakes Jessie had made herself—he didn't want to speak out of fear words would somehow spoil the day. He'd been more than a little concerned that despite Jessie's promise to help, she would bail on him when the hard work began.

But it seemed he'd worried for nothing. At Andrea's suggestion, he'd written down the list of chores and presented it to Jessie to let her pick which one they'd do first. To his surprise she'd chosen the replacement of the tie post, the hardest job.

They'd worked side by side digging out the concrete base of the old post. He'd used a pickax to loosen the dirt and she'd scooped it out with a garden trowel. He thought for sure they'd be there forever digging out that old broken post when Andrea suggested Jessie take a break and help her mix up some lemonade. By the time they'd returned with the frosty glasses, Tom had the post stump and concrete base pulled from the ground.

Now as the sun crept up to midmorning, Tom stood beside the replacement post while Jessie shoveled concrete into the hole at the post's base. Jessie had cement smeared on one cheek and more concrete scattered on the ground than in the post hole, but damned if she wasn't having a great time. And Tom had to admit, he hadn't had so much fun with chores since he was a boy, working alongside his own father.

It was all Andrea's doing. She'd worked some magic to motivate his stubborn daughter into a willing partner in today's chores. He was pretty certain that if he'd been the one to ask Jessie for a hand yesterday, not only would she have refused, she would have made a big noisy scene in the process.

Or would she? That brief look of joy on Jessie's face when Andrea had told his daughter he'd needed her help still tugged on his heart. He tried to remember the last time he'd asked Jessie to work with him. He recalled dimly that she used to tag along with him everywhere when she was four and five. Lori was often gone for hours at a time and Jessie was just too young to be left alone.

Then Jessie had burned her arm and everything changed. At first he'd been so overwhelmed by guilt and grief, he had to put some emotional space between himself and his daughter or he'd go mad. Then the physical aspects of Jessie's care consumed him—the hospital stays, the doctor visits. By the time they'd gotten some normalcy back into their lives, he had no idea how to rebuild his relationship with Jessie.

Somehow it'd seemed easier to hire old Mrs. Keller from town to keep an eye on Jessie during the day. When it became too much for the elderly woman early this school year, Tom had let her go, assuming Jessie was old enough to stay in the house by herself while he was out working the ranch.

He heard the front door shut and looked over his shoulder to watch Andrea as she approached with three more glasses of lemonade. Some of her dark hair had escaped from her braid, the silky strands framing her face. Her white tank top, tucked into worn denim jeans, shaped every curve, bared her shoulders temptingly. He wondered how warm her skin would feel.

"Dad?"

Andrea smiled as she neared, then set down the glasses on a wooden bench he'd set up beside the barn. She picked up one glass and offered it to him. A faint smile still curved her lips and he wondered if they tasted of lemonade.

"Dad!"

His head snapped back to Jessie. She leaned on her shovel, her head tipped up toward him. She thrust out her lower lip. "You're not listening."

"Sorry." He took the lemonade from Andrea with a brusque nod of thanks. "What did you want?"

"Is that enough?" Jessie poked the concrete piled high around the post with the shovel.

"That's plenty." He gulped down half the lemonade and handed the glass back to Andrea without looking at her. Then he grabbed his level and laid it along the post to make sure the braces hadn't shifted. "Looks good. We just need to crown the concrete and we're done."

As he bent to show Jessie how to smooth the top of the concrete, he glanced up at Andrea. She gripped his lemonade glass in both hands, her gaze fixed on the icy contents. When she set his glass aside, he could swear she was blushing. That he might have been the cause sent a shiver through him. Then he gave himself a mental kick in the pants for letting his imagination run away with him like that.

He rose and brushed off his hands. "We'll leave it until tomorrow, then pull off the braces."

"What's next?" Jessie asked.

"You tell me." Tom took off the ball cap shading his eyes and swiped the sweat off his forehead. "Where's the list?"

"I gave it to Andy," Jessie said. "For safekeeping."

Andrea rubbed her hands on her jeans, then pulled the folded paper from her back pocket. With a wink for Tom, she handed the list to Jessie.

Jessie studied the list as if it were the Rosetta stone. "Let's see…" A loud bang from the barn brought Jessie's head back up. She turned to him. "Sounds like Trixie's done with her breakfast. Can I turn her out in pasture before we do the next thing?"

"Sure. Go ahead."

Handing the list back to Andrea, Jessie raced for the barn. Tom could hear the chink of Trixie's halter and Jessie's high voice as she talked to her pony.

"I ought to turn out Sonuvagun and the colt," he told Andrea.

Andrea slipped the list back into her pocket. "Can I help?"

For a moment all Tom could think about was the way Andrea's jeans hugged her backside. He shoved his cap back on his head. "The colt's a handful, but Sonuvagun's a good old boy. You can lead him out."

They passed Jessie and Trixie as they went inside the barn. Heads hanging out of the stall fronts, the gelding and colt watched as they approached. The five pregnant mares, awkward and heavy with their precious foals, just flicked an ear in passing interest.

Andrea headed over to the first mare's stall and peeked inside. She glanced back over her shoulder at Tom, her eyes wide with amazement. "She's huge."

Tom moved up beside her. "This close to foaling, they have a tough time getting comfortable."

She was so close, Tom would only need to lean slightly to his right and their arms would brush. He could see if her skin felt as warm as it looked.

"Poor thing. When is she due?"

Wisps of hair framed Andrea's face, begging him to smooth them back. She turned to him, her expression expectant, and for a crazy moment he wondered if she wanted him to kiss her. Without conscious will, his head tipped down toward her as her gaze locked with his.

Then her question registered and he took a step away from her. "Any time in the next couple of weeks. I'll likely be sleeping in the barn pretty soon." He crossed the barn aisle to Sonuvagun's stall, grabbed the gelding's halter. "Let's get these horses turned out."

As he buckled the halter on, Tom kept his back to Andrea, then handed her the lead rope without much more than a quick glance to be sure she had a good grip on it. A brief explanation of how to lead a horse from the left side, then he went for the fractious colt. He didn't let himself think about how Andrea might have interpreted that slight dip of his head.

But for the rest of the workday, even as he mucked out stalls and dealt with his overtired daughter's crankiness, his mind returned again and again to that same image. Andrea's gaze locked with his, her face turned up to him, her lips parted in invitation.

Chapter Five

Tom had just set the colt loose in the round pen Monday morning when he heard Jessie's first scream. He dropped the colt's halter and lead rope and made for the gate, unlatching and latching it again in record time.

Jessie's second scream blasted from the house as he ran pell-mell across the yard, but what he heard made him slow his pace, not speed it up. He knew that sound—it was rage and defiance, not pain or fear. He'd nearly slowed to a walk by the time he reached the front porch steps and it was just as well. He was able to jump back just as hurricane Jessie exploded from the front door, hurled herself down the steps and raced toward the pasture with one last rebellious, "No!"

Tom was still frozen on the top step when Andrea appeared in the doorway. Her face set and determined, she took a deep breath, then pushed open the screen door. She glanced his way without missing stride as she made a beeline for the pasture.

Tom descended the stairs after her. "Wait." She didn't slow. "Andrea, wait."

He took her arm, the first time he'd let himself be so close to her since the workday began. He let go quickly, not about to give himself the chance to enjoy the feel of her skin. She immediately moved on, headed straight for Jessie, now standing out in knee-high grass beside her grazing pony.

Just as Andrea reached the pasture fence, Tom tried again. "Come on, leave her be."

Andrea whirled toward him. "Leave her be? She just threw her writing book across the room. Flat out refused to do the assignment I gave her. Not to mention screamed in my face."

Turning back to the fence, she bent to squeeze between the rails. Tom grabbed her arm again. "Andrea."

She straightened and glared at him until he let go of her arm. But at least she stayed put.

Tom looked out over the pasture at Jessie. One arm slung over her pony's back, she leaned against Trixie. Head down, shoulders hunched, Jessie looked beaten down and in a world of hurt.

"What was the assignment?" Tom asked.

"I asked her to write a paragraph. One paragraph."

Now Tom understood. "She hates to write."

"So I've gathered," Andrea said wryly.

"It's hard for her. To hold the pen, to write the letters."

"Unless she's using the pen to draw a picture of her horse."

It was nothing more than the truth, but Tom felt compelled to defend his daughter. "That's different."

Andrea stepped closer, head tipped back to look up at him. "How?"

Now there wasn't much more than a foot between them. He'd done so well the last few days keeping his distance from her. But his attraction for her pulled him constantly, more inexorable than gravity.

She was so close. It wouldn't take any effort at all to stretch out his fingers and brush her hand. Or he could bend down ever so slightly and press his lips against her silky hair.

"How is it different?"

Andrea's question brought him out of his daze, back to his senses. He dragged his gaze from Andrea and back to Jessie out in the pasture. His daughter scrubbed furiously at her face as if wiping away tears.

He felt low and despicable, fantasizing about Andrea when he ought to be thinking of his daughter and her interests.

"Tom?" Andrea pressed.

Jessie looked up at that moment and her gaze flicked from him to Andrea, then back to him. She knew they were talking about her.

Placing a hand lightly on Andrea's shoulder, he schooled himself against his predictable reaction as he urged her away from the pasture fence. They walked past the barn and toward the round pen, out of Jessie's line of sight.

The sorrel colt wandered the round pen, his nose in the dust. The colt's head shot up when they approached and he ambled toward them.

He ought to be working the colt, not arguing with Andrea. He ought to be doing just about anything besides finding excuses to be with her, to touch her.

Tom leaned against the pipe panel of the round pen.

"You have to understand how much pain Jessie's had to endure."

Andrea stood beside him, slender back against the metal pipe, shoulder nearly brushing his arm. "Of course it hasn't been easy for her."

Her voice seemed to tease his ear, her innocuous words somehow sensual. Tom shook his head, startling the colt who'd come up beside him. The two-year-old stud took off bucking and kicking, proclaiming his virility with an arched neck and raised tail.

Tom felt a little like the colt just then, as wrong-headed as those feelings might be. Resolute, he returned his focus on Jessie. "After the fire it took her months to learn to use her right hand again."

Andrea sighed, the sound seeming to brush along his spine. "But you can't let her get away with murder."

Get away with murder? Anger burst inside him, washing away the soft, dangerous feelings. Andrea might as well have chucked a bucket of ice water over his head.

"What the hell are you talking about?"

"Her table manners are atrocious. She mouths off at every opportunity. And you know how she ignores her chores."

Heat rose in his face. "She's been doing her chores."

"She mucks out stalls, does the evening feeding— anything to be around the horses. But clean her room? Clear the breakfast table?"

A little tug of guilt started up inside him. He thought of all the times he'd cleaned up after Jessie because it was easier than nagging her. "She deserves a break once in a while. Especially with writing, when it's so hard for her."

"She has to write. There's no getting around it."

Andrea pushed away from the round pen rail, paced in front of him. "And you have to let things be hard for her sometimes."

He shook his head, wishing he could shake off Andrea's cool logic as easily. "I can't stand to see her struggle."

She stilled, put her hand on his arm. "I know. Because you love her. Because she's been hurt. But don't you see? You'll hurt her more letting her have her way."

Andrea's touch sent a warmth up his arm, the sensation both comforting and arousing. He wanted to pull away, to hold her close. He wished he could change the past so that Jessie was never burned and alter the future so she would never feel pain.

In that moment he did the wisest thing—he backed away from Andrea to give himself some breathing space. "You're the teacher. You do what you think is best." He ducked through the rails of the round pen. "I have work to do."

He picked the halter up from the dirt where he'd dropped it and buckled it out of the way on the rail. Andrea still stood there, looking as if she wanted to say more. Tom turned his back on her. Facing the colt, he sent the young horse galloping around the pen.

They hadn't settled a thing.

Andrea dawdled by the round pen gate as Tom worked the colt, considering whether she should try to continue the discussion. He'd acknowledged her authority as teacher, had as much as given her free rein. But he had no intention of changing his own interaction with Jessie. Which would mean the nine-year-old would live by two sets of rules—Andrea's firm, her father's lax.

As Tom stopped the colt in its tracks with a subtle motion of his hand, then sent it careening in the other direction, Andrea realized he enforced a tougher code of discipline with his horses than he did his own daughter. Not that he let Jessie run slipshod. But little girls were slippery things, much more difficult to understand than horses. And smart little girls like Jessie knew all the tricks for getting her way—with sugar on the good days and spit and vinegar on the bad ones.

With a sigh, Andrea turned away from the round pen and headed for the pasture. If she wasn't so mixed up inside about Tom, if she wasn't burning for him one moment and aching for him the next, she might be able to get through to him. She'd had these discussion with parents in the past, advising them of behavior problems, recommending courses of action. She'd done her best with Tom, but when he was close to her, she couldn't think and all her reasoned arguments jumbled inside her.

She ducked through the pasture fence rails and walked through the thick grass toward Jessie. For now, she'd deal with the daughter. As complex as the workings of Jessie's mind were, she was a simpler problem to unravel than Tom.

Jessie's expression turned mulish as Andrea reached her side. Andrea ignored the sour look. "You have three choices," Andrea told the little girl. "Write the paragraph yourself. Dictate the words to me and I'll write them down. Or use your dad's computer."

"And if I don't?"

Andrea was ready for that response. "You don't ride

your pony. Not today, not tomorrow. Not until you write the paragraph.''

Jessie's jaw dropped in indignation. ''Dad won't—''

''Dad will. I'm the teacher. I make the teaching decisions.''

Andrea held her breath, waiting for Jessie's next argument. The little girl stared down at her feet, hidden in the tall grass. When she finally answered, Andrea could barely hear her. ''All right,'' she muttered. Then she stomped across the pasture back toward the house.

Her spine was as straight as her father's, just as stiffened with pride and stubbornness. There was nothing easy or soft about either Jarret.

Watching Jessie slip through the fence rails, Andrea felt a warmth spread inside her. The toughies always caught her heart the quickest. The affectionate kids, the ones generous with hugs and kisses were appealing, but the lost and hard-edged children never failed to move her.

As she followed Jessie toward the house, she glanced over at Tom, still in the round pen. There was an edge to him as well, not as sharp, but even more dangerous than his daughter's. If she let him, Tom Jarret would steal her heart, too.

By Thursday morning, Tom was worried Jessie would make herself sick with excitement. Between the prospect of a trip to the capitol and a day devoted to her friend Sabrina, Jessie couldn't stay still long enough to eat her breakfast, let alone brush her hair or get her shoes on and tied. When she knotted her laces and couldn't work them free, she nearly blew up like a spooky colt until Andrea suggested she wear sandals.

He might be better at hiding it, but he felt just as

prickly as his daughter. The moment Andrea swung herself up into the cab of his truck and sat beside him on the bench seat, the very air seemed ready to explode. Even when both girls were in the back seat, chattering like magpies, Tom's awareness of Andrea scraped along every nerve.

As they reached Interstate 80 and headed west to Sacramento, the girls quieted down, coloring books open on their laps, shared crayons on the floor between them. In the silence, Tom wondered if Andrea could hear his pounding heartbeat in the small space of the truck cab. It was all he could do to keep his hands on the wheel instead of reaching for her.

He could feel her gaze on him, but he resolutely kept his focus on his driving. Her soft voice, however, was impossible to ignore. "Are you worried about the mares?"

He gave himself permission to glance over at her, then dragged his gaze back to the road. "I've got my cell. Jim will call if they start showing signs." He'd arranged to have one of the local high school kids keep watch on the mares for the day. Irritation still lodged in his gut over how Jim had given Andrea the once-over.

"They usually foal at night, though, right?"

Why was her voice so damned sweet? He tightened his hands on the steering wheel. "Yeah, they do."

Jessie leaned forward in her seat. "But Trixie had her baby out in pasture, right smack-dab in the middle of the day. By the time we called Sabrina's dad, Trixie was all done." Sabrina's father was the local vet.

"I shouldn't have dragged you out today." Andrea turned toward him, the motion bringing her infinitesimally closer to him. "We could have waited until the mares foaled."

Her scent drifted toward him, like a beckoning finger urging him to follow it to its source. Hell, he had to get a grip on himself or he'd be bonkers by the end of the day.

He cranked up the fan on the AC, hot under the collar despite the relatively cool spring day. Andrea still gazed up at him, no doubt waiting for a response.

He breathed in the refrigerated air, and his head cleared a bit. "I checked all the mares this morning. None of them were showing any signs."

He was just patting himself on the back, congratulating himself for reclaiming his good sense, when Andrea gave his arm a squeeze. "Look!"

He tugged his arm away to break the contact, then peered out the window to where she pointed. A bald eagle soared above them alongside the highway, flanked by a pair of red-tailed hawks. The hawks were good-sized birds, but the eagle dwarfed them.

Her voice was soft with wonder. "That's so amazing." She turned in her seat. "Jessie did you see?"

The girls started up their chatter again as they searched the sky for the eagle. Sabrina spotted it out the back window of the truck, and she and Jessie followed the bird's path until the curves of Interstate 80 took them out of sight.

A smile of pleasure still lit Andrea's face. "Thanks."

He glanced over at her. "I didn't put the eagle there."

"No, but…" She laughed. "Thanks anyway."

Tom felt something tighten in his chest. Andrea managed to pull him every direction all at once, without even trying. She'd turned him inside out in little more than a week's time spent with them. What would she do to him by the end of the school year?

Damned if he didn't look forward to finding out.

* * *

Keeping one eye on the girls playing hide-and-seek amongst the stone pines of Capitol Park, Andrea gathered up the trash from their bag lunches and tossed it into a nearby garbage can. A couple hours touring the capitol building, visiting the State Senate and Assembly rooms and the county displays, was about all the girls could stand before begging to stop for lunch. They'd bought sodas and cookies from the basement cafeteria to supplement the lunches they'd brought and headed outside to enjoy the exquisite spring day.

Andrea sat on a nearby concrete bench and lifted her legs to sit cross-legged. She'd felt such a lightness inside her since she'd seen the eagle soaring overhead on Interstate 80. In all the traveling she'd done throughout California and the surrounding states, she'd never seen anything like it.

But it wasn't just the eagle that filled her with a bubbling joy. It was the man she'd shared it with, the man who dominated her thoughts, jumbled her emotions. It was a delightful confusion that left her breathless.

And yet… Two years ago she'd felt the same way about a man—excited, edgy with anticipation. Her heart ready to burst from her chest. She'd surrendered to those feelings, and made choices that had led her to disaster.

Another quick check on Jessie and Sabrina, then she scanned the park for Tom's return. When the girls had tired of wearing their backpacks, he'd offered to put them back in the truck. The parking garage was just around the corner up 10th Street.

Jessie caught sight of him before Andrea did and ran excitedly toward him through the trees, Sabrina on her heels. As he bent to listen to what his daughter had to say, Andrea could see him search the park, no doubt looking for her.

He straightened when he found her and headed toward her. Jessie and Sabrina raced on ahead.

Out of breath, Jessie grabbed Andrea's hand, pulling her to her feet. "Dad said we could go to Old Sac."

"Old Sacramento," Tom clarified. "If you don't mind."

She only minded that when he was near, she couldn't put two thoughts together. She didn't like how much she enjoyed his company, how much pleasure it brought her to be with him.

She shrugged, wishing she could shrug off her fascination for him as easily. "Okay with me."

His gaze narrowed, as if he'd heard the hesitation in her tone. "We could do it another time."

Jessie tugged at her father's arm. "No, now! Today!"

One look from Tom quelled Jessie's demand. Her lower lip thrust out, she turned away, arms crossed over her chest.

Tom brushed Andrea's shoulder with his fingertips. "It's an easy walk from here."

Why did he have to touch her? Despite the briefness of the contact, although he'd certainly meant nothing by it, her body reacted as if he'd touched her with passion.

She took a deep breath to still her trembling. "Why not? Sounds like fun."

Jessie whooped and did a little dance, then she and Sabrina raced for the corner of 10th and L Street. Tom shouted out after them, "Don't cross the street without us!" With another light touch on Andrea's shoulder, Tom urged her to follow the girls.

He sighed, hands shoved into his jeans pockets. "Sometimes that little girl makes me crazy."

The daughter was a safer topic of conversation than the father. Focusing on Jessie to keep her mind off Tom seemed a wise course. "Her emotions do seem all over the map at times."

They reached the corner where the impatient girls waited for them. The moment the light turned green, Jessie and Sabrina flew across the street. The girls slowed once they'd reached the other side, impeded by the lunchtime downtown crowd.

As she and Tom followed, Andrea made sure she kept Jessie and Sabrina in sight as the girls navigated the busy sidewalk. "What was she like...before?"

"Before the fire?" He said it matter-of-factly. "She was—" he let out a long, slow breath "—softer. Happier. More energy than you'd ever expect in one little girl."

They reached K Street and turned left, then continued along the pedestrian mall. "She hasn't lost the energy," Andrea said.

"No." Tom took her arm briefly to steer her around a pack of teenagers. "But now she seems to focus it all toward being angry."

A light rail train glided up the center of K Street and pulled up at a stop. Passengers entered and exited the train.

Jessie dashed toward them at a dead run. "Can we take the train, Daddy?"

"Maybe on the way back."

Jessie glowered at Tom and mutiny threatened to erupt. Then Sabrina reminded her that the toy store was just up ahead and Jessie skipped off with her friend again.

"It's really okay to say no sometimes," Andrea said.

"I know." He shook his head with impatience. "Of course, I know. Before, it was easier. I was the tough one, the one who laid down the law. It was her mother—"

He cut off the word as if it tasted foul in his mouth. His face was set and Andrea knew he wouldn't continue unless she pressed him. The storm brewing in his eyes almost forestalled her, but she wanted to understand what was tearing at this family.

Because of Jessie. Because she'd do a better job as a teacher if she comprehended what went on beneath the surface. Not because at times her heart ached for Tom and the pain he still wrestled with.

"What about Jessie's mother?" she prompted.

He didn't want to answer. For a moment Andrea saw the same nascent mutiny in Tom's face. They were two of a kind, one wounded by fire, the other by guilt.

"Lori treated Jessie like a little doll," he said finally. "She'd dress her up, fix her hair. Jessie loved it."

They reached the enclosed Downtown Plaza and slowed as the crowd thickened. "It's hard to imagine Jessie enjoying dress-up."

"She was Lori's pretty little girl. Jessie put up with the lace and frills just for the chance to be with her mother."

A look at her father for permission and Jessie went inside the toy store with Sabrina. Andrea and Tom waited outside, watching the girls through the shop windows.

"And then…?" Andrea prodded.

"And then, the fire," Tom said, his voice bitter. "And Jessie wasn't pretty anymore. At least according to Lori."

Andrea gasped, appalled. "She didn't tell Jessie that."

"No. She was self-centered and vain, but Lori had at least that much heart." He laughed, a harsh sound. "She kept it to herself. But Lori knew that what she'd done…"

Jessie raced up to them, a toy train in one hand, a hot pink yo-yo in the other. "I want these, Daddy."

Tom stared down at his daughter, looking a bit lost. He didn't want to say yes, but he couldn't say no.

Andrea didn't think—she just jumped in. "Pick one."

Jessie glared at her. "What?"

Andrea stood her ground. "Pick one toy to buy and put the other one away."

"You don't get to decide," Jessie said with a toss of her head. "My dad does."

Tom took both toys from Jessie's hands. "You heard Andrea. You get one, or none."

Jessie simmered like a volcano, outrage plain on her face.

But Tom didn't wait for the explosion. "None, then." He stepped inside the store. "I'll just put these away."

"No!" Jessie shouted. "I want the train!"

"Fine." Tom turned back to Jessie. "Put the yo-yo away while I pay for this." He handed her back the toy.

Jessie stared at her father as if he'd grown a second head. Then she tossed her head and said huffily, "Come on, Sabrina." The girls made their way back to where they'd found the yo-yo.

Tom watched her go. "You always seem to get it right."

Andrea knew better. "Only sometimes."

* * *

In the end, Tom bought two toys—the train for Jessie and a stuffed pony for Sabrina. When Jessie asked him if he'd buy the toy for Sabrina, Tom glanced over at Andrea, then felt a little foolish looking to her for permission. But he was beginning to realize Andrea was right—he was no good at saying no to Jessie.

In Old Sac, the girls ran themselves ragged, dashing from store to store and talking a mile a minute. Jessie wanted treats from every candy shop, but Tom had enough sense to know what that much fudge would do to his high-energy daughter. The worst crisis came when the usually unflappable Sabrina burst into tears when she realized she'd lost her pony. Jessie demanded he buy Sabrina another one right away. Andrea saved the day when she found the stuffed toy back in the last candy shop they'd visited.

When Jessie clamored for a ride in one of the horse-drawn carriages that ambled through town, Tom was more than willing. He was more exhausted following two nine-year-old girls around Old Sac than he'd ever been working colts all day.

When they settled into the carriage, the girls sat up front with the driver, and Tom helped Andrea into one of the seats in the back. They sat opposite each other in the sideways facing seats, Andrea's knees brushing his in the small space. The girls' lightning-pace chatter, the driver's memorized spiel describing points of interest in Old Sac, the clatter of hoofbeats on cobblestone all faded in the close intimacy of the carriage.

He knew he shouldn't stare, but with her nearly in his lap, almost close enough to kiss, he couldn't seem to tear his gaze away. One of her knees had ended up between his and he struggled with the urge to run his hand up along her leg, to feel how warm she was beneath her denim jeans. Almost as if she'd read his mind, color rose in her cheeks and she shifted away from him. Her knee bumped his as she slid toward the front of the carriage and put a bit of space between them.

He wanted to pull her back toward him, but instead forced himself to scoot toward the rear of the carriage. He groped for a safe topic of conversation. "Think we ought to have dinner before we head back?"

He heard the edginess in her voice when she answered. "I don't know if the girls are hungry after all that candy."

The kind of hungry he felt would get him into trouble. He flexed his hands, trying to shake off the tension. "Traffic's bad this time of day. It'd be better to wait before driving back."

"Then dinner's fine." She locked her fingers in her lap. "I'm sure the girls will eat something."

Every word she said seemed to have a double meaning, seemed to answer an entirely different, unasked question. His mind kept suggesting interpretations of their innocent conversation that kited off into far too intimate territory.

He'd ridden unbroken colts that had given him a smoother ride. If the carriage tour didn't end soon, he'd have Andrea in his arms, his mouth on hers.

The instant the carriage pulled to a stop, he was on his feet. Andrea rose at the same time he did, then swayed a bit when the driver climbed down and rocked the carriage. He had to reach for her to steady her; it would have been rude not to give her a hand. But when his fingers wrapped around her hand, the carriage jostled again as the girls descended and Tom pulled her almost into his arms.

Her hands flew up to his chest as she sought her balance. Her fingers pressed into his skin through the thin knit of his T-shirt and he gulped in a breath. She didn't step back immediately, just tipped her head back and gazed up at him. In that moment, he knew he'd lost every shred of willpower to resist kissing her.

He should have been grateful when Jessie hollered up at him to come on. It was absolutely the right thing for Andrea to pull away and let the driver help her down. Kissing Andrea was absolutely, positively the wrong thing to do.

But he couldn't help but wish he'd gotten at least one little taste.

Chapter Six

Andrea stared at the stout bay mare standing patiently in the round pen and gave serious consideration to turning around and heading back to the house. When she'd first agreed with Tom that learning to ride was a great idea, she hadn't thought through just how big a horse was and how far off the ground she'd be when she climbed into that saddle. Now, stepping into the stirrup seemed an impossible task.

"Need a leg up?" Tom asked, standing too close behind her.

Since the field trip two days ago, Andrea's awareness of Tom had intensified, until she could focus on little else. That moment in the carriage replayed in her head like an endlessly looping movie clip—her hands spread across his chest, his heat seeping into her palms, Tom with his head bent down…

Thank God Jessie had interrupted. Another moment,

and she would have thrown her arms around him, let him kiss her.

If that was what he'd intended at all. Maybe that look on his face was only surprise when she touched him. Maybe he was only helping her keep her balance in the carriage.

It didn't matter to her imagination what Tom really intended to do. Fantasies had taken root in her mind, pulled and teased her every time she and Tom were in the same room. Thankfully, Tom spent most of Jessie's school time outside or Friday's lessons would have been nonsense.

Andrea returned her focus to the placid mare. The bay horse stood stolidly in the center of the round pen, waiting for her to climb into the saddle. Although Tom maintained a polite distance between them, her nerves jangled with expectation that he might touch her.

Andrea took a quick look over her shoulder at Jessie, who sat with her friend Sabrina on the front porch steps. Sabrina had spent the morning with Jessie and now the girls waited for Sabrina's mother to take them over to their house for the afternoon. Which would leave her and Tom alone for hours.

Don't think about that, Andrea told herself. Think about the horse. Think about climbing into the saddle.

She lifted her left foot as high as she could, but somehow her jitters made those last few inches up to the stirrup an impossible stretch. She tried to hike her leg up higher, but that made her sway. She grabbed the back of the saddle just as Tom put a hand on her shoulder to steady her.

He had to stop doing that. Stop being so courteous. He should have stepped back in the carriage, let her fall to the floor. He should have let her land in the dust at the mare's feet. No more helping hands. No more touching.

But even as she thought that, he'd bent and put his hands around the calf of her right leg. "Bend your leg, I'll help you up."

Without thinking, she did as she was told, her right hand going to his shoulder for security as he straightened and lifted her level with the horse. She had only to move her left toe slightly forward to slip it into the stirrup. She swung her right leg over the saddle and there she sat, secure on the sleepy mare.

She clutched the saddle horn, still feeling the imprint of Tom's fingers on her right leg. "Now what?" Her voice broke a little between the two words.

Tom lifted the leather reins from the mare's neck. "Take these."

She took the loop of leather from him with her right hand, still keeping a death grip on the saddle horn with her left. "Okay. Now what?"

"It's hard to believe you've never been on a horse." Tom's smile scrambled her brains, the light in his blue eyes wiping away every shred of common sense.

She struggled to regain a modicum of equilibrium. "I've spent more time in the city than out in the country."

"Even cities have riding stables." He nudged her leg out of the way and pulled on the strap that tightened the cinch. "Even people who don't know one end of a horse from the other have gone out on trail rides."

"Not me." And as she looked down at the dirt under the mare's feet, she saw one good reason she'd never climbed on a horse. She was too darn far off the ground.

"Hang tight," Tom said as he walked away.

Panic flared up inside Andrea. He wasn't going to

just leave her alone in the round pen, was he? She watched his broad back retreating. The mare huffed out a long sigh.

What looked like a long dog leash was draped over the round pen rail. Tom grabbed it and headed back toward her.

He clipped the end of the long leash on the mare's bit. "Sweetpea is about the quietest horse on the place. But we'll be a little extra safe and put her on the lunge line."

Tom stepped back, clucking with his tongue as he paid out the lunge line. The mare plodded off, her head low, her ears limp on either side of her head.

For the first several steps, Andrea strangled the saddle horn with both hands, the reins gripped tight. But the mare didn't do anything scary, so she let go of the tension in her muscles, bit by bit.

"That's right, relax," Tom urged her. "Just let your body move with the horse."

She did as he suggested, allowing her hips to match the mare's motion. Keeping a firm grip on the reins, she took her left hand off the saddle horn and let her right hand rest there lightly, just in case.

"I'm going to urge her to move out a little bit," Tom said from the center of the ring. "I want her to walk a little faster."

Another cluck and the mare quickened her pace. Andrea tensed and the mare slowed. Swallowing against her fear, Andrea relaxed and the mare moved along freely.

Sabrina's mother pulled in just then and the girls raced toward the car. After settling Jessie and Sabrina in the back seat, Mrs. Fox called out, "I'll bring Jessie back after dinner." Tom waved in response, then Mrs. Fox pulled out.

Leaving her and Tom alone. Without realizing it, Andrea tightened her legs on the horse and the mare began to trot. Andrea grabbed the saddle horn in a panic.

"You're fine," Tom said soothingly. "Pull back on the reins and sit deep in the saddle."

She followed his instructions and Sweetpea immediately slowed to a stop. She grinned over at Tom, exhilarated that the mare had responded to her. "That was fun."

His smile back at her bounced her insides around more than the horse had. "Ready to try a jog on purpose?"

She couldn't answer, couldn't pull her gaze from his. The excitement that had simmered inside her since the field trip to Old Sac threatened to bubble up, spill over whatever barriers she'd tried to use to contain it.

If she answered Tom yes, what was she agreeing to? Conquering her fears on horseback or accepting the sharp attraction between them? She could almost see an answer in the single-minded focus on Tom's face.

Her response came out in a whisper. "Yes."

She let her gaze linger on Tom only a moment more, then squeezed the mare lightly with her legs. The horse moved off at an easy jog, bouncing her only slightly in the saddle.

"Lean back a little," Tom coaxed. "Let your hips move along with her."

Andrea released the tension in her back, let her spine rock with Sweetpea's motion. Acutely cognizant of Tom's presence in the middle of the round pen, she forced herself to center her awareness on the horse between her legs.

She fixed her gaze on the mare's black-tipped mahogany ears, on the leather reins clutched in her hands, on the warmth of the sun on the back of her neck. Each time she was tempted to turn and look at Tom, to slide from the horse's back and into his arms, she returned her focus on the mare.

Tom's soft voice drifted toward her. "You're one animal. Those are your legs moving across the ground, one heart beating inside you both."

Tom's words and the mare's gentle pace mesmerized her. She released her hold on the saddle horn, let her hand rest on her thigh. So many of the little girls she'd taught had been enthralled by horses, would talk about them endlessly, drew picture after picture. Now she understood their fascination.

"Ready to try a lope?" Tom asked.

Sweetpea flicked her ear toward him just as Andrea glanced his way. She nodded and took hold of the saddle horn again.

"Touch her with your outside leg," Tom said. "The one nearest the rail."

Andrea did and Sweetpea stepped into a rocking chair lope. Accustomed to the gait within a few strides, Andrea let go of the saddle horn. As the sweet spring air brushed her cheeks, she remembered the fanciful image she'd created the morning she'd first seen Tom. Now she could fill in all the details—the feel of the horse thundering across the meadow, the cowboy sitting behind her with his arms wrapped around her.

Except it wasn't an anonymous cowboy anymore. It was Tom, and she knew what his touch felt like, how his heat soaked into her body when he stood near her. Her fantasy couldn't hold a candle to what she knew the reality would be.

"Pull her up," Tom said, pulling her from her thoughts.

A light tug on the reins and Sweetpea slowed to a jog, then a walk, before halting. Tom walked toward her and unclipped the lunge line. He wrapped up the line and hung it on the fence, then returned to Sweetpea's side.

He rested one hand on the mare's withers, and tipped his head back to look at her. "Ready to try it without a net?"

All she could think about was how close his hand was to her leg, how easy would be for him to stroke his fingers along her thigh. Annoyed with her rampant fantasies, she shifted in the saddle, startling Sweetpea. The mare tensed and threw her head up, throwing Tom's hand off the withers.

"Maybe next time," Andrea said breathlessly. "I think I'm ready to get off."

He backed away so she could swing her leg over the horse. She slid to the ground, then handed him the reins.

"I should go. Your sister and I are going over to Marbleville for some shopping."

She took a step away from him, but his steady stare stopped her as surely as the reins had halted the mare. It might as well have been her wearing Sweetpea's bridle. Tom only needed to lock his gaze with hers and she would follow him anywhere.

Tension strung itself between them, knotting Andrea's insides, urging her closer to Tom. She edged nearer to him without even realizing it, until they were nearly toe to toe. Her exquisite awareness of him sharpened, heightened, grew in brilliance. He dropped the reins and let the obedient mare stand on her own, then closed the distance between them.

His hands cupped her shoulders, burning her through her T-shirt. She thought she'd die if he didn't kiss her. She could almost feel his gaze on her lips as a tangible touch and she moaned softly with impatience.

He leaned toward her, close enough to feel the stroke of his breath on her cheek. He was so near, she could almost taste him.

Then suddenly he tore his hands from her shoulders and whirled away from her. He stomped across the round pen, muttering what sounded like a few choice profanities. The spring breeze riffled through her hair, its coolness bringing her to her senses.

"Oh, my God," she whispered. Trembling, she grabbed for Sweetpea's saddle, steadying herself by gripping the leather.

"I'm sorry," Tom said roughly, his back still to her.

"Me, too." She shook her head. "I mean, I don't know how…we shouldn't have…"

"No, we damn well shouldn't." He turned toward her now. "I'm the one at fault, not you."

"Why are you…"

"Because I shouldn't have touched you," he said savagely. "I should never have gotten close enough to…" He drew a hand over his face. "I swear I'm going crazy." He lifted his head and blew out a sharp whistle.

Sweetpea ambled toward him, stepping carefully to avoid the reins dragging in the dirt. When she was within reach, Tom grabbed the reins and led the horse from the round pen and toward the barn.

Rooted to the spot, Andrea watched as he and the mare disappeared inside the barn. It took her a few moments to get her feet working, to get her knees to bend.

She set off toward her apartment, sensation still jangling along her nerves, heating her skin.

Once she'd showered and changed, she had to force herself to leave the foreman's quarters, fearing she'd see Tom in the yard. But if he was nearby, he was keeping himself scarce. She made it to her car and down the drive without catching so much as a glance of Tom. But she could still feel him.

Hidden in the shadows within the barn, Tom watched Andrea drive away with a mixture of relief and frustration. The heavy ache low in his body throbbed and pulled at him, making clear thought impossible.

Thank God Sweetpea could just about untack herself. As it was, he'd annoyed the horse mightily when he'd tried to take the saddle from her back without releasing the cinch first. She'd raised her back leg and nearly cow-kicked him, something the well-mannered mare would never do ordinarily. A couple of bites of carrot and she forgave him, obligingly standing still while he loosened the cinch and slid the saddle from her back.

He never would have guessed teaching someone to ride could be an erotic experience. He recalled Lori's first sessions in the saddle. She hadn't liked the smell or the flies or the way the horse bounced her around. Around the fifth or sixth ride, she'd broken a nail when the gelding spooked and nearly unseated her. She'd jumped off and never climbed into a saddle again.

But Andrea… She'd been a little scared. She'd sat pretty stiff on Sweetpea's back the first few times around the pen. But she'd listened to his coaching, let herself trust the horse. After the first couple minutes, you would have thought she'd been riding forever.

He could still see the way her body had moved along

with the mare's, the two of them one creature. It wasn't much of a mental stretch to imagine Andrea riding him instead of the mare, the motion of her hips in the rhythmic movements of sex.

That was when he really lost it. He knew he'd have her in his arms, knew he'd be kissing her, touching her. How he'd stopped himself in time he didn't know.

He turned Sweetpea out in pasture with Sonuvagun and the other mares, then headed for the colt's paddock. An hour spent schooling the randy two-year-old would pull his mind off Andrea and the near miss in the round pen. The sorrel colt always took more focus than Sonuvagun or the mares, and he sorely needed that kind of distraction. After he worked the colt, he could replace some pasture fence he'd been meaning to get to.

But dealing with the colt's tantrums didn't dull his agitation, nor did wrestling with field fencing and T-posts calm him. The work just tired him out and tore down his defenses. His exhaustion only made it easier, later in the shower, to imagine Andrea with him, her smooth curves slick with soap, her warm skin slipping against his.

And the cold shower after barely dampened the fire.

"Is that the last of them?" Andrea asked Beth as Tom's sister juggled several department store bags in her arms.

"Unless you'll let me take that cute little sundress you bought at Hattie's." Beth looked down at her generous hips. "Of course, I wouldn't be able to get it past my knees. But it would look great hanging in my closet."

Andrea laughed as she shut the trunk of her car. She'd really enjoyed the afternoon spent with Beth.

Tom's complexity baffled her, her attraction for him always leaving her breathless and edgy. But his uncomplicated, easygoing sister soothed and cheered her.

Beth dashed across the street with her packages and gave one last wave before she ducked inside the Hart Valley Inn. Andrea checked her watch—nearly seven. She could head back to the Double J and nuke one of the frozen meals she had stashed away in the small fridge in her apartment. Or she could have dinner at Nina's Café.

Her stomach rumbled, making the decision for her. She grabbed her purse from the back seat of the car, then headed for the café. Nina Russo, standing by the cash register with Nate, her three-year-old son, greeted Andrea with a smile. Nina motioned her toward an empty booth, and Andrea sat at the table with a sigh, pleasure over the afternoon still lingering.

Just as she opened the menu the waitress brought her, the café door jingled, signaling the arrival of another customer. Andrea looked toward the door and her ease vanished in an instant. Every nerve stood at attention as Tom stepped inside and scanned the café searching for a place to sit.

When his gaze passed right over her, relief battled with disappointment inside Andrea. But then he stopped, snapped his head back in a double take. His eyes locked on her, as if there were no one else in the busy café.

Even as she mentally urged him to sit somewhere, anywhere else, her face betrayed her and she smiled at him. He kept his gaze fixed on her as he threaded his way through the crowded café.

When he stopped at her table, his mouth curved in a faint smile. "I can't seem to shake you." His tone seemed more bemused than irritated. "I thought you and Beth would have dinner together in Marbleville."

"So you didn't expect me to be here." She said it lightly, her own smile still lingering.

His gaze drifted down to her mouth. He might as well have touched her, stroked her lips. Heat rose in her cheeks.

She gulped in a breath of air and her words came out in a rush. "Beth had to prep for Sunday breakfast." Her explanation sounded inane. "So we had to get back."

He shook his head and took a step away from the table. "I don't want to disturb you. It's your night off. You probably want to eat alone."

A moment ago, that was exactly what she wanted. But now that he was here, she didn't want him to leave. "Please...have dinner with me."

He hesitated, then slid into the booth across the table from her. When she offered the menu, he shook his head.

"Nina hasn't changed the menu since her folks owned the place."

When the café owner spotted Tom, her face lit up and she sashayed over to their table. Every male in the place stopped eating or drinking or talking to watch the voluptuous Nina as she moved through the room.

But she had eyes only for Tom. "Your usual, honey?" she asked, her smile more an invitation than a welcome.

Were Tom and Nina romantically involved? Andrea felt an ache inside at the prospect.

Color rose in Tom's face and he wouldn't quite meet Nina's direct brown gaze. "Yeah," he muttered. "Thanks."

After a wink at Tom, Nina turned her friendly smile toward Andrea. "You're Jessie's new teacher, aren't you?"

Irritated that she cared so much about the relationship between Tom and Nina, Andrea forced an answering smile. "I am."

"We all love that little girl." Nina put a proprietary hand on Tom's shoulder and gave it a squeeze. "Just like we love her daddy."

Nina might as well have thrown down the gantlet. Tom edged away from the café owner far enough that Nina's hand dropped. "Andrea's doing a damn good job." He met Nina's gaze. "You be sure to let everyone know."

Andrea could see the longing in the other woman's face, then Nina pasted on a smile as she turned to Andrea again. "What can I get for you, hon?"

Andrea ordered and Nina hurried off, shoving her order pad at one of her waitresses as she passed her. Then Nina took Nate by the hand and disappeared into the kitchen with her son.

Tom let out a heavy sigh, his expression troubled. "You'll like the meatloaf. Nina makes it herself."

Raising her water glass to her lips, Andrea took a sip. "Were you two ever—"

"No." Tom locked his hands on the table. "We dated a few times in high school."

Andrea glanced toward the kitchen. "It's obvious she still cares for you."

His jaw worked as he stared down at his hands. "I've flat out told her I'm not interested. I don't want or need a woman in my life." His head swung up and his gaze met Andrea's. "I got my fill with Lori."

Mort Gibbons from the Pump 'n' Go passed their

table on his way out and Tom smiled and waved in greeting. Then he grabbed his water glass and downed the contents. "So how's Jessie been doing this week?"

With the door securely shut on his relationship with Nina, Andrea pulled her thoughts to Jessie. "The writing is coming easier since she started using your computer. I'm still insisting on handwriting practice."

He nodded, then shook a few pieces of crushed ice into his mouth. He chewed the ice, the motion of his jaw and throat as he swallowed drawing her gaze. She wondered if his cheek would feel rough or smooth against her palm. His sandy colored hair looked damp in back, so he'd probably showered before he'd come out to dinner. But had he shaved, too? Her fingers itched to find out.

When she lifted her gaze to meet his, she realized he'd asked her a question and waited for an answer. She felt heat rise in her face. "Sorry. You said something?"

"Is it working? Teaching Jessie, I mean."

If she ignored the fact that she couldn't seem to stop the rampant fantasies about Jessie's father. "We have our ups and downs. But I think we're working together pretty well."

Another slight nod of his head. "The trial period is pretty much over. I want you to finish out the school year." He shook the ice in his glass. "If you're willing."

"Of course." She could handle her attraction toward Tom; she'd done fine so far. She'd avoided the kiss earlier today, surely she could steel herself against reacting to his touch. "I'd like to continue teaching Jessie."

"Great." He set down his water glass, picked up his

knife. He tapped the knife against the table, the staccato seeming to ratchet up the tension between them.

Andrea picked up her water, sipped at it, relishing the coolness against her palm. When she saw the waitress approaching with their meal, she puffed out a sigh of relief. At least now she could focus on something other than the man across the table from her.

Andrea poured ketchup onto her plate next to the meatloaf while Tom cut into his steak. He was right about the meatloaf. It was savory and spiced perfectly. As she chewed a mouthful, she felt a pang inside, remembering her mother serving her the same meal—meatloaf and mashed potatoes—for her sixth birthday. It had once been her favorite.

She felt the pull of tears in the back of her throat and took another sip of water to wash them away. Glancing over at Tom, she was relieved to see his attention on his steak and baked potato rather than on her.

She took another bite of meatloaf, found she could swallow it without that tightening in her throat. "Beth and I talked quite a bit about you and Jessie. But she never mentioned grandparents."

Tom poked at his baked potato with his fork. "Jessie doesn't have grandparents."

"They're all gone?"

He cut his steak, drank from his refilled water glass. "My mom died when I was seven. My dad passed away six years ago. Jessie barely remembers them."

"But your ex-wife's parents—"

"They don't come around." He spat out the words. "Not since Lori left."

As bedeviling as Jessie could be, she was still a love and Andrea couldn't imagine her grandparents wouldn't want to know her. "But does Lori—"

He sawed away at his steak. "Drop it, Andrea."

"But surely her mother—"

"Change the subject."

"I just wanted to know—"

He dropped his fork and knife with a clatter, fixed his gaze on Andrea. "Lori breezes in here maybe two times a year. She's run through the allowance her folks give her, so she comes to squeeze me for a few bucks. She gives Jessie a pile of gifts Jessie can't use, pats her on the head, then goes on her way." His face set, he dropped his gaze to his plate, attacked his steak again.

Andrea sat there, appalled—at herself for digging at Tom's wounds, at Lori for her cruelty toward her daughter. As lost as she felt all those years dragged from place to place as a child, she had at least one constant—her mother. Even while suffering the loneliness of a friendless life, she never doubted her mother's love.

"Tom." She said his name softly, but he didn't look up until she laid her hand on his. "She knows you love her."

He swallowed against some emotion as gratitude flickered in his stormy gaze. "When she's mad at me…"

"Even then."

His throat worked again. "But sometimes—"

"She knows." Andrea stroked the back of his hand. Some of the tension in his face seeped away.

He set down his fork and covered her hand with his. "How do you always know what to say?"

She thought she would melt under his gaze. Then he squeezed her hand and drew his away, picking up his fork again. She dropped her own hand into her lap, then took another bite of mashed potatoes. With emotions wrenching her in every direction at once, she wasn't sure she could eat much more. But the pleasure of Tom's company, the steady chatter of the café crowd soothed her, filled her with a sweet and unfamiliar feeling.

In that moment, with Tom smiling across the table at her, with the savor of her delicious meal still on her tongue, she felt at home. For nearly the first time in her life, she felt as if she belonged.

Chapter Seven

The tantalizing fragrance of fresh-baked brownies beckoned Tom the moment he stepped into the house with the saddlebags. Even as his mouth watered in anticipation of a taste, his imagination played out a picture of Andrea pulling a pan from the oven, then turning to him with a beckoning smile.

As he entered the kitchen and set the saddlebags on the table, he saw his fantasy wasn't far off, although it was Jessie at the oven, carefully sliding the brownies from the rack. Andrea hovered over her, shutting the oven door when Jessie straightened. Thick oven mitts on her hands, Jessie carefully placed the pan on top of the stove.

Jessie sagged against the counter with a grin and tugged off the mitts. "I did it all by myself, Daddy. Did you see?"

He reached over and squeezed Jessie's shoulder. ''I did, sweetheart.''

Jessie turned to Andrea. ''Can I go change into jeans for the ride?''

''Sure, sweetie,'' Andrea said. ''I'll clean up.''

Jessie raced from the kitchen and thundered up the stairs. As Andrea carried the mixing bowl and measuring cups to the sink, Tom grabbed a towel. Sometimes the temptation of being close to her was more then he could resist. He was grateful for the excuse of drying dishes beside her.

She had her long hair pulled back in its usual braid, but some had escaped and curled around her ears. Her jeans faithfully followed her every curve from waist to ankles. Her pale-blue tank top left her shoulders bare and exposed a sprinkling of freckles. He couldn't suppress the sharp image of tasting those chocolate-brown spots on her skin.

He watched her swish the mixing bowl in soapy water, the motion of her delicate hands mesmerizing. When did washing dishes become such an erotic act?

As she set the rinsed bowl in the drainer, he tore his wayward thoughts away from Andrea's body. ''That was quite a feat,'' he said as he wiped the bowl. At Andrea's questioning look, he continued, ''Getting Jessie to take the brownies from the oven.''

''I bribed her.'' Andrea fished a measuring cup from the sink. ''She gets the first brownie from the batch.''

Tom put the bowl away in the cupboard beside the stove. ''I know it took more than the promise of a brownie. Jessie's scared to death of being burned again.''

Handing over the rinsed measuring cup, she turned to him. ''We've been working up to it for a few days now. We started with a cold pan and cold oven. I made sure she knew what parts of the oven were hot and how the mitts would keep her hands safe.''

He set aside the dry one-cup measure. ''But why?''

''It was her idea. She knew we'd be baking brownies for the trail ride. She wanted to be able to do it all herself.''

Another miracle wrought by Andrea. How was it she saw exactly what Jessie needed? She'd only been here a couple weeks, yet she knew more about his own daughter than he did.

''Sometimes it seems like I'm just no good as a parent. Half the time I don't see what's right in front of my nose.''

''You're a wonderful father.'' Andrea put a hand on his arm, her palm still damp from the dishwater. ''But you're with her all the time and it's harder to see the changes. It could be that a month ago taking a hot pan from the oven would have terrified her. Today she was ready.''

He covered her hand with his, gave himself a moment to enjoy her touch before she pulled away to finish the dishes. He waited until she'd washed the remaining items and let the dishwater drain before he resumed drying.

''Speaking of ready,'' he said as he put away the last of the measuring cups and spoons, ''are you okay with the ride today? We'll be on horseback at least a couple hours.''

She dried her hands on a paper towel, then tossed it in the trash under the sink. ''You might have to peel me out of the saddle. But I'm game.''

A clatter on the stairs announced Jessie's return. She

entered the kitchen like a rocket. "Are the brownies ready to cut?"

"They're still a little warm," Andrea said, handing over the oven mitts. "Bring them over to the counter."

Tugging on the mitts, Jessie picked up the brownie pan reverently and carried it to the counter next to the sink. Andrea pulled out a plastic knife and placed it in Jessie's hand. While Andrea coached, Jessie cut the brownies into jaggedy portions that could only charitably be described as squares.

Jessie looked up at Andrea. "Can I have mine now?"

When Andrea nodded yes, Jessie poked the plastic knife under the largest brownie in the pan and pried it out. She sat at the kitchen table, and took her first bite. "Yummy," she said around a mouthful of brownie.

Andrea poured Jessie a glass of milk, then directed Tom to get the sandwiches and fruit from the refrigerator. He had only the faintest of memories of his mother and father together in the kitchen, but what he did recall filled him with a sweet warmth. What would it be like to have a woman as a companion, as an emotional partner rather than just in the physical sense? He'd never experienced that with Lori and certainly not with the women he'd been with since.

As he helped Andrea fill the two sets of saddlebags with their picnic lunch, he realized she was exactly the kind of woman who would share every part of herself with a man. Even for him, someone who had no interest in any kind of commitment, that promise was a nearly irresistible lure.

When he lifted the filled saddlebags from the table, his gaze met Andrea's across the kitchen table. Even with Jessie chattering away about their upcoming ride, a taut thread of connection snapped between him and

Andrea. Her brown eyes seemed molten, her soft lips begged him to stroke them with a fingertip. It took an effort to pull away, to walk from the kitchen and out of the house.

He hung the saddlebags over the round pen rail, then headed into the barn to bring out Sonuvagun and Sweet-pea. No matter what he did, his attraction for her never seemed to fade. Sometimes it seemed he'd never last the few weeks between now and the end of school without giving in to his body's urging.

But he wouldn't give in. Because Andrea was different than the other women he'd been with the past few years. He sensed that for Andrea, sex would be more than the physical release his previous partners sought. For her, the act would be a prelude to forever.

And forever with a woman was the last thing he wanted.

Her rear was sore, her legs ached, but none of that seemed to matter. The meadow she and Tom and Jessie passed through was so exquisitely beautiful, Andrea barely noticed the pain of sitting in the saddle. The emerald grass rolling in indolent waves, the china-blue sky, the oaks with their gnarled branches dotting a meadow that stretched from horizon to horizon—it was all like something in a dream.

The horses walked lazily through the knee-high grass, heads down, occasionally stealing a mouthful as they forded the ocean of green. Jessie, who'd kept up a nonstop monologue on her pony most of the way out, had finally lapsed into silence. Andrea soaked up the warmth of the noontime sun, the quiet occasionally broken by birdcall or the soughing breeze.

Riding Trixie just in front of them, Jessie turned in her saddle. "Can I trot on ahead again?"

"Just to the mine," Tom answered. "And don't you dare go inside."

Jessie made a face, but she gave her dad a reluctant "Okay." Then she gave Trixie a kick and the little mare trotted off willingly. Sonuvagun popped up his head and looked ready to follow, but Tom held his gelding back. Sweetpea barely twitched an ear as the pony increased the distance between them.

Tom reined Sonuvagun right up next to her, so close his denim-covered leg nearly brushed hers. If she switched the reins to her left hand, she could have reached out to touch his tanned arm, to test the texture of his skin.

If she was completely out of her mind, that is. She ought to be focusing on riding the horse, on the soreness along her thighs, the sun baking her shoulders. But her every thought seemed to circle back to Tom beside her—his hand instead of the sun warming her shoulders, his touch soothing her aches, his body between her legs instead of the horse....

Knock it off! she scolded herself. Her fantasies of Tom seemed to go further every day, became ever more real and sexual. Her attraction for him had become a living thing that wouldn't leave her alone, gave her no peace. Her every nerve seemed to tingle with energy, a readiness she fought to ignore.

And the gorgeous day only added to the torture. The faint breeze on her skin, the fragrance of wildflowers mingled with Tom's scent, teased her with a sensual barrage. If she hadn't been certain she'd promptly fall off, she would have galloped the stolid mare across the meadow, just to escape the conflicting sensations.

Jessie's presence acted as only the slightest of buffers. Too impatient with the walking pace Tom had set out of deference to Andrea's inexperience on horseback, Jessie went off alone as far as she could while still within eyesight. That left Andrea unprotected from her longings.

"That girl was born to be on horseback," Tom said softly as he watched his daughter.

Eager to talk about something, anything to distract herself from the muddle of emotions inside her, Andrea asked, "How long has she been riding?"

"Since she was two." Tom laughed. "She demanded I put her up on Sweetpea. She rode her bareback, holding tight to Sweetpea's mane while I led her around the round pen."

She could picture Jessie, with that same intense expression as Tom's, all her single-minded attention on the horse she was riding. What would it be like, Andrea wondered, to have all of Tom's focus on her.

She'd stumbled into dangerous territory again. Shifting in the saddle, she gave Sweetpea an inadvertent squeeze with her legs. The mare woke up and trotted a few steps. That gave Andrea something to think about besides Tom, although bringing the mare back to a walk took little effort.

"How about you?" Tom asked when he caught up with her. "What's your passion?"

You. The answer popped into her mind uncensored, but she had enough good sense to keep the word from slipping from her lips. "Teaching. Reading. I sew a bit." She smiled over at Tom. "I have a quilt I've been working on for years. I ought to pull it out while I'm here."

"You didn't mention traveling. As a passion, I mean."

It hadn't even crossed her mind. "Well, that one goes without saying." Yet, in that moment, the thought of moving on when Jessie's school year ended tightened a knot in the pit of her stomach.

They topped a rise and Andrea could see Jessie up ahead beside an outcropping of rock. The little girl had dismounted and now leaned against Trixie while the pony grazed. Never one for photographs and the memories they triggered, Andrea longed in that moment to capture the image of Jessie beside her pony, standing in the knee-high grass.

"What do you like about it?" Tom's voice drew her from her reverie.

"About traveling?" She groped for a response, but all the usual reasons rang false. She plowed ahead anyway. "It's fun to meet new people, see new places. Every day's an adventure." She winced at the trite cliché.

"But what about the people you leave behind?"

The softly spoken question hung there while the answer clutched at her insides. She'd always convinced herself she felt no regret in severing ties when she moved on, but when she thought of leaving Tom and Jessie, the sense of loss threatened to overwhelm her.

With a cluck, she urged Sweetpea back into a trot and guided the mare toward the knoll up ahead where Jessie waited. She wished she could leave behind Tom's question just as easily.

"Come on, you guys," Jessie called, as Tom asked Sonuvagun for a little more speed. The gelding jogged along, quiet as you please, his nose to Sweetpea's tail. Jessie, impatient and antsy, nearly danced around her pony.

"I'm starving," Jessie declared. "What took you so long?"

She'd been waiting for all of about five minutes, but Tom knew that could be an eternity to Jessie. He dismounted and started untying the blanket from behind the saddle, one eye on Andrea still up on Sweetpea.

Andrea dragged her right leg slowly across the mare's back, then lowered herself carefully to the ground. She had to be mighty sore and she would probably feel even worse tomorrow. He'd have to give her some liniment when they got back to the ranch, and recommend a long, hot bath. It didn't take much of an imagination to conjure up the image of Andrea in the tub, his hands on her, soothing her aches.

He turned his back on her and bent his head to the blanket. Once he got it untied, he tucked it under one arm and unclipped the saddlebag. Andrea already had hers off and had headed over to where his anxious daughter waited.

"Where should we eat?" Andrea asked.

Jessie stepped over to a flat spot beside the crag of massive boulders. "Right here. Put the blanket down, Daddy."

"Hold your horses, Jessie," Tom said as he shook out the blanket. A nearby oak tree spread its massive branches over the spot, shading them from the growing warmth of the day.

As soon as he set down his saddlebag, Andrea busied herself with pulling out sandwiches, sodas and brownies. She emptied everything onto the blanket, made sure the plastic bag of baby carrots was within Jessie's reach, then settled down beside his daughter. Tom lowered himself to the blanket between them, his back to a granite boulder. As small as the blanket was, his knee nearly rubbed up against Andrea's.

As a distraction from her nearness, Tom resumed their earlier discussion. "Andrea was telling me why she likes traveling."

A large bite of butter and jelly sandwich lodged in her cheek, Jessie's eyes lit with excitement. "Andy's been to eight different states, Daddy. She's been to Disneyland *and* Disney World."

Andrea edged a bit away from him, moving to the corner of the blanket farthest from him. Had she sensed the nagging attraction he felt for her? Damn it, the last thing he wanted was to make her uncomfortable.

As she nibbled on a corner of a tuna sandwich, she sat Indian style, her knee only inches from his again. "We lived in Florida for a few months and Southern California for almost a year."

He took a big bite of his ham and cheese, then took a swig of soda to wash it down. "You must have friends all over, then."

Her gaze dropped to her sandwich. "A few."

Reaching across the blanket, he snagged a handful of carrots from the bag. "How do you keep in touch?"

Andrea pinched off a bit of sandwich with her fingers, but she didn't eat it. "We're all pretty busy."

When Jessie grabbed for the brownies, Tom put out a hand to stop her. "Three carrots first."

Her face screwed up in disgust, Jessie picked through the bag for the three smallest carrots. Nose wrinkled, she chomped them down, then attacked the brownies again.

Chocolate smeared across her cheeks, Jessie leaned

back on the blanket with a sigh. "That was the best lunch ever. Except the carrots," she amended.

Andrea finished half her tuna sandwich, then wrapped the other back up in plastic wrap. She picked up the bag of carrots and, just as Jessie had done, sorted through for the three smallest. When she caught Tom watching her, color rose in her cheeks. Tom laughed and she grinned in response.

"Okay, I'm not big on carrots either," she admitted.

She popped them into her mouth, and chewed them one by one. He wanted to laugh again, because she was so good for his daughter, because her smile lifted his spirits.

He took two more from the bag himself, then handed them to Jessie. "Go ahead and give the rest to the horses."

Jessie jumped up, only too glad to dispose of them. He watched her quickly count the contents of the bag and just as quickly divide the carrots fairly amongst the pony, mare and gelding.

"She's doing well with her math," Tom said.

Andrea nodded. "She likes it best." She pulled the foil packet of brownies toward her. "Would you like some?"

There was nothing suggestive in the question, but his overactive mind was always ready to fill in the blanks. He took a rich, dark square from the foil, appalled to see his hand tremble a bit.

He bit into the still-warm brownie, trying not to wonder if her mouth would taste as sweet. He ought to keep his eyes off her, but he couldn't seem to resist watching her.

"Daddy!" Jessie's cry saved him from his own weak will. "I have to…you know."

"Go around to the other side of the rocks," he told her. "No one will see."

Andrea began to clean up, gathering up the remains of the sandwiches and the empty soda cans. He took the trash from her and stuffed it away in the saddlebags. A little ashamed of how often he let his fingers brush hers, he enjoyed the contact nevertheless.

When everything had been picked up, she sat back on her heels and tipped her head up to his. On one knee, ready to rise from the blanket, he realized he had only to lean slightly forward and he could kiss her. Her lips parted as if in anticipation, in invitation. As wrong as he knew it would be, as sternly as he lectured himself that he was misinterpreting her signals, he very nearly gave in to the lure.

She pushed herself to her feet, and her voice shook as she called out, "Jessie! Are you done?"

Silence from the other side of the shielding boulders. Tom stood and shouted, "Jessie!"

Still no answer. He headed around the pile of rock, Andrea close behind him. "Where could she be?" she asked as they reached the other side and saw no sign of Jessie.

"The mine shaft." Fear crept up his spine as he bent to look inside the black cleft in the boulders. "She knows she's not to go inside, but..."

Rock had tumbled down to block the opening to the mine shaft, so there wasn't enough room for even Andrea to squeeze inside. Tom couldn't see much farther than a few feet into the adit. "Jessie!"

He tried to push aside one of the smaller boulders, but it wouldn't budge. The hillside dropped off sharply just beyond the mine opening, and oaks clung to the steep slope. He thought he spied a large enough branch to use as a lever to push the boulders aside and was about to go after it when he heard the clatter of rock. Jessie popped out from behind a manzanita below, and started up the hill.

Relief giving way to anger, Tom scrambled down the hill, his feet slipping on the loose rock. "Damn it, Jessie, where were you?"

"I just came down a little ways," Jessie said, her tone aggrieved. "Girls need privacy, okay?"

He took a breath, forced himself to calm down. She was right, of course. She hadn't gone far, she'd been perfectly safe. But guilt stabbed at him. He'd been so focused on Andrea, on kissing her, he was oblivious to his daughter.

He waited for Jessie to pass him before turning to follow her. "Time to go."

When he reached the top of the hill, Andrea fell in beside him. "She's okay, Tom."

"Yeah." But when he thought about what Lori had been up to when Jessie had been burned four years ago, his gut churned.

They rounded the rocks to their picnic site, then packed up the saddlebags and blankets on the backs of the horses. Jessie hopped up on Trixie, then reined the pony around to wait for them.

Andrea stood beside Sweetpea, her left hand holding the reins, her head dipped down toward the stirrup. She laughed and shook her head. "I'm not sure I can lift my leg high enough to get on."

He'd have to help her up, which meant he'd have to touch her. Dropping Sonuvagun's reins, he came up beside Sweetpea. Andrea bent her right knee as he'd taught her and he hoisted her into the saddle as quickly as he could. He didn't allow himself even a moment to enjoy the feel of her leg in his hands.

Andrea grimaced a little as she settled into the saddle. ''I may not be able to get down again, but at least I can make it home.''

She smiled at him, her brown eyes bright with humor and the ache of guilt inside him washed away. With nothing more than a look, she'd lifted his spirits and made him feel so damn good about himself.

He ought to be scared to death. But all he felt was happy.

It was well past midnight when Andrea jolted awake from a restless sleep. She groaned as she turned over in the bed, revisiting every single twinge of pain in her abused muscles. Who would have thought sitting on the back of a horse would wreak such havoc with her body?

Just as Tom wreaked havoc with her peace of mind. It seemed she couldn't be near him without playing out a hundred encounters in her mind, sensual thoughts she had no right to entertain. Sometimes she felt like a spider's prey, wrapped in soft, unbreakable threads of desire that would trap her sooner or later.

Moving slowly, she eased herself up from the bed. A quick check of the clock told her she could down another couple painkillers. With the soreness eased, she might have a chance to fall back asleep. That is, if she could keep at bay the sharp images of Tom's touch, the heat of his gaze.

She'd just washed down a dose of acetaminophen when she heard a clatter from the barn. It was loud enough that she realized the noise must have been what woke her. Her apartment was close enough to the horses that she heard the occasional nicker or bang of a hoof during the night. But even to her inexperienced ear, this sounded different, the irregular rapping setting off an alarm.

She grabbed a satin robe to cover her scanty nightgown, then slipped her feet into the sandals she kept by the door. She'd take just a quick look into the barn, then go alert Tom if there was anything amiss.

She shut the door quietly behind her, then waited a few moments at the top of the stairs to let her eyes grow accustomed to the darkness. A nearly full moon lit the yard between the barn and house, making it easy enough to make her way down the stairs. Along the way, she heard the clatter again and the soft whinny of one of the horses.

A light flared on outside the barn and she gasped in surprise. She remembered Tom had told her the flood lamps were motion sensitive, but she hadn't gotten close enough yet to trigger them. The crunch of footsteps on gravel quickly revealed whose presence the lights had detected.

He'd only pulled on blue jeans and left the button undone to boot. The play of dark and light defined the muscles in his arms and chest, made the trail of hair leading down to that undone button a dark path that begged to be touched. As he strode across the yard, Andrea couldn't hold back a soft murmur of appreciation.

He couldn't have heard her; the sound had been barely a whisper, hardly more than a breath. And she still stood in the shadows, most likely invisible to him with the flood lamp glaring in his eyes. But he turned toward her anyway, unerringly seeking her out. The set of his shoulders, the tight grip of his hands, the alertness in his gaze told her he'd found her.

She stepped from the shadows into the light.

Chapter Eight

He thought his heart would hammer its way from his chest. The sight of Andrea in a satiny robe that hung barely past her hips, the expectancy in her face, her stillness as she waited for him to…he wasn't sure what, but it involved heat and skin against skin and soft, dark moans. Every square inch of his body screamed in readiness, urged him to reach for her.

Then the *rat-a-tat-tat* from the barn, the noise that had dragged him from sleep, sounded again, jolting his attention from Andrea. He pulled in a breath of the cool night air, then another, doing his best to chill his heated thoughts.

He couldn't quite shake off his restless energy, never mind relax a certain part of his anatomy that pushed against the placket of his jeans. Thank God for the distraction of the horses.

Andrea moved up beside him as he headed for the

barn, shivering a little in her skimpy robe. He absolutely wouldn't think about what she might be wearing under it.

"I heard the noise, too." She wrapped her arms around herself. "What is it?" Her voice shook and he wondered if it was the cold or something else.

He thrust aside the possibilities. "I think I know. Let's see." He unlatched the barn door, then stepped back to let her go in first. He turned on one set of the overhead lights, heard the horses shift as the light woke them.

He was pretty sure of what he'd see when he took a peek in Honeybee's stall. The broodmare had been the first to get in foal last spring and the one closest to her due date. It was a little early, but not more than a week or so.

He looked over the stall door and saw exactly what he'd expected—a gangly bay foal struggling to gain its feet, its tiny hoofs making a racket against the wood lining the stall.

Gesturing to Andrea, he ushered her closer to the stall. "Come take a look."

She went up on tiptoes to see over the stall door and her breath escaped in a soft gasp of surprise. A smile lit her face and when she turned to him, he felt like a hero for showing her this small miracle.

"It's so tiny," she said, gazing in awe at the foal, now standing on its spindly, wobbly legs.

"Good-sized for a newborn. She'll be bigger than her mama when she's done growing."

Andrea leaned a little closer to him. "Is she supposed to be so skinny?"

He wanted to tip his head down, bury his face in her soft hair. The silky brown strands hung loose, freed of their customary braid. He could imagine the way her hair would feel slipping through his fingers, stroking the backs of his hands.

He had to struggle to remember her question. "She'll fill out quick enough."

Barely keeping to its feet, the foal staggered over to Honeybee and nosed around under the mare's belly. This was Honeybee's third foal and she'd done a good job cleaning up the little filly. She stood patiently as the newborn rooted around for her mama's milk. When the foal finally latched on and began to nurse, she flapped her little stub of tail from side to side, announcing her contentment to the world.

Andrea laughed at the foal's little flag of a tail. "It's hard to believe she'll be as big as her mother some day." The words came out high and breathy.

He could barely take a breath himself. She leaned toward him, just the slightest bit and her soft fall of hair swung to brush against his hand. He ordered himself to pull away, but there was no way in heaven or hell he could convince himself. Instead he drew his hand down the length of her hair, letting the satiny stuff spill across his hand and wrist.

He cupped her shoulders and turned her to face him. If she'd resisted, he could have let go, stepped away from her. But she eased toward him willingly, her head tipped up, her lips parting. He tried to tell himself that wasn't invitation he saw in her face, that kissing her would be a terrible mistake. But when she whispered his name, so quietly it might have been a chance puff of breeze, he knew he was lost.

He bent slowly, giving her every opportunity to pull away. But instead of backing off, she seemed to melt under his touch, stepping even closer. He curved one hand behind her neck, the other dove into her hair. She reached for him, her fingers curling around his bare arms, her heat burning him.

The bliss of that contact was eclipsed by the first touch of his mouth to hers. His rapidly beating heart shifted into even higher gear, until it was a constant thundering in his ears. Her mouth was impossibly soft, incredibly sweet. He could have stood there forever, brushing his lips across her mouth, feeling the pressure of skin against skin.

He dipped his tongue inside, took a tentative taste of her. Her moan sizzled along his nerves, sent heat arrowing through him. Desperate to have her closer, he slid one hand down to the small of her back and pressed her body against his. He felt ready to explode, his lungs full of her scent, her taste on his tongue, the silk of her skin and the satin of her robe slipping across his chest.

With the speed and power of a freight train, he was hurtling past the point of no return. He had to quit now, had to pull back. If he didn't put on the brakes, they'd be plunging toward an intimacy he knew damn well neither one of them was ready for. It was time to stop.

After one more kiss.

She was drowning in sensation, every nerve burning with the pleasure of Tom's touch. She wanted to rip the clothes from her body and his, feel nothing between them but heat. Even as her mind told her she shouldn't, the exquisite delight of his nearness drugged her into passivity.

From somewhere inside her, she mustered up enough will to tense her arms against him. For a moment, he ignored that token resistance, his tongue dipping farther inside her mouth. That sweet invasion nearly destroyed her resolve, urged her to ease even closer. Finally, she backed her head away, pushed gently against his arms again. This time he let go immediately and stepped away from her.

He stared down at her, the brilliance of desire still illuminating his eyes. Gazing up at him, Andrea felt weak, and had to grab hold of the stall door to keep from swaying.

"Are you okay?" His voice was low and rough.

She could only nod. She covered her mouth with a shaking hand, wishing she could wipe away the last few minutes. "We shouldn't have—"

"No, we shouldn't." He passed his hand over his face. "Hell."

She took a step toward the door. "I should go."

"Yeah." Shoving his hands into his pockets, he stared down at the brick lining the barn aisle.

She backed another step toward the exit. "Good night, then."

"Good night." He swung his head up to look at her, the heat lingering in his gaze pinioning her to the spot. "Andrea…"

She didn't want to talk about what had just happened, didn't even want to think about it. She forced herself to take another step away.

"Andrea," he said more softly and she froze again. "You won't…Jessie still…" He looked away then back at her. "She needs you. Please don't leave."

It hadn't even crossed her mind. Yet it was exactly what she ought to do. Suddenly cold again, she wrapped her arms around herself. "We can't ever—"

"No," he agreed readily.

"Because it isn't right."

This time he responded more slowly. "It isn't right."

She thought she heard a question in his tone, but she avoided considering what that might mean. "It's clear we have…feelings for each other." She shivered, remembering the hot passion of his kiss. "We just don't act on them."

The half light of the barn shadowed his face, hid his expressive eyes from her. She held her breath waiting for an answer, the silence broken only by the shuffling of the foal, the soft sough of a breeze just outside the barn, the horses breathing.

She didn't want to get nearer to him, but she had to drive her point home. "You can't touch me anymore." Even three feet away, she thought she could feel his heat. "Because when you do, I can't…" Can't think, can't stop, can't resist. She took a gulp of air. "Just don't."

She still couldn't see his eyes, but she caught the brief nod of his head. Suddenly she felt so cold, her teeth chattered. She turned on her heel and rushed out of the barn. She broke into a run across the yard, then dashed up the stairs to her apartment. She couldn't get inside quick enough.

Stripping off her robe as she headed for the tiny bedroom, she dropped it to the floor before climbing back in bed. There weren't enough covers on the bed to stop her shaking, so she grabbed another from the closet. When she began to sweat under the heavy bedclothes, even as she continued to shiver, she realized it wasn't cold but reaction that made her body quake.

She flung off the covers again, crazy with restlessness. Old instincts crowded in and a sudden urgency to escape flooded her. She wanted to pack up everything she owned and run for her car, then drive down the road away from here.

She remembered seeing a feral cat trapped in a cage once. It had flung itself against the wire walls confining it, again and again, uncaring of the pain, just desperate to flee. She felt like that cat, on fire with the fear of the trap.

But she had to stay. Because of Jessie.

Her own childhood had been filled with broken promises, with her mother's well-intentioned vows. *We'll stay longer at the next town, sweetheart,* her mother would say. *To the end of the school year, I promise. And you'll make a ton of friends there.*

But then her mother would pull up roots again after a few short months, and Andrea would have to abandon her fledgling friendships. After enduring that pain, she'd vowed to always stand behind her word given to a child.

She relaxed her hands gripping the sheets, shoved off the excess blankets and straightened the covers. If she could just get comfortable, she knew she could fall asleep again. Her turbulent emotions had exhausted her.

But one temptation nagged her, even though she knew she was better off not knowing. She had to see if the light was still on in the barn, if Tom was still awake. If he'd gone off to his own bed, she was certain she could quell the thoughts of him roiling in her mind.

Finally, she gave in. She sat up on the edge of the bed and twitched aside the curtain on the window facing the yard. Just one peek, that was all she needed.

The sight of him, standing just outside the barn, struck her chest with the force of a fist. Arms crossed over his chest, he'd flung his head back as if he gazed at the stars. The faint light from the barn revealed little of his face, but there was loneliness in the set of his shoulders. She could feel his longing as keenly as her own.

She watched him for far too long, until her eyes burned, and her body ached with stiffness. She didn't turn away until he walked back inside the barn. By then, any hope for sleep had vanished.

She did succumb when dawn sent a gray light into her window, dropping her into muddled dreams more tiring than her wakefulness. By the time her alarm rang, jarring her from sleep, the bright light of morning set off a throbbing in her head.

As she pushed herself upright and slapped off the alarm, everything that had happened the night before rushed in to greet her. She groaned, huddling in her bed. It was going to be a long day.

Her head bent down to the eggs she was scrambling for Jessie's breakfast, Andrea had to force herself to turn and face Tom as he entered the kitchen. She fixed a smile on her face and tossed out a cheerful good morning before returning her attention to the eggs.

She prayed he would leave it at that. But he crossed the kitchen and took the bowl and fork from her hands, then set them aside on the counter. She felt his gaze, knew she had to meet it, but it was still an effort.

His gaze didn't waver from her face. "I lost control last night."

Heat rose in her cheeks. "We both did."

He shook his head. "But I should have known better. Touching you…kissing you…"

She swallowed against a dry throat, took a breath. "I won't be here much longer. Five more weeks."

"I won't touch you again. I swear it."

She should feel relieved, should be able to release the tension that gripped her. But his avowal only tightened the edginess inside her.

He turned away from her, opened the refrigerator. By the time Jessie appeared in the kitchen, her blouse buttoned wrong and her hair an unbrushed mess, he was seated at the table with a glass of milk and Andrea was serving up the scrambled eggs.

She would have immediately sent Jessie upstairs to get the tangles out of her hair, but she didn't want to be alone in the kitchen with Tom again. So she told the little girl to take care of her hair and the smudges on her cheeks right after breakfast. By that time, Tom would be outside working.

But the moment Jessie heard that Honeybee had had her foal, Andrea knew Jessie's hygiene would have to wait. The little girl shoveled in her eggs at mach five, ate her toast in three bites, then thundered out of the kitchen. When Tom hollered, "Stay out of Honeybee's stall!" Jessie yelled, "Okay!" before she slammed the front door.

Jessie's eagerness to see the foal had done what all Andrea's mental lectures had not—distracted her from the aftermath of Tom's kiss. Tom seemed to be more at ease as well, smiling at her across the table before he rose and cleared his and Jessie's dishes.

"Think you'll get any work out of her today?" he asked as he rinsed the dishes.

"Not likely." She set her plate and glass next to the sink. "I'll have to change the lesson plan to Foal 101."

"You go on ahead. I'll finish these."

A moment ago, she wanted nothing more than to put some distance between them. But now that the explosiveness between them had been defused, she was reluctant to leave.

She put her hand out, touched him fleetingly on the

arm. "That little girl of yours is a love. I'm so glad for the chance to teach her."

She could see the pride in his face as he scrubbed her plate, then set it aside to rinse. "We're glad to have you."

The glow his words kindled inside her stayed with her all day, as she and Jessie sketched the spindly little foal in the barn, as they pored over the filly's lineage, tracing it back four generations. Later, when they made horse cookies from a recipe Jessie downloaded from the Internet, Tom's expression of confidence still warmed Andrea.

Last night, her every instinct had shouted at her to escape. Today, her heart ached to stay forever even though her longings for a home here would be impossible to fulfill. She would simply have to box up every sweet moment inside her, carry it to ward away the inevitable loneliness later on.

Tom's touch was forbidden, but Jessie's wasn't. When the little girl gave her a Heimlich-strength hug after they'd pulled the last batch of horse treats from the oven, Andrea relished the rare moment of tenderness. Even when Jessie gave her arm a punch afterward, Andrea felt honored that the little girl had bestowed the same rough gesture of affection as she gave her best friend Sabrina.

That night at supper, Jessie talked a mile a minute, her conversation peppered with references to the foal and how special she was and how the filly seemed to like her best. She informed Andrea that even though her dad would pick out the name that went on the foal's papers, he always let her choose what they would call the filly around the ranch. She was trying to decide between Cassie and Molly, two of her most favorite names.

The excitement of the day wore on Jessie and she nodded off as she and Andrea were taking turns reading from one of the *Narnia* books. Before she went up to bed, she exacted a promise from her dad that Sabrina could come spend the night this weekend so she could see the new foal. Andrea didn't doubt Jessie fell asleep the moment her head hit the pillow.

Tom walked her out to the porch, holding her sweater for her so she could put it on. The temperature had dropped with the sunset, brushing her cheeks with the same chill as in the early morning hours.

The sweater wrapped around her, she turned to Tom. "Good night."

"Good night."

She expected him to go inside, but he moved down the stairs as she did. "I have to check the foal."

"Cassie," she corrected him.

"Cassie." He crossed the yard with her, then hesitated before turning toward the barn. "Andrea…"

"Yes?"

A faint smile on his face, his gaze met hers. "Never mind. See you in the morning." He turned and disappeared inside the barn.

His unfinished thought tantalized her, but she had to shake it off if she had any hope of getting any sleep tonight. She took a long shower, the warm water draining her energy, filling her with lassitude. Sinking gratefully into bed, she'd barely pulled up the covers before drifting off.

Her dreams were gentler, sweeter, saturated with images of Tom. Unconscious, she let herself do everything she wouldn't while awake—touch him, kiss him, whisper lovingly to him. She visited a paradise she didn't even know she yearned for, certain she could put it aside when she woke.

But despite her best intentions, her longing for heaven followed her into day.

Thirty-six hours after the kiss in the barn he figured he'd recovered pretty well. He could still recall the feel of her mouth on his whenever he thought of her—which was a good part of his day, but not every waking hour. Now and again, he'd be able to push her aside in his mind and get a little work done without images of Andrea playing themselves out like a movie.

Truth be told, his work was going to hell in a handbasket. Sonuvagun, the most good-natured gelding on earth, was getting cranky because his addle-brained rider couldn't get even the simplest reining patterns right. The colt, taking advantage of his mental lapses, was having a field day in the round pen, bucking and kicking his way through his training sessions. And just that morning he'd nearly skewered himself on a T-post as he was attempting to repair some pasture fencing.

It was just a matter of forbidden fruit. Knowing Andrea was Jessie's teacher and therefore off limits made her that much more irresistible. If she'd been any other woman—Nina for instance, or that saleswoman from Sacramento he'd spent some time with last year—her kiss wouldn't have haunted him so.

He just had to buckle down and focus on his work rather than what had transpired in the barn two nights ago. If not, he risked ruining a perfectly good colt or landing his butt in the dirt when Sonuvagun lost his patience and dumped him.

And he'd start right now, with the colt who had so

far this morning ignored his every cue. The young horse, lathered up from racing around the round pen, stood facing him, sides heaving. His sorrel coat was dark with sweat and now that he'd gotten all his wiggles out, looked completely tuckered out.

He clucked and the colt flicked an ear toward him. Another cluck and the horse stepped toward him, closing the distance between them. When the colt reached him, it butted its head against his chest, as if to ask, "Can we be done now?"

Tom led the colt to the wash rack and wrapped the lead loosely around the tie post there. The day's round pen work was a loss, but the colt's sweaty coat gave him a good opportunity to practice getting washed down.

Tom knew it wasn't just his inattention that had the colt riled up. His open mare—a gray maiden he hadn't bred last year—had come into season yesterday. Although he kept the colt well away from the mares, the stud could sense the mare's readiness. His mind was on procreation, not education.

As he hosed off the colt's legs, he heard the front door open and footsteps on the porch. He didn't have to look up to know the measured steps were Andrea's and not Jessie's. As much as he tried to resist the temptation, he watched her approach, his gaze taking in everything from the soft hair framing her face to the sneakers on her feet.

He'd never much noticed what women wore, but Andrea's tank top—a pale pink that set off the light tan of her shoulders—and white denim shorts teased his imagination. Would her legs be paler above the modest hemline of her shorts? How soft would her skin feel under the straps of the tank top?

The colt began pawing at the concrete pad of the wash rack, bringing Tom's attention back to the task at hand. He grabbed a large sponge and wet it before shutting off the hose and setting it out of the way.

Andrea gave the colt's hind end a wide berth as she reached the wash rack. "It never would have occurred to me to give a horse a bath."

"I don't bother unless I'm showing." Tom laid the wet sponge on the colt's back and the horse skittered aside as far as the lead rope would let him. "Rocket would just as soon be dirty."

A whinny from the barn caught the colt's attention and he screamed back, dancing at the end of the lead. Andrea stepped a little closer to the colt's head. "What's the matter with him?"

"Watch it!" Tom grabbed Andrea's shoulder and pulled her back just as the colt struck out with one of his front feet. "He's asking his lady love for a date."

"His lady love…oh." Andrea's cheeks colored when she saw the evidence of the colt's excitement.

It had been a long time since he'd been embarrassed by the antics of a randy colt, but with Andrea near, the colt's natural urgings got all tangled up with his own. He was a man, not a stud colt, and he could reason out why he ought to keep his body's urges to himself. But damned if he didn't feel as out of control around Andrea as the colt did around a ready mare.

Grabbing the colt's lead rope, he gave it a sharp tug, tightening the stud chain around the young horse's nose and reminding him to behave. Luckily, the mare quieted down, cutting short her attempt at seduction. The colt remembered how tired he was and let his head droop again.

Tom went back to sponging the sweat from the colt's

coat. "Was there something you wanted?" Even that simple question sounded suggestive.

"No." Her voice trembled a bit. Because of the near miss with the colt or something else? "Jessie's finishing up lunch and I just wanted to stretch my legs. I should be getting back."

She backed away, keeping a safe distance from the colt. When she headed for the house, he watched her retreat, beguiled by the sway of her hips in the snug denim shorts.

By the time she'd disappeared back inside the house, he realized he was clutching the sponge tightly to his chest. He had squeezed it so hard, water had soaked through the front of his T-shirt and was dripping into the waistband of his jeans.

He could swear the colt was laughing at him.

"I don't have to!" Jessie shouted, slamming her hands down on the kitchen table.

Andrea felt the beginnings of a headache building between her eyes and she was sorely tempted to let Jessie win this battle. It was nearly three, the time they quit lessons for the day. She was still rattled by her encounter with Tom in the yard earlier, not to mention the lingering after-effects of the kiss in the barn. Maybe it just wasn't that important that Jessie practice her cursive handwriting today.

Except that she'd already let it slip longer than she'd intended. Andrea had made it clear to Jessie she would write at least one page of cursive every Thursday. With the filly's arrival early Thursday, today's usual lessons had been swept aside. Although she'd been mostly successful getting Jessie back on track today, the day's curriculum still revolved around little Rosie.

But despite the lure of writing a poem about the foal in longhand to practice the dreaded cursive, Jessie had gone beyond obstinate to downright pigheaded. "I don't want to," she insisted. "It's too hard."

"No harder than it was last week and you did fine then."

Jessie glanced over at the kitchen clock. "It's three o'clock. School's over."

Pain digging into her brow, Andrea wanted to agree, but she had to stick to her guns. "Not until you finish the cursive."

Jessie crossed her arms over her chest, her body language declaring her refusal. Steps on the porch and the sound of the front door announced Tom's arrival. That was the last thing Andrea needed, both because his presence would scramble her belabored brain even more and because he would probably give Jessie a free pass.

He entered the kitchen and paused in the doorway, taking in Jessie's surly expression. "What's up, Jess?"

Jessie turned to her father, aggrieved. "She's making me work when school's out."

"Is that right?" Tom asked mildly.

Andrea took a breath, trying to calm her jangly nerves. "She needs to do her cursive practice for the week."

"I can't," Jessie said. "It's too hard."

Tom stared down at his daughter. Andrea caught her lower lip in her teeth, anticipating a fight.

"I know it's hard, Jess." He crossed his arms over his chest, as implacable as his daughter. "But you do as Andrea asks or Sabrina won't be spending the night tonight."

Jessie gasped in outrage as a spurt of gratitude burst inside Andrea. Tom winked at her, then crossed to the sink for a drink of water. He ignored Jessie's jabbering as she moaned and groaned about the injustice of it all.

Setting aside the glass, he turned to Andrea. "Let me know if she hasn't finished by five. I'll want to give Sabrina's folks plenty of warning."

Openmouthed, Jessie watched him leave, then gave Andrea the evil eye. A bit more token resistance, then Jessie slid paper and pen closer and settled down to work.

As Jessie carefully penned her assignment, Andrea stepped over to the kitchen window. As she watched, Tom entered the barn, then emerged a few moments later leading Sonuvagun. He tied the horse, then set about grooming the gelding and tacking him up.

It was such a little thing, standing up for Andrea in the face of Jessie's rebellion. But it meant so much more—that Tom respected her judgment, that he'd taken to heart her recommendation that Jessie needed a little tougher handling sometimes.

As if he sensed her observing him, he looked over his shoulder in her direction. A smile flashed on his face before he returned his attention to his horse. That smile eased the last of Andrea's tensions, and warmed her the rest of the afternoon.

Chapter Nine

On the front porch, Andrea waved goodbye as Jessie and Sabrina drove off with Sabrina's mom. She sagged against the porch rail, exhausted after a night and day spent riding herd on two lively nine-year-old girls. She'd been on her own with the two since early this morning when Tom had gone into Sacramento to pick up a horse trailer he'd taken in for repairs. He'd called her midday to say he would be running some errands and that he'd be back by five. It was a quarter past and he hadn't made it home yet.

She felt a niggling of worry, a holdover from those nights as a child spent alone, waiting for her mother to get home from a late shift. Her mom always walked in the door within twenty minutes of the promised time, but during those twenty minutes, Andrea's vivid imagination played out a hundred scary scenarios. When she heard her mother's key in the lock, the frightening images dispersed—until the next time she was alone at night.

Andrea checked her watch and dithered over what to do. Should she go shower and head into town for dinner? She could leave a note for Tom, let him know about Mrs. Fox's impulsive invitation to have Jessie over for the night. Or should she wait until he got home before leaving?

Waiting won out, hands down. She tried to tell herself it was simply good courtesy to tell Tom in person where Jessie was and to inform him of her plans for the evening. She wasn't buying her own reasoned explanation, though. She'd missed Tom terribly all day and wanted a chance to spend a few minutes with him.

She didn't like to think about how important he'd become to her. She'd much rather call it hormones, physical attraction. But that didn't explain the sheer pleasure she felt when he smiled at her across the breakfast table.

She descended the porch steps, ready to head for her apartment for her shower when a cloud of dust from the gravel road caught her eye. Her heart thudded into hyperdrive in anticipation of seeing Tom's truck top the rise. When his pickup came into view, she wrapped her arms around her middle, as if to hold her joy inside.

He covered the last leg into the yard slowly, towing the big three-horse trailer behind him. When he pulled up by the round pen, he looked hot and exhausted, his sweaty hair plastered to his head. Still she ached to throw her arms around him.

He opened the truck door and stepped out, shoulders sagging. He reached inside for his cowboy hat, then slammed the door. When he turned to face her, it took everything in her not to run to him.

He walked slowly toward her, a smile spreading on his face as he neared her. "God, it's good to be home."

Her fingers itched to stroke his cheek, to ease the tiredness in his eyes. "Bad day?"

"Just long." He looked around him. "Is Sabrina still here?"

"Mrs. Fox just left with both of them. Jessie's spending the night. I hope that's okay."

"It's fine." His hands on the brim of his hat grew restless, turning the Stetson over, slapping it against his leg. "What do you say we—" He looked off toward the barn, toward the house, down at his feet. Finally he directed his gaze up at her. "Would you like to go out to dinner?"

It was like being handed a wonderful and completely unexpected gift. "I would love to."

"I thought we could…" He fidgeted with his hat again. "We could go over to Marbleville. The Italian place is pretty good."

She locked her hands together to keep from touching him. "I just need to shower."

"Me, too." His boots scraped on the gravel as he shifted his feet. "Meet you out here in…thirty minutes okay?"

"Perfect."

She waved awkwardly as she stepped away, then had to force herself to walk rather than race to her apartment. She wanted to look back over her shoulder, to see if he was watching her, but she kept her gaze resolutely forward.

She showered quickly, her hair covered by a cap since it didn't need washing. Deciding what to wear took more time. She'd been living in jeans, T-shirts and shorts since she'd arrived, but tonight she wanted something different, something nicer. She had few choices as far as dresses were concerned, most of them were the businesslike wardrobe she had worn in the class-room.

But then she remembered the sundress she'd bought in Marbleville with Beth. With its full ankle-length skirt and simple bodice, it was dressy without being seductive. The diffuse floral pattern in blues and lavenders had made her feel feminine and pretty when she'd tried it on in the store.

She unbraided her hair and brushed it until it shone, then pulled it back on either side with two mother-of-pearl combs. A bit of lipstick, a touch of eye shadow and she barely recognized herself. When was the last time she'd dressed herself up like this?

A shiver of fear settled into her belly and she pressed a hand to her middle. She'd last worn a frilly, feminine dress for Richard. She'd bought the lacy confection especially for him, because he hated seeing her in anything but dresses. She'd worn it the night he proposed.

Just a week before, he'd refused to take her out unless she changed out of her slacks and into a dress. She should have taken that as a warning. Instead she'd gone out to buy a dress to please him.

It wasn't even the same dress, but she felt a sudden urge to tear it off, to throw it away as she thought she had all her old memories of Richard. But she loved the dress, had chosen it because she adored the iris print, the ruffled petals, the long, graceful green stems. She reminded herself that Richard wouldn't have approved of the dress—he would've wanted the bodice cut lower and the hem above her knee.

Smoothing her hair back one more time, she grabbed up a small handbag and hurried out the door. She saw

Tom seated on the porch steps, elbows on knees, hat hiding his face. When he heard her footsteps on the stairs, he rose and turned toward her. He took off his hat, revealing hair still damp from his shower and a look of wonder on his face.

My God, she was beautiful.

He'd told himself a thousand times he had no business thinking of his daughter's teacher as anything but a competent employee, but in that moment, that lecture seemed like utter nonsense. He'd never known anyone who was so bright, sweet, kind and honest. Andrea was everything Lori had never been—caring, responsible, without a duplicitous bone in her body. Where Lori could never be trusted, he felt completely confident that he could always rely on Andrea's straightforwardness.

He'd had the day away from her to do some thinking. While he still saw the wisdom in steering clear of an intimate relationship with Andrea, there was no reason they couldn't become closer friends. Even though she'd be moving on in a month or so, he would like to keep in contact with her. Because Jessie surely would want to, but also because of his own growing attachment.

They could be friends without stepping outside those bounds. He had at least that much self-control.

But as she stepped out into the yard and approached him, that resolve seemed to scatter with the breeze skittering past them. With her hair lying loose around her face, the soft dark strands like a cape around her shoulders, the modest dress faithfully following her slender curves, she might as well have walked from a dream.

His navy polo shirt suddenly seemed too warm, his khaki slacks too constricting. He would have taken off his hat and fanned himself if he wouldn't have felt damn silly doing it. Instead he smiled and gestured her toward the pickup.

He had to help her up into the cab, so he had to take her hand, didn't he? If he let his fingers linger on hers, it was just to be certain she was secure in the truck. If he hurried around the front to climb into the driver's side, surely it was just so she wouldn't be kept waiting.

But when he sat beside her, shut the door and breathed in her scent, nothing made sense anymore except the way she smelled, the softness of her skin. It took three tries to get the key in the ignition, then he fumbled with the gear shift when he tried to put it into drive.

He headed up the gravel drive toward the county road, wincing when the truck lurched over a pothole. ''Sorry. Meant to get the road graded this spring.''

She grabbed the seat as the pickup jounced again. ''I'm fine.''

Even the sound of her voice seared across his nerves. If he didn't get a grip on himself, he'd be parking the truck and pulling her into his arms. A big mistake.

So he focused on navigating the rough gravel drive, then the county road, only slightly better maintained than his own. Dust followed the pickup in a high, roiling cloud, announcing their passage.

Driving the county's rural roads had never bothered him much; he liked the fact that civilization was still held at bay in Hart Valley. But with Andrea beside him, all dolled up for a night out with him, he felt a little embarrassed by the rustic countryside.

''Pavement's just up ahead,'' he told her, although she knew as well as he did. ''It'll smooth out then.''

''I'm fine,'' she assured him. ''I don't mind the bumps.''

Tom glanced over at her, took in her smile. Of course she didn't mind. Warmth spread inside him at the realization.

He turned his attention back to his driving as they finally reached pavement. "Lori hated it."

Andrea turned in her seat so she faced him. "The roads?"

Braking for the stop sign ahead, he let the old memories crowd back in. "The roads, the dust and heat in the summer, the mud and rain in the winter. She hated the flies, the snakes, even the damn raccoons when they dumped the trash cans."

"I'm with her on the snakes," Andrea said, her tone laced with humor.

He pulled onto the access road to Interstate 80, then gave her a quick look. "We don't get too many snakes."

"Glad to hear it."

God, he wanted to stroke her cheek, see how the tipped up corner of her mouth would feel against his fingertips. Instead he kept both hands on the wheel as he drove up the ramp onto Interstate 80.

"She just couldn't live here." As he said the words, he realized it was the first time he'd admitted it and a tiny little part of himself forgave her. "She grew up in the Bay Area. Hart Valley might as well have been an alien planet."

"How did you meet?" Andrea shifted in her seat and her tantalizing fragrance seemed to fill the cab.

He inhaled Andrea's scent, wishing he could wash away the pain of the past with her sweetness. "I was in my third year at UC Davis. I'd gone over to San Francisco for spring break. She'd just dropped out of school and was as wild as they come."

He still remembered the rush he'd felt when the most beautiful woman at the frat party came on to him. She'd walked right over to him, wrapped her arms around him and kissed him before she'd even given him her name. He'd thought he'd died and gone to heaven.

The smell of tequila on her breath, the soft slur of her words as she whispered raunchy suggestions in his ear should have warned him off. But when she pressed herself even closer, her hands groping, lust took over and fogged his brain.

"She was everything I wasn't—sophisticated, rich." Recalling his starry-eyed devotion to her, he laughed ruefully. "I'd spent my life on a ranch. We always had enough to get by, but when you run cattle, there isn't much left over for luxuries. And Lori was used to luxury."

It didn't take her long to run through the modest allowance his folks had sent him. He'd had to double up his work hours, cut corners to have enough to entertain her on the weekends he went into San Francisco.

But nothing he'd done had ever been enough.

He turned off on the Marbleville exit, slowed for the red light. An edgy energy prickled along his arms, made it hard to sit still. "She never had to work for anything. Her parents gave her whatever she asked for, then along comes this big dumb rancher ready to take up where her folks left off."

"But you loved her." It wasn't quite a question.

"How the hell would I know? I was so damned young." A bitterness he thought he'd cast aside long ago welled up in him. "And so damned stupid."

"Naive, I'm guessing," Andrea suggested.

When the light turned green, he turned left, crossing over Interstate 80 and into Marbleville's Old Town. The

small public parking lot was full and he had to circle it
a couple times before he spotted a car about to leave.
He parked the truck, shut off the engine.

"I should have known better." He rattled the keys in
his hand. "She was wrong for me. All wrong."

She reached across the truck cab, laid her fingers
lightly on his arm. "Not everything was wrong."

It took him a moment, then he understood her meaning. "Jessie was the only good thing to come out of
it."

Digging up the past had set up a burning in his gut.
He shoved upon the door, climbed out. Rounding the
truck, he tried to box those feelings up again.

But as soon as he took Andrea's hand to help her
from the pickup cab, everything stirred up again. A
yearning threatened to overwhelm him—to take Andrea
in his arms, to hold her close, to take what comfort he
could from her.

Yet that would expose his soul far more than he could
bear. So when Andrea stepped from the truck, he let go
as soon as he could. As they walked to Vincenzo's Ris-
torante, he made sure to keep a foot of space between
them on the narrow sidewalk.

By the time they'd taken their table in Vincenzo's
he'd had himself convinced he had his emotions reined
in again. But he hid behind his menu, unwilling to face
Andrea, knowing she could unravel his control with one
empathetic look.

The food was as delicious as promised, but for much
of the meal, Andrea wondered if she'd ever get more
than two words in a row out of Tom. She knew talking
about his ex-wife hadn't been easy for him. But if she'd
known the discussion of Lori would throw such a dark

cloud over him, she would have changed the subject as soon as it came up.

She'd wanted nothing more than to enjoy the evening. She wouldn't allow herself to think of this time with Tom as a date, as any kind of romantic interlude. But she deserved the opportunity to relax in the company of another adult.

She'd just about given up when Tom looked up from the lasagna he'd barely touched. "I've been pretty lousy company, haven't I?"

"Well…" Stalling, she took a bite of her chicken piccata. "You've been a bit quiet."

She tried to keep a straight face, but then the corner of his mouth quirked up and she burst out laughing. The bleakness that had weighed him down finally seemed to lift and his easy laughter joined hers.

He grinned at her. "You are so good for me."

A flush rose in her cheeks at his unexpected praise. "Thank you."

His gaze roamed her face, his scrutiny setting off sparks inside her. When his attention returned to his dinner, she let out a breath of relief.

"So…" He picked up his fork and took a big bite of lasagna. "How's Jessie's writing coming along?"

"We've made some progress." She scooped up some capers with a morsel of chicken. "She's happy enough using the computer. Cursive practice, though…you know how much she hates that."

"Because it hurts her?" He tapped his fork on the edge of his plate. "Because of the burn?"

She considered carefully how to answer. "Using her right hand might always be uncomfortable for her."

"But…?"

"But…she draws. She weaves friendship bracelets

for Sabrina. I've seen her roll out horse cookies until her hand was cramping and I had to tell her to stop."

He stared at her, and she had to resist squirming under his steady gaze. "You're saying it's just an excuse, then."

She wouldn't sugarcoat it. "Yes."

His jaw tensed. "She just needs to apply herself."

Those were loaded words; she could hear it in his tone. "Is that what her teacher said?"

"The principal." His mouth relaxed in a ghost of a smile. "The Battleaxe."

Based on what Jessie had told her, Andrea would love to go a few rounds with the infamous Mrs. Beeber. "Jessie's been through plenty. You both have."

She touched the back of his hand lightly, needing the brief connection to be sure he truly listened to her. Sensation shivered up her arm in response and for a moment she couldn't remember what she'd been about to say. "I wouldn't dare minimize what you've been through. But you can't let it shape your life, either."

"Have I?" The challenge in the question was unmistakable.

But she wouldn't rise to the bait. "Only you can answer that one."

He continued to stare her down for several long moments, the stubborn set of his jaw so like his daughter's. "I've done my best."

"You've done a great job," she assured him.

"Her suffering just tore my heart out. For a long time I just couldn't say no to her."

He was a strong man, a proud man. Yet she could imagine how Jessie's agony had brought him to his knees.

She reached across the table, laid her hand over his.

"How did it happen?" she asked quietly. "You've never said."

He turned his wrist, enclosing her hand in his. She injected every bit of comfort she could in the contact.

She wanted to look away from the raw pain in his eyes, but she kept her gaze locked with his as he spoke. "I was away for the day, up in Redding. I'd gone to check out a filly—Honeybee."

"Who was at home with Jessie?"

"Lori." He swallowed. "And the ranch foreman."

His grip on her hand tightened. "The power went out. We had high winds and…" He shook his head. "Lori didn't realize it at first. She was…busy."

Emotions flickered across his face—rage, guilt, despair. She wished she'd never asked him, yet sensed that telling her what had happened to Jessie might relieve some of the pain.

"Jessie called for Lori all through the house." His gaze grew distant, as if he'd traveled back to those agonizing moments. "When she wouldn't answer, Jessie found a flashlight. The batteries were nearly gone. I'd meant to change them…"

Another layer of guilt added to the burden. His fingers tensed again. "She knew she wasn't allowed to use matches, but she was so scared of the dark—" His voice broke. "She lit the match okay, got the candle going."

The hardest part was coming. Andrea placed her other hand over his as he continued. "She tried to reach for something on the other side of the table. The sleeve of her sweatshirt caught the flame."

He shut his eyes. "When she screamed, Lori finally heard. I was just pulling in as Jessie ran from the house,

her arm on fire. Lori was just coming from the foreman's apartment.''

His eyes snapped open. ''I should have been there. I
never should have left.''

''You had no way of knowing what would happen.''

''But I knew about Lori and the foreman.'' The muscle in his jaw flexed. ''I pretended I didn't, but...'' He
uttered a crude oath. ''I should have been there to protect her.''

She had to find a way to soothe him, to ease the hurt.
She raised his hand to her cheek, rested it against her
skin. Then she turned her head, pressed her mouth
against his fingers.

She'd meant to comfort him, to communicate to him
how much she cared about him, about Jessie. But as her
lips brushed against his knuckles, as she felt the taut
skin against her mouth, heat exploded inside her.

Too much heat. She told herself to pull away. She
lowered her hands to the table, but she couldn't let go.
Her fingers just nestled more securely within his.

His blue gaze mesmerized her. She couldn't have
looked away if her life depended on it.

''Andrea...'' He said her name in a low, urgent tone.
''Sometimes when I'm with you...''

She swallowed, her throat dry as dust. She sensed
what was coming next, what door he might be opening.
It had tempted them both nearly from the time she'd
first arrived at the ranch, had intensified whenever they
were near enough to touch. The kiss in the barn had
threatened to blast the door open, but they'd stopped in
time. His naked emotions, laid bare as he recounted
Jessie's tragic accident, battered on the door now.

She ought to lock it securely, ought to declare here
and now that any kind of intimacy between them would

be a huge mistake. She told herself that a hundred times a day. But it always came back to this—a touch she couldn't resist, a promise she couldn't defend her heart against.

"I want to touch you," he murmured, his voice so low no one beyond their own table could hear. "I want it so damn bad. But I wanted her, too."

"I'm not Lori."

"No, you're not. Thank God for that."

"But it would still be a mistake."

He nodded, although he didn't seem quite sure. "Because of Jessie."

"Yes." She hesitated, then shook her head. "No. Let's not blame it on Jessie."

A trace of irritation flickered in his eyes. "Meaning?"

He wouldn't want to hear the truth, that he wasn't near enough ready to trust her, to trust any woman enough to become involved beyond the sex act. No matter how close they became physically, he wouldn't let her anywhere near his heart.

Not that she wanted to be that close to him. Since Richard, she'd realized she couldn't commit to a man any more than she could commit to a place.

With an effort, she pulled away, dropped her hands in her lap. "I know why it would be wrong for me. You'll have to find your own reasons."

The words came out more harshly than she'd intended, so she sought a way to soften them. "I genuinely like you, Tom. Can we just leave it at that?"

His gaze on her concealed more than it revealed. She desperately wanted to know what lay behind those vivid blue eyes. "That was why I asked you to dinner," he said finally. "Because I like you. I'd like us to be friends."

Friends. An ache started up inside her. The one thing she'd longed for most, all her life. A friend. And a home.

She'd never have a home. But a friend...

She smiled, let herself brush her fingers across the back of his hand. "I'd like us to be friends."

"And when you go..." He glanced away, then back at her. "Jessie will miss you. I will, too."

"I'll write. I'll call." Even as she promised, a hollowness opened up inside at the thought of leaving. "I won't forget either one of you."

"Good." He nodded. "That's fine." Yet as he returned to finishing off his lasagna, she sensed his disappointment.

She hadn't given him enough. She had somehow let him down. Yet it seemed there was nothing inside her worthy enough to give him.

Just yourself, a voice whispered. Give him yourself. That's enough.

She tried to thrust aside the notion, tried to refute it with a long list of her shortcomings. But the thought persisted, throughout dinner, during the drive home and long into the night.

Chapter Ten

In the weeks that followed their night out, the atmosphere between Andrea and Tom crackled like an imminent lightning storm. He never touched her—except as they passed each other in the kitchen putting supper on the table, or as he helped her into the saddle before a ride, or as he took a bucket of grain from her when she helped to feed the horses.

When he spoke to her, he was always polite, but Andrea always sensed a thread of urgency in his tone, a roughness that both thrilled her and frightened her. Because she felt that same urgency shimmering between them, ached to hear that roughness whispered against her skin.

Jessie wasn't as much of a distraction as she could have been. She'd suddenly decided she loved to write and spent hours at the computer crafting wonderfully imaginative stories. And when Andrea brought home a book of calligraphy that included intricately illuminated letters, Jessie unexpectedly fell in love with cursive. She brought her single-minded focus to the art of penning neat, carefully drawn handwritten sentences, the first letter of each paragraph a glory of intricate color and design. If Jessie's subject matter still revolved entirely around horses, Andrea couldn't fault her painstakingly crafted result.

Even as the sensual barrage set her every nerve on edge, the growing closeness between her and Jessie stabbed at her when she thought about leaving the little girl behind. Her fondness for Tom was so tangled up in their attraction she wasn't certain how she felt about him. But Jessie had made a place in her heart that would be impossible to dislodge when it was time to move on.

Two weeks from today. The Friday after next. It was all she had left.

A leaden weight in her stomach, she neatly stacked the schoolbooks on the coffee table in the living room, making everything tidy for the weekend. Jessie was upstairs in her room, finishing the last hour of the school day with *The Lion, the Witch and the Wardrobe.*

When she couldn't find another thing that needed straightening, she climbed the stairs to Jessie's room. The door was slightly ajar, but she rapped on it before poking her head in. Jessie lay on her stomach, stretched out on her bed, propped up on one elbow. She wore a short-sleeved T-shirt today, something she'd been doing more often as she shed her embarrassment over her burn scar.

Jessie finished the page she was on, then looked up at Andrea. "Hi."

Andrea ached to sit beside Jessie, to enfold her in her arms. How was she ever going to leave her?

She forced a smile. "I'm going back to my place. When you're done, make sure you log your pages."

Andrea had persuaded Tom to reward Jessie for every hundred pages read. The inducement had transformed an indifferent reader into a voracious consumer of books. Luckily, the Marbleville County Library was well stocked enough to feed Jessie's new habit.

"Okay," she said a bit absently as she returned to the fantasy land of Narnia.

Backing from the room, Andrea swung the door almost shut as it had been. Her gaze strayed down the hall to the room next to Jessie's. So far, she'd resisted the temptation to look inside Tom's bedroom, had lectured herself numerous times that she had no right to intrude on his privacy. But today, the lure just seemed too great.

Surely Tom was busy in the barn or in the round pen. He rarely came inside in midafternoon, and then only for a drink of water or to grab a quick snack. She'd have enough time to peek inside the forbidden zone and finally satisfy her curiosity.

She tiptoed down the hall, although Jessie was too engrossed in her book to hear her and Tom was nowhere near. Feeling a bit like a teenage girl stealing a quick look inside the boy's locker room, she nudged open Tom's bedroom door and stepped inside.

The no-frills, utilitarian furniture she'd expected—an unornamented oak dresser, a king-sized bed with a plain, matching headboard and well-used quilt. Mismatched nightstands on either side, one with a lamp, the other a clock radio. A straight-backed chair draped with a couple T-shirts and a pair of Wranglers.

The amount of clutter fit a man that spent far more of his waking hours working outside than inside the four walls of his bedroom. She saw a pair of sneakers, one upended by the dresser, the other peeking out from under the bed. Several white socks lay scattered across the hardwood floor. A hoof-pick sat next to a hairbrush on the dresser.

She couldn't help herself; she moved through the room picking up socks, carrying the sneakers to the closet, ordering the brush, nail clippers, and pocket change on the dresser. A glass-fronted display case beside the dresser needed a good dusting and its smudged windows a thorough cleaning, but she hadn't the right supplies. Maybe she'd check with Tom, see if he minded her giving his room a good going-over.

Her hand on the quilted bedspread, ready to twitch it more neatly over the pillows, she suddenly realized her intrusion into Tom's private space was as intimate as touching him, as kissing him. Images burst inside her, of Tom stretched out under those covers, reaching for her, beckoning her to join him.

She dropped the covers as if they'd burned her and backed away from the bed. When she turned, her gaze fell on the glass-fronted display case, its dirty windows barely revealing its contents. What would a man like Tom keep on display? Maybe it was something Lori had left behind, although she couldn't imagine him keeping any of his ex-wife's belongings.

Too compelled by curiosity to resist looking inside, she crossed the room and knelt in front of the case. What she saw through the beveled glass surprised her—model horses in every color and pose, from a spindly-legged foal to a wild, rearing stallion.

Her fingers itched with the temptation to open the doors for a closer look. She'd just wrapped her hand around the ornate brass pull when the tread of booted feet finally caught her attention. She was barely on her feet when Tom strode into his room, tugging his T-shirt from his jeans.

He'd been about to pull the shirt over his head when he saw her. "What the hell are you doing here?"

Heat rose in her cheeks. "I'm sorry. I shouldn't have… I was just… I was trying…" Her mind scrambled for an excuse, but came up empty.

He let the hem of his T-shirt drop over his jeans, looked around him. "You cleaned my room."

"Just a bit. Put a few things away, that's all."

He nodded, angled away from her a bit. The T-shirt nearly covered the front placket of his jeans, but still she could see an unmistakable bulge. That his body might be reacting to her presence in his room sent a sizzle of sensation up her spine.

She tore her gaze away, back up to his face. She had to think of something, anything else than what it would feel like to press her hand against that ridge. "Would you like me to clean in here?" she blurted out. "Dust and keep things straightened up?"

He stared at her, his blue eyes a mystery. "No, thank you."

"I'd be glad to do it," she rattled on. "Maybe in the afternoons when we're done with lessons."

He shifted, pulled at his T-shirt. "That wouldn't be a good idea."

"Would mornings be better?" she persisted, feeling like a runaway train. "Before we start the school day?"

"You shouldn't be in my room, Andy."

He said it softly, without censure. His using her nickname for the first time ratcheted up the tension in the room.

She wanted desperately to touch him, have him touch

her. She didn't know if she could walk past him out of the room without giving in to those desires.

Looking away from him, her gaze returned to the display case. "Are the horses yours?" she asked, hoping he would move away from the door.

He did, keeping a wide berth as he circled behind her. She had the impression of a prowling mountain lion, investigating its prey.

"They were my mother's," he said, reaching past her to open the cabinet doors. "They're Breyer models. She collected them as a girl."

Exquisitely aware of him just behind her, Andrea went down on one knee to look inside the open case. A rearing Appaloosa stallion towered over a white mare and its foal. A sorrel gelding trotted briskly on another shelf beside a black and white paint.

She admired a bay quarter horse, modeled in the same sliding stop she'd seen Tom execute on Sonuvagun. "Does Jessie play with them?"

"Not yet." He knelt beside her and his shoulder rubbed against hers. She smelled horse on him and his own scent of a hardworking man. "I told her she can have them when she's twelve. She has to show me she can take good care of them."

When his shoulder rubbed against hers again, she sensed it hadn't been accidental. A glance up at him confirmed what she'd guessed—that he was as consumed with the attraction between them as she.

She sat back on her heels, opening some space between them. He did the same. Still she could feel heat coming off him in waves.

"Sometimes," he said hoarsely, "it seems a forgone conclusion."

She wanted to pretend she didn't know what he was talking about. She shook her head. "We shouldn't."

"So we keep saying. And yet…" He reached across the chasm they'd set for themselves. He nearly touched her; she could swear she felt the stroke of his fingers against her cheek. But then he rose to his feet and stepped away.

"The tractor broke down. I need to head over to Marbleville for a part. I was just coming up for a shower."

She closed the cabinet doors, wishing she could shut off her feelings for Tom as easily. "Jessie and I are done for the day. I was about to head over to the apartment."

"Okay." Another tug of his T-shirt, another attempt to cover what she had no business thinking about.

She stood and headed for the door, stopped just before she slipped out. "I'll stay out of your room."

Arms crossed over his chest, he nodded. Then, as she turned to go, he called out, "Andy."

She stepped back into the doorway, knowing she shouldn't, but helpless to do anything else. "Yes?"

He opened his mouth, then closed it again, looked down at his toes, then back up at her. He swallowed, his throat working. Finally, he spoke. "I'm probably asking for trouble."

"What is it?"

He uncrossed his arms, shoved his hands into his pockets. "Did Jessie tell you about the silent auction tomorrow night?"

"She did. She said Beth is letting her and Sabrina stay at the inn for the night."

"Will you go with me?" The words spilled out, as rushed as any teenage boy's first invitation to a girl. "There's dinner before the auction and dancing after."

She could think of nothing she would want to do more. "I'd love to go with you."

He grinned and Andrea thought her heart would burst from her chest. "That's great." In that moment, the boy the man had been stood before her. Her heart leaped higher, beat faster.

Feelings suddenly swamped her, emotions she couldn't hold inside. She stumbled back a step, turned away. "I have to go."

Hurrying down the hall, then down the stairs, she could feel Tom's gaze on her. She thought he might have called her name again, but she didn't dare go back. She ran from the house and across the yard toward her apartment. As she pelted past them, the mares out in pasture bobbed their heads up and one of the foals galloped off around its mother, kicking up its heels.

Finally inside her apartment, the door shut behind her, she sagged into the battered sofa, gasping for breath. She let the feelings come now, let herself examine them, try to understand them.

When she'd met Richard three-and-a-half years ago, she'd been so reluctant to trust him. Although she'd sensed a wrongness, everything seemed right on the surface and her logical mind had persuaded her he was exactly what he seemed. It was only later she realized her instincts were sharper than her mind.

But with Tom, no matter how many layers she peeled away, she saw only a good man with the best intentions. A man who would stand beside those he cared for, who would be a rock and an anchor.

A man it would be so easy to give herself to. A man it would be so easy to love.

She covered her face with her hands. She wasn't in

love with him. She absolutely wasn't. Because she wouldn't let herself.

She couldn't.

Tom tipped his head back in the shower, letting the cool water stream over his heated body. It was a futile gesture, thinking he could wash away memories of Andrea's scent, the silky texture of her hair, the satin of her skin. He'd done his best to keep his hands off of her since their kiss in the barn, but somehow touching her had become as urgent and necessary as breathing.

Wetting his hair, he rubbed bargain brand shampoo into it. He imagined washing Andrea's hair, working the shampoo from the scalp to the ends, exploring her body along the way. He'd rinse the soap away carefully to keep it from stinging her eyes, then he'd kiss her face, sipping up drops of water along the way.

He wrenched the hot water faucet shut, then swallowed back a yelp as icy water pummeled him. It didn't much help his body's response to the tantalizing images of Andrea, but it gave him something else to think about while he finished washing.

Feeling the pressure of time, he dried quickly and pulled on a clean T-shirt and jeans. As much as he might want to tell himself he needed to hurry before the auto parts store in Marbleville closed, he knew he simply wanted to be there and back before supper. Suppertime had become a treasured ritual, golden moments spent reviewing Jessie's day, sharing an intimate glance with Andrea across the table.

As he grabbed his change off the dresser, he had to smile when he realized Andrea had stacked the coins. He should have felt invaded by her presence in his room, yet he felt only a rightness, as if she'd belonged there. Something he'd never quite experienced with Lori.

Striding down the hall, he poked his head into Jessie's room. She lay on her back, book splayed beside her on the bed. Hands hooked behind her head, she stared at the ceiling.

"Jess?"

She started, then sat up so quickly she knocked the book to the floor. "Yeah?"

He couldn't help but wonder what she'd been daydreaming about. "I'm going into Marbleville. Andy's over in her apartment if you need her."

She stared at him for several moments, again piquing Tom's curiosity. Her words came out in a rush. "Can I go with you?"

She hadn't willingly accompanied him on an errand in at least a couple years. Usually, he saved up his chores in town for times she was in school or over at Sabrina's.

He felt wary and pleased all at once. "You might get bored."

"So what?" She clambered from the bed and grabbed her sneakers. "I won't die."

Had space aliens kidnapped his daughter and left an imposter in her place? He was half tempted to check her forehead for fever. "Company would be great."

Shoving feet into sneakers in record time, Jessie raced past him and took the stairs two at a time. She had the front door open before he'd even reached the bottom.

Her hand on the door, she waved him past her. "Can we bring home take and bake pizza for dinner?"

"Fine with me." He stepped aside to avoid her headlong rush down the porch steps. "We ought to let Andrea know we're both going and that we're bringing home dinner.''

Halfway to the truck, Jessie changed course quick as a cutting horse going after a cow. ''I'll tell her.''

Standing by the pickup, Tom watched as Jessie yelled for Andrea and banged on her door. From his vantage point in the yard, he caught just a glimpse of Andrea when she answered, heard only fragments of the brief conversation between her and Jessie. Then Jessie clattered down the stairs and sprinted over to the truck.

''She said she'll make a salad to go with the pizza,'' Jessie said as she climbed into the truck. ''Yuck.''

Tom put the truck in gear and headed up the bumpy gravel drive. ''Vegetables are good for you,'' he told Jessie, the rote words giving him time to redirect his thoughts away from Andrea.

But as they reached the county road and jounced along toward where the pavement started, Tom realized Jessie had an agenda, one that would keep his mind firmly on his daughter's teacher.

It started with an innocent enough question. ''So, Dad…do you like Andrea?''

He took a breath, knowing he had to tread carefully. ''Sure, I do. She's a great teacher.''

''But do you really like her?'' Jessie persisted. ''Not just as a teacher.''

''You mean as a friend?'' he asked, intentionally obtuse.

''Yes.'' Jessie shook her head. ''No. Well, sort of.''

As he pulled onto Interstate 80, Tom knew exactly where this conversation was going. He would have given his right arm not to have this discussion with his daughter. He didn't know himself how he felt about Andy; how could he tell Jessie?

"I like Andrea quite a bit," he allowed. "As a friend, as well as a teacher."

Jessie digested this, sitting in silence until they'd reached the Marbleville exit and he braked for the red light. Just as well he was at a standstill when she blurted out her next query.

"Do you like her enough to marry her?"

A piano could have fallen on him in that instant and he wouldn't have noticed. He'd been pretty sure what Jessie had been dancing around, what she really wanted to know. It didn't prepare him any better for the forth-right question.

Watch your step, he told himself as he turned right at the green light. "People don't usually get married if they just like each other."

"But they could sometimes?" The hopeful note in Jessie's voice squeezed Tom's heart painfully.

He pulled into the parking lot of the Marbleville Center and negotiated the lanes over to the auto parts store. Once he'd parked the truck he turned to Jessie. Wistful longing warred with expectation of disappointment in her upturned face. He hated to add one more heartbreak to the string she'd had to endure.

"Jess…" He sensed whatever he said would hurt her. "What Andrea and I feel for each other isn't the same as what a man and woman feel when they want to marry." He winced inwardly at the partial lie, but he wasn't about to explain to his nine-year-old daughter about lust. "Since she came to be your teacher, we've become friends, but that's all."

Jessie looked away, her lower lip thrust out. He expected her to lash out with rude and angry words. When he saw tears glittering in her eyes, he felt like the worst father in the world.

But he couldn't pretend to love Andy or marry her just because his daughter wanted him to. That would be repeating his error as a twenty-two-year-old, marrying Lori when he'd mistaken sexual attraction for love.

With her back to him, Jessie swiped away tears with the heels of her hands, then looked over her shoulder at him. "What about the auction? Did you invite her?"

Jessie had been pestering him about it for a week, but he'd managed to sidestep a commitment. Until that afternoon, when he'd encountered Andrea in his room. The invitation had issued itself, seemingly without conscious intent.

"She'll be coming with us," he told Jessie.

"With you, you mean. I'm going with Sabrina." Jessie crowed with delight. "You're taking Andy on a date. That makes you more than friends."

What could he say? Any more argument over the semantics of it and Jessie would be sure there was something brewing between him and Andrea. Better to cut the conversation short.

Because any more talk and he'd be stepping into a lie. He knew damn well he and Andrea had long ago bypassed friendship and stumbled into much more intimate territory.

They climbed from the truck, Jessie skipping on ahead of him toward the auto parts store. What seemed so simple to a nine-year-old befuddled him beyond reason. He longed for even a tenth of Jessie's wisdom.

Chapter Eleven

Andrea stood before the mirror in her tiny bedroom dressed in her bra and panties, a pile of rejected clothes on the bed behind her. It seemed her entire wardrobe had morphed into either hooker attire or the staid uniform of a schoolmarm. She had nothing to wear to the silent auction and dinner dance that hit the middle ground between overly suggestive and downright matronly.

She shook her bangs from her eyes and turned to face the mountain of garments on the bed. Maybe she ought to wear jeans and a T-shirt. It wouldn't be nearly dressy enough, but at least she'd feel confident she wouldn't be showing off any more leg or baring more shoulder than usual. She'd be just plain old Andrea, the same ordinary person Tom saw every day.

Sinking onto the edge of the bed, Andrea propped her chin on her hand. Who was she fooling? No matter what she wore, the scintillating attraction would crackle between her and Tom, real and tangible. She could wear a suit of armor and still feel Tom's gaze straight to her soul. There was no protecting herself from him, even if she wanted that protection.

They were rushing toward something powerful, something inevitable. The only way to avoid that destination would be to pack up and go before Tom came calling for her.

She considered that option for about a quarter of a second before rising to dig through the pile of clothes again. She unearthed a raspberry-pink shell that teamed perfectly with a floral print skirt still in the closet. A little wrinkled from the wrestling match on the bed, the light, slippery silk top would need a bit of touching up.

Fifteen minutes later she pulled on the shell and tucked it neatly into the waistband of the skirt. She felt feminine and pretty, even more so when she added a pair of dangly earrings in raspberry and navy and a delicately beaded Y-necklace.

She'd just pulled the band from her braid when a knock sounded on the door. Her gaze flew to the bedside clock—all her indecision over what to wear had made her late. Her half-unwoven braid tangled in her fingers, she hurried for the door.

She tugged on the knob, realized she'd locked it, then fumbled with the lock for a moment before opening the door a crack. Tom stood on the landing, heart-stoppingly gorgeous in a dark-gray suit, crisp white shirt and silvery tie. If her hair hadn't been a mess and her feet bare, she would have stepped outside and wrapped her arms around him.

As it was, she shook her fingers loose of her braid

and tossed the long strands back over her shoulder. "Can you give me another couple minutes?"

"Jessie's champing at the bit, but I think I can hold her off. Just come down when you're ready. We'll wait in the truck."

"Be right down," she gasped, then shut the door.

She combed out her hair in record time, then made small braids on either side that she pinned back with a sterling silver clasp. A little blush, just a touch of eye shadow and lipstick and she declared herself ready. She was halfway out the door before she realized she was still barefoot, then it took a full minute to locate her navy sandals.

She trembled as she descended the stairs and crossed the yard. She couldn't see Tom's face through the glare off the truck's windshield, but she wondered if he watched her, and if he liked what he saw.

Then the driver's side door opened and Tom emerged. He walked toward her, closing the distance between them just beyond the truck.

He took her hand. "I…you…" He shook his head, laughed. "Sorry. No words."

Turning his back to the truck and Jessie's eager eyes, he lifted her hand, pressed his lips to her fingers. He released her hand, but rested his fingers lightly on her bare shoulder, guiding her to the truck.

The passenger door popped open before he could touch it. Jessie poked her head out. "You look bee-yoo-ti-ful. Doesn't she, Dad?"

"She does," Tom assured his daughter.

At Jessie's smug smile, Andrea sent Tom a questioning look. He shook his head. "Later."

On the drive into town, Jessie kept up a rapid-fire monologue, rarely allowing the adults room to wedge in so much as a word. Her unending chatter ping-ponged between glowing testimonials of Andrea's teaching prowess and well-embellished stories of Tom's superhuman acts as a rancher and trainer extraordinaire.

Jessie dominated the conversation right up until Tom parked the truck in the Hart Valley public lot. Then the nine-year-old barely waited for Andrea to open her door before she squeezed from the back seat and dashed across the parking lot toward Sabrina just arriving with her parents.

Before Andrea could slide from the truck, Tom was there to help her down. Her hand still resting in his, she asked, "What was that all about?"

Tom looked a bit chagrined. "That was a nine-year-old girl's version of matchmaking."

"Match—" Suddenly Andrea understood. "Oh."

"She brought it up yesterday. I didn't know what to say." He stepped in close to her, fingertips stroking the line of her braids. "How can I explain to a nine-year-old what I don't understand myself?"

"Tom…" She covered his hand with hers, then pulled it gently from her face. "I'm not here much longer."

A muscle tightened in his jaw. "Not as Jessie's teacher."

She tried to tug her hand away, but he wouldn't relinquish it. "Two weeks before school's out."

He caressed the back of her hand with his thumb, and heat blossomed, spilled up her arm. "Can we just deal with tonight? Let the future be for now?"

As he continued to stroke her hand, just with that simple motion of his thumb, she wanted to melt right there into a puddle at his feet. "Tonight," she agreed.

A smile curved his lips, lit his eyes. Then he laced

his fingers with hers and they joined the crowd heading for the Hart Valley Inn.

As Tom stepped inside the inn with Andrea, pride at having her at his side swelled within him. Damned if he didn't want to strut like a peacock. The most incredibly beautiful woman in the county—hell, in the entire state of California—was smiling up at him, her arm linked with his.

When she slipped away from him to greet his sister, Beth, he followed, unwilling to let her stray far. Not even the look of speculation in Beth's face could keep him from reclaiming Andrea's hand.

"You've outdone yourself this year, Sis," he said, gesturing to the silent auction items arrayed throughout the lobby.

"Folks have been especially generous." She shot a pointed look down at his hand enfolding Andrea's. "I'm glad you both could make it."

He refused to rise to the bait. "See you later," he told Beth as he nudged Andrea away from his sister's scrutiny.

They wandered toward the armoire, two shelves of which Beth had cleared to make room for auction items. Andrea admired a tall, etched glass vase flanked by a bottle of wine from a local winery and a stack of cookbooks from a bookstore in Marbleville.

"How does this work?" she asked as she ran a finger down the pile of books.

He imagined that finger drifting down his body, leaving a path of fire. "There's a bid sheet for each item. You write your name and your bid on the sheet, then hope no one comes after you with a higher price."

She smiled up at him, her delight obvious. "But I can bid again?"

"Until they call time. Last one on the list wins."

"And where does the money go?"

He couldn't resist smoothing a wisp of hair behind her ear. "Some goes to the Hart Valley Library, some to the high school, some to the park maintenance fund."

She shivered at his touch, but when his hand drifted down to rest behind her slender neck, she didn't move away.

Reaching for the pen accompanying the bid sheet for the vase, she wrote her name below the last bidder, then upped the price by a dollar. "This is fun." The words came out soft and breathy.

She took his hand, towed him over to the bookshelves where more items were displayed. "Let's see what else there is."

When she let go of his hand, he stood behind her, cupping her shoulders. "Careful you don't go broke."

She craned her neck behind her to give him a haughty look. "Do you think I have no self-control?"

He knew he hadn't an ounce of willpower where she was concerned. Brushing a kiss on her brow, he murmured in her ear. "I think your eyes are bigger than your pocketbook."

She pretended indignation, the light of humor in her soft brown gaze. As they moved along the bookcase, he followed her, still standing behind her. Occasionally she would lean back against him, her head against his chest. Somewhere along the line, his arms had stolen around her, his hands linked at her waist.

"Are you sure?" he asked as she reached for yet another bid sheet on the bookcase. "I think you're up to twenty-five dollars so far."

"I'm good for it."

He looked back at the armoire where Nina stood watching him with Andrea. A needle of guilt stabbed him at the longing in Nina's face.

When Andrea followed his gaze, Nina quickly looked down at the bid sheets in front of her. "Maybe you ought to talk to her."

"We've talked enough."

Andrea turned to face him. "You said you'd told her you weren't interested in a relationship. Yet here we are."

"What's between you and me is none of Nina's business."

Her brow furrowed as she lifted her hand and laid it lightly against his chest. "What *is* between you and me?"

Nothing. Everything. He shook his head. "I don't know." Yet somewhere within him, he knew that was a lie. He was just afraid to put a name to it.

At the armoire, Nina scribbled furiously, then moved away, head high. "I think Nina just outbid you on that vase," Tom told Andrea, glad for the change of subject.

"No way," Andrea said as she hurried back to the armoire.

Tom let her go, giving himself some breathing room. Andrea's question rolled around in his mind, nagging at him. There was one answer—he wanted her, plain and simple. He wanted to touch her everywhere, undress her, thrust inside her until they both reached ecstasy.

He wouldn't be satisfied with a one-night stand with Andrea, as he'd been with other women. And he sensed his passion wouldn't flare and then die away to ashes as it had with Lori. There were too many complexities, too many layers in the connection between him and Andrea. He'd never be able to explore them all, even if she stayed past the end of school.

He knew they were both spiraling in toward a cataclysm, an explosion of desire. He could put on the brakes, bring their headlong tumble toward each other to a stop. It would be best for all of them, especially his daughter who wouldn't understand Andrea's inevitable goodbye.

Nina stood across the room, looking a little lost. Her gaze met Andrea's and he expected the two of them to turn a cold shoulder on one another. But Andrea threaded her way through the crowd in the lobby and approached Nina.

He hadn't a clue what they would have to say to one another, but before long, Andrea was holding Nina's hand as the café owner swiped away tears. Andrea's kindness astounded him, moved him. She gave Nina a hug, then made her way back to him.

He'd just as soon not know what they'd said, but he could see from the determination in Andrea's face that she would tell him. In an effort to waylay her, he spoke before she could. "They're starting to seat for dinner."

She saw through his ploy, but she went along to the banquet room willingly enough. They wall of noise as they entered prevented conversation; they would have had to yell to be heard over the racket. The mass of bodies made navigating the room difficult and he had to pull Andrea close to shoehorn them through the tightest spots.

Halfway across the room, he spotted Jessie waving at him from one of the children's tables in the corner. She and Sabrina sat with Nina's son Nate and several other squirming kids, ready for their dinner of hot dogs and hamburgers. The adult tables were filling quickly and it took some doing to find two empty seats together.

She let him pull out her chair, waited until he'd seated himself, then leaned close enough so that only he could hear. "Nina wanted you to know—she doesn't still love you."

This was the last thing he wanted to discuss, but he knew there was no getting around it. "She doesn't?"

Andrea shook her head. "It's what she wanted from you. A home and family."

He wondered at the trace of desolation in Andrea's tone, wished she'd turn to him so he could see her eyes. "It's not as if there aren't other men in town to give her that."

Reaching for her water glass, she brushed the condensation with her thumb. "She was stuck on you. I think she isn't anymore."

It was almost as if Nina's loneliness had transferred to Andrea. He put his hand against her cheek and tipped her head up toward him. "What is it?"

Mystery dwelt in her face, behind her chocolate-brown eyes, teasing him to unravel it. Her expression, already serious, became more pensive.

"I think I helped her let go of what she knew she'd never have," she said.

"All that in five minutes?" He tried to make it a joke, but the humor fell flat.

She fixed her steady gaze on him. "We both agreed that wanting something, even wanting it desperately, won't make it happen."

The simple statement punched the air from his lungs. She'd spelled out exactly what he'd insisted all these years—that he'd never again entangle himself with a woman. Lori had taught him a harsh enough lesson that commitment led to pain and heartache. He'd convinced himself he needed nothing from a woman beyond physical release.

But that was a lie, and Andrea had stripped it bare. It denied the part of him, deep inside, that ached to build something with a woman.

But not just any woman. With Andrea.

An inexplicable anger surged up and he had to take a drink from his water glass to tamp it down. Emotions buffeted him—longing, confusion and ever-present desire. He zeroed his thoughts onto the one thing he did understand—the physical.

He set down his water with a shaking hand. "There's still the attraction between us."

Her eyes widened, but she didn't look away. "Yes." The word was barely a whisper. "I want you, Tom."

Heat burned in his groin at her frankness. If they hadn't been in a packed banquet hall he would have kissed her, plunged his tongue inside her mouth to taste her. As it was, he grazed a kiss across her brow, then let her go.

The graduating class of Hart Valley High, twelve students in all, had begun to circulate around the room, delivering the salad course. That gave Tom something to do with his hands besides touch Andrea. He could grip his fork, lift bites of lettuce and tomato to his mouth, as he discussed the rising price of crude oil with Mort Gibbons to his left.

Threads of Andrea's conversation with J.C. Archer, owner of Archer's Bakery, drifted toward him, Andrea's light voice weaving in and out of J.C.'s deep bass. They were comparing notes on the best way to knead bread and how to assure a flaky pie crust. He didn't give a damn about pie crust, but he couldn't help himself from straining to hear every word Andrea spoke.

By the time the main course of barbecue chicken arrived, he thought he'd go mad. How could he be expected to sit so near to Andrea and not pull her into his arms, run his hands over her body, taste her mouth, the pulse in her throat, the scent on her wrist? When a wild impulse fountained up to swipe the dishes from the table and take Andrea there, he knew he'd better get out and clear his head.

He shoved his chair back, drawing the curious gazes of everyone at the table. "Be right back," he muttered, then strode from the banquet hall and out of the inn.

As he stepped out onto the sidewalk, he caught sight of Jessie and Sabrina seated on the bench out front. They must have wolfed down their dinner if they were already out here.

Jessie giggled at something Sabrina had said, then saw him and a guilty flush rose in her cheeks. "Hi, Daddy."

He could guess what she and Sabrina had been talking about and it only added to his turmoil. "Forgot something in the truck."

He headed toward the parking lot, then cut through it toward Deer Creek that ran along behind the Main Street businesses. It wasn't much of a creek, in fact it dried to a trickle by high summer, but with the whole town inside the inn, he'd have some privacy here.

Or so he thought. He was shocked to find his sister, Beth, seated on a creekside rock, puffing on a cigarette.

"I thought you gave those things up."

She just about jumped a foot, then scowled up at him. "I did. This is the first one in months." She took another drag, then ground it out on the rock. "It's for medicinal purposes."

He laughed and lowered himself to a nearby tree stump. "You'll have to explain that one to me."

She waved a hand toward the inn. "I love doing the annual fund-raiser, but it drives me crazy every year. It was either the cigarette or run screaming through the banquet hall."

"Then I'll forgive you this once."

"You won't tell Mark?"

He drew an imaginary zipper across his lips. "Your secret's safe with me."

If he thought his promised silence would exempt him from Beth's nosy nature, he was sorely mistaken. "Speaking of secrets…"

"Drop it, Beth." He tried to quell any further probing with a stern look.

But Beth was immune. "What's going on between you and Andrea?"

No way was he answering that one, even if he knew. "Nothing."

Her gaze narrowed. "Are you two…?"

He felt heat rise in his cheeks. "None of your business."

"Then you are."

"We're not!"

"But you want to."

"Beth!" He jumped to his feet, paced along the streambed away from his overly inquisitive sister. Returning to her, he stabbed a finger at her. "It's none of your damn business!"

The curiosity in Beth's face gave way to an unsettling flash of understanding. "Oh," she said.

Oh? What the hell did "oh" mean? He would have

asked, but he wasn't sure he wanted to know. "I'm going back inside," he told her.

"Okay." She just gazed up at him steadily, amusement mixed with pity in her face. "Save me a dance."

"I don't dance," he told her firmly. "You know I don't dance."

Dimples creased her rounded cheeks. "Uh-huh. Just save me one."

His dirty look didn't so much as put a dent in her private glee. He was getting mighty perturbed by the females in his life, from his prickly, matchmaking daughter to his loon of a sister.

Shaking off the notion that Beth knew something he didn't, he headed back through the parking lot, up Main Street and into the inn. Jessie and Sabrina were in the lobby, a game of Twister spread out in the middle of the lobby floor. Some of the kids playing with Jessie and Sabrina were her main tormenters at school, yet Jessie was holding her own amongst them.

Her body tangled with Sabrina's on the Twister board, she grinned at him as he passed through the lobby. Amid all his confusion over his daughter's teacher and the roil of emotions inside him, one certainty shone—Andrea had healed his daughter, had nurtured her back into feeling good about herself. Here was proof.

As he stepped back into the cacophony of the banquet hall, his gaze went straight to Andrea. Either she was looking for him or she sensed his return because her brown eyes found him.

And as he neared her, he realized his sister was right. He *would* be dancing tonight. Because there was no way in hell he could pass up a chance to hold Andrea in his arms.

Chapter Twelve

He's like a keg of dynamite, Andrea thought, a thrill shimmering through her body. One touch and he'll explode.

He'd returned to the table almost more volatile than when he'd left. It wasn't anger she sensed brewing behind Tom's stormy blue gaze, but something at once thrilling and terrifying. And nothing more than a stroke of her fingertips would bring it rushing to the surface.

The tables had been cleared and now she helped clear the banquet hall for the dancing. While Tom and the other men hefted the heavier tables and carried them to the storage room in the back, Andrea, Beth, Nina and Arlene from the Stop 'n' Go toted chairs to the wheeled carts where they were stacked upright. Even Jessie, Sabrina and the other youngsters assisted, making a race out of sweeping the floor with push brooms.

There was no question that she would dance with

him. As the crowd had lingered over dessert, Beth had announced on the P.A. that it was time to ready the banquet hall for the dance. Tom had reached for Andrea's hand under the table, linked his fingers with hers. Her gaze had flicked up to his face, and she had seen the turbulent emotions there. Whatever silent question lay there, she answered yes without hesitation. Because she was willing to take whatever Tom offered her.

The last chair on the cart, ready to be wheeled into the storage room, Andrea searched the hall for Tom. He and one of the other men—Beth's husband Mark?—was wrestling the last of the tables into place in storage. The uncanny connection between them must have alerted him that she watched him because as he stepped from the storage room, he sought her out, locked his gaze with hers. Warmth flooded her from the center of her body outward.

She dimly heard someone speaking to her, then felt a hand on her shoulder. She turned to see Beth behind her. "Sorry. What was that?"

Beth smiled. "I said, the silent auction ends in five minutes. You ought to check your bids."

Andrea welcomed the chance for some space to breathe. She returned to the lobby, and made a circuit of the room, revisiting the auction items she'd chosen. She'd been outbid on several and had a chance to reconsider which of the sundry odds and ends she really wanted.

She picked up a pen, ready to scribble a higher bid on the vase and the stack of cookbooks, when it hit her exactly why she coveted them. A vase overflowing with handpicked flowers, a shelf full of cookbooks, their recipes tried and tasted and loved over the years, made a home. As did the cozy afghan knitted in rose and pale pink, the snowy-white tea set decorated with delft blue flowers, the cookie sheets bundled with a basket of whimsical cookie cutters. Every item she'd chosen was more suited to a woman putting down roots than a rootless wanderer like her.

Let Nina win the vase, she told herself. Beth has more use for the cookbooks. Yet even as she lectured herself, she wrote her name again on the various sheets and upped the bid, intent on winning them.

She'd written her name the last time just as the high school seniors started around the lobby, gathering up the bid sheets. The winning bidders would be tabulated and posted in the lobby. They could pay for their choices and pick them up anytime in the next two weeks.

Two weeks. The deadline loomed like an impenetrable wall. On this side were her last few days with Tom, with Jessie. Her last few days to experience what home felt like before she picked up everything she owned and moved on to the next dot on the map. Except this time she would be bringing with her souvenirs of Hart Valley—a tea set, a hand-knitted afghan, a crystal vase etched with bearded iris.

A warm hand spanned the small of her back and she looked up into Tom's brilliant blue eyes. "The music's started. Come dance with me."

Mesmerized by the promise in his honest gaze, by the heat of his touch, Andrea let him draw her close, lead her back into the banquet hall. A bluesy piece filled the room with languid melody and they joined the couples dancing slowly in the center of the room.

He held her left hand with his right, his left arm at her waist pressing her body against his. She felt every inch of him from knees to chest and the contact nearly stole her breath.

He gently tucked her head beneath his chin. "I don't dance."

His whispered words sent sensation dancing up her spine. "I don't either."

"I had to hold you."

The rawness of his confession sent liquid warmth from her center down her legs, weakening her knees. A throbbing ache started up inside her, and she wanted to nestle even closer to him. He urged her hips toward him and she felt his rigid flesh press against her.

She was on fire. She couldn't hear the music anymore, was blind to everyone but Tom. His fragrance, the feel of his crisp suit jacket against her cheek, the very sound of his breathing overwhelmed her senses. Her feet might as well have been moving on thin air for all she felt them.

The music changed, grew lighter, faster, but Tom's motion didn't change. He drew her into a quiet corner and she was grateful the lights had been dimmed and that the crowd was more focused on the dancers than on them. She tipped her head back to look up at him, saw the glitter of desire in his eyes and she shivered.

He brushed the pad of his thumb across her cheek. "I want to take you home."

She nodded. He bent, feathering kisses along her cheek, her temple, her brow, back down, closer and closer to her mouth. By the time his lips grazed hers, she thought she would go mad with anticipation.

He drew back slightly, his mouth close to her ear. "I need to check on Jessie, make sure she and Sabrina are settled in their room."

She barely had breath enough to speak. "Yes."

He loosened his hold on her, let her step away from him. She shivered from the chill she felt at losing his warmth. One last touch along her cheek and he headed out in search of his daughter.

He couldn't have been gone more than five or ten minutes, but it seemed endless as she waited for him. Her rational mind made a token effort to scold her, to persuade her not to take the perilous step she'd committed herself to, but to her heart it was just so much noise. If she was sure of nothing else tonight, this one thing she was certain of—no matter how much pain might come later, she would take this time with Tom.

Then she caught sight of him striding toward her, skirting the crowd of dancers. Once he'd reached her side, he took her hand, led her from the hall, then through the lobby. Outside in the cool evening air, he laid his arm across her shoulders, bringing her into his warmth and safety.

At the truck, he helped her up inside, then leaned in to cover her mouth with his, tasting her briefly with the tip of his tongue. She wanted more of him, but he broke the contact and shut the door, then went around to the driver's side. After tossing his jacket and tie in the back seat, he settled behind the wheel. She slid across toward him and belted herself in beside him, her hand on his thigh.

The play of muscles beneath the smooth fabric of his trousers as he drove fascinated her and she ached to explore. But at the slightest movement of her fingers, his hand covered hers.

"Don't," he rasped out. He raised her hand up for a quick kiss before placing it in her own lap. "I'd like to make it home in one piece."

She kept her hands to herself, satisfied that she

aroused him as much as he did her. The drive back to the Double J seemed endless, the turmoil inside her growing unbearable.

When they finally pulled onto the rutted gravel drive to the ranch, Andrea felt ready to scream with impatience. Her body shook with wanting him, her hands itched with the need to touch him. The truck couldn't stop quickly enough.

The moment he shut off the engine, he pulled her into his arms and brought his mouth down on hers. She opened to him immediately, moaning deep in her throat when his tongue thrust inside. As close as he held her, it wasn't close enough. She wanted to be inside him, a part of his soul, his essence.

With a groan of impatience, he pushed her back on the seat, angled his leg between hers. As awkward as it was, she would have let him take her there, so frantic she was for his body. But even as his hand cupped her breast and his thigh pressed against the vee of her legs, he reared back, gasping for breath.

"Not here."

He levered himself off of her, opened the driver's side door. She slid across the seat toward him, and his hands circled her waist to help her down.

She had to take a gulp of air to speak. "Where?"

"My bed. I want you there."

Heat streaked up her spine, at the same time pooling low in her body. Sensual images flooded her, in expectation of what would come. She pushed them aside. She wanted the now, to experience each moment as it came.

It seemed to take forever to get inside. In the living room, he kicked off his boots as she tossed aside her sandals.

No more waiting; she had to touch him. She grabbed

his shirt, tugged it from his slacks. At the same time, he ran his hands under her raspberry shell top, easing it off her as he stroked her sides. He unclasped the barrette from her hair, let the silky strands fall around her shoulders.

He drew back, his hot gaze falling on her lacy pink bra. His hands curved around her body, he moved them up until they rested just below the scraps of lace. His thumbs brushed the underside of her breasts, driving the air from her lungs. Then he teased her nipples and she groaned, her knees turning to water.

Her head lolled back as he continued to graze the pebbled tips of her breasts with his thumb. His intense gaze never left her face, watched as pleasure washed over her.

One hand left her breast, easing down her body, hesitating briefly at the elastic waistband of her skirt. Then his fingers dove inside, stroked her belly, found the top of her panties. He drew a lazy line across the silky edge, all the while still flicking his thumb across her breast.

"I thought you wanted me in your bed," she whispered.

"Soon."

He bent his head, touched his lips to hers. After the heated rush on the way here and in the truck just before they'd come inside, he seemed in no hurry at all. His deep kisses had become soft touches, his caressing hands taking their time.

Her tongue laving the seam of his mouth, she invited him to do the same. But he just kept up his featherlight kisses. "You're torturing me," she told him.

"Not yet." His fingertips slipped past the barrier of her panties. "Now I am," he murmured against her mouth.

With that, his hand moved lower, briefly cupped the crisp curls shielding her femininity, then drew back. Down again, this time to trace the cleft with one fingertip. Again, his finger dipping into the moist folds.

Her nails dug into his arms, but she didn't care. It served him right for driving her crazy this way.

"You are heartless," she gasped out, then moaned, long and low, when his finger slipped fully inside her.

She would have collapsed, but he hooked one arm behind her knees and the other around her shoulders. He carried her up the stairs, to his room, to his bed where he laid her on top of the faded quilt.

His blue gaze dark and intent, he unfastened his cuffs, the top three buttons of his shirt and stripped it off over his head. Unbuckling his trousers, he shoved them off his hips. His thumbs hooked into the waistband of his shorts.

She went up on one elbow, placed a hand over his. "Let me."

His arms went lax at his sides. She sat at the edge of the bed, her hands shaking so badly she wondered if she'd be able to follow through. She let herself enjoy the feel of his skin first, her palms exploring his smooth chest, the ridged musculature of his flat belly. Rising to her feet, she brought her hands higher, to his shoulders, his strong neck, back down to his hair-roughened arms.

He was like a gift, a cherished precious gift she had never in her wildest dreams imagined receiving. Only one more bit of wrapping to remove and his body would be all hers.

If she had the nerve. She sat back on the bed, skimmed her hands down his sides to the soft cotton at his hips. The hard bulge pressing against his shorts at once frightened and thrilled her.

His head tipped down, his hot gaze bored into her. ''Well?'' The trace of a smile curved his lips, but his tight-fisted hands told her his control was wearing thin.

She started with just the tips of her fingers. They slid past the band of elastic, tugged it slightly away from his skin, inched it down slowly. His shorts snagged on his swollen flesh and she used a gentle finger to free it, allowing herself to stroke the tip as she did so. He gasped in a breath as he grabbed her shoulders and hung on tight.

She'd never been so bold. Sex with Richard had been rushed and awkward, far more for his pleasure than hers. She'd never felt this explosion of heat inside her at watching a man's excitement.

Not any man. Tom. He'd fascinated her, captivated her from the moment she first saw him on Main Street. Feeling the textures of his skin under her fingers, tasting his kisses, listening as his breath caught when she stroked him—it was bliss. And paradise still lay ahead.

When his shorts fell to his feet, he took charge again, pressing her back on the bed, urging her hands up above her head. He reached for her skirt, threw it aside, then nudged her bra straps from her shoulders. A flick of his fingers and the bra was loose, then impatiently discarded.

Certainly he would dispatch her panties as quickly, but he seemed intent on teasing her as she had him. He tucked his thumbs under the sides of her panties, his fingers wrapping around her thighs. Then he brought his hands together, until his thumbs tangled in the soft curls at her center. He started up his torture again, his thumbs stroking enough to bring her to the edge, but not enough to take her over.

When she could stand it no more, she nudged his

hands aside and pushed the panties off herself. He laughed, the soft sound dancing on her skin.

He moved up over her, his rigid arms keeping their bodies a frustrating few inches apart. "Tell me what you want."

"Everything," she whispered, her hands restless on his back. "Now."

"Soon."

Lowering himself to his elbows, he cradled her face with his hands and finally kissed her the way she wanted. His tongue thrust inside her mouth, writhed against hers. She ached for so much more—to be filled by him, surrounded by his warmth, his strength. To fulfill him in every way, in ways he'd never imagined.

One strong hand moved swiftly down her body, to her cleft where his finger pushed inside her. "You're so hot," he whispered against her mouth.

"Tom…" She couldn't be still when he touched her that way. Her legs thrashed on the bed, tangled with his.

His palm pressed against her sent her spiraling higher, higher. He lowered his head to her breast, grazed the lip lightly with his teeth.

Her eyes flew open as the first wave crashed over her. Her hips thrust up against his hand, instinctively seeking more contact, more sensation. Her body pulsed around him with a last rush of ecstasy. Shuddering, she sank back onto the bed.

He tasted her breast one last time, then lifted his head, his smile satisfied. Still trembling, she laughed. "How can you look so pleased with yourself when you haven't…" She shifted slightly, trapping his still heavy flesh between their bodies.

His breath caught, but his smile lingered. "Because you have. Because I will."

Tom knew if he didn't put some space between them, their lovemaking would come to an abrupt end. He levered himself away from her, both for some breathing room and to reach for the nightstand drawer. He pulled out a foil square, ripped it open.

When she held her hand out for the protection, he knew he risked a less than ideal end if he let her sheath him. Even still, he wanted her hands on him. He gave her the condom, sat back on his heels. He had to grit his teeth, dig his nails into his palms to resist his body's imperative.

As she stroked him, cupped him, took her damn sweet time at the task, she knew exactly what she was doing. God love her, she was enjoying every moment of it. Payback for the way he'd teased her. It was agony and ecstasy all at once.

She must have sensed how he teetered near the edge because she finally finished, drew her hands away. Now it was his turn to drive her mad, to take her to the precipice and over the top.

She opened her legs, inviting him inside. Her gaze locked with his, he could watch her every response, another layer to his passion. He thrust in slowly, letting her get used to him before he buried himself completely.

As he filled her, a moan started up low in her throat, vibrated through her body. He had to stop, drag in a breath. He wouldn't be able to prolong this as it was, not this first time at least. But he wanted to give her as much pleasure as he could.

Her legs wrapped around him, taking him deeper.

Dredging up the last of his self-control, he began to move, drawing himself out, then back in, a slow rhythm. A flush rose in her cheeks, the hue of her desire notching up his own excitement. Her hair lay like silk over his arms, her scent filled him.

Her breathing quickened and his own heart hammered in his ears. He held back as she reached higher and higher, her half-lidded eyes dark with her passion. She threw her head back as she came apart in his arms, the clenching of her body impossible to ignore. He exploded inside her, sensation riding on every nerve, burning every inch of his body.

Afterward, he lay in her arms, like a phoenix too weak yet to rise from the ashes. His full weight was on her, but for the moment, he couldn't move.

"I'm too heavy," he murmured against her neck.

"You're not," she whispered back, her arms, her legs wrapping around him more tightly.

Still, he eased himself from her body. "Give me a minute." He rolled from the bed, headed for the bathroom to clean up. As quickly as he could, he returned and lay beside her, pulled her into his arms.

She snuggled up against him, her backside spooning into him. She chuckled as his flesh rose half at attention. "Ready for round two already?"

He nuzzled her hair, the flowery fragrance of her shampoo tantalizing. "Soon."

She sighed, the sound singing along his veins. "When will Jessie be back tomorrow?"

He didn't want to think about his daughter, not yet. Because thinking of Jessie reminded him how soon Andrea would be leaving, and the thought of Andrea out of his life was impossible to conceive in that moment.

He held her more tightly, banishing the future from his mind. ''Mark is dropping her off at ten.''

Another sigh. ''I can't be here.''

Alarm erupted within him and for an instant he thought she meant she couldn't be at the ranch any longer, that she had to leave. His passion-scrambled brain had made him that crazy. He had to take a breath, remind himself she meant only that she couldn't be in his bed when Jessie returned.

Rising up on his elbow, he kissed her cheek, brushed his lips against her ear. ''We have hours before then.''

She turned in his arms, facing him, raising her mouth to his. ''What about sleep?''

His lips pressed against hers, his tongue dove inside her mouth. ''You're all I need.''

In my arms, he reminded himself, in my bed. There was no place for her in his life, at least not beyond the end of school. He would be saying goodbye then, letting her go.

I don't want to let her go!

The realization slammed into him, shocked him to the core. This wasn't Lori walking out on her husband, her child. This was Andrea, Jessie's teacher, whose commitment to him and his daughter was only to stay through the end of the school year.

''Hey.'' Her soft voice finally registered. ''I do have to breathe, you know.''

He immediately relaxed his constricting hold on her. ''Sorry.'' Brushing his mouth against hers, he traced a line of kisses along her jaw to her ear. ''Now, where were we?''

Her hand drifted down his body, found his swollen flesh. ''Here,'' she murmured.

Her touch drove everything from his mind but pleasure.

* * *

Sleepy and sated, Andrea watched as the first light of dawn sifted through the curtains covering Tom's bedroom windows. Tom's steady breathing behind her told her he still slept. She couldn't blame him considering the number of times they'd made love.

Despite the soreness between her legs and her tired, aching muscles, she knew he had only to kiss her to rouse her again. Her hunger for him was a revelation. Tom had satisfied her over and over, until she fell back, exhausted in his arms. Until the hunger rose again.

She'd felt nothing even remotely close with Richard. She'd kept herself distant from her fiancé, never willing to truly give herself to him.

Now she understood why. She never loved Richard, had never given her heart to him. He had only touched the facade of who she was. He had never reached her core, her essence.

She'd given everything to Tom. She trusted him utterly, was willing to expose the most vulnerable part of himself. Because he was a good man, an honorable man.

Because…something deep within her struggled to the surface. She refused to let it rise. She cared more deeply for Tom than she had any other man. Respected him, admired him. That was all, no more. She didn't—

"Are you awake?"

At the rumble of his voice, she started, yanked from her turbulent thoughts. Turning, she faced him, smiled. "Is there something you wanted?"

His answer was in his mesmerizing eyes. He eased her back into the pillow, dipping in to take her mouth, his tongue thrusting inside. Her body's response surprised her, so quickly did he arouse her beyond bearing. Voracious for him, she skimmed her hands over his body, absorbing his heat, his groans of pleasure. The rough and muscular, the smooth and sensitive, every part of the man who enfolded her in his arms thrilled her.

She might as well have never reached her peak several times that night. Her climax thundered through her body in tandem with his, profound and soul-shattering. It seemed pieces of her scattered into space, then took their own sweet time floating back to coalesce again as herself.

Limp with satiation, she let her head loll back against his shoulder. His fingers wove through her hair, smoothing it between her breasts.

"Andrea." The quiet murmur of her name sent a shiver through her. She shifted to look up into his face.

He swallowed, the motion of his throat drawing her gaze. Taking a breath, he opened his mouth, shut it, took another breath.

Alarm prickled inside her. "Tom, what is it?"

He rose to look down at her, one hand curved around her face. "I want you to stay, Andy. Don't leave when school's over."

Joy burst inside her, flooding aside her brief misgivings. "Stay? With you?"

"Yes. I mean…" Incomprehensible emotion flickered in his eyes. "With Jessie. She'll be heartbroken if you leave."

Pain lanced her, striking the breath from her lungs. She looked away, wishing she could crawl inside herself.

He'd made no promises before they'd made love and

she'd asked for none. She had no right to feel he'd wrenched her foundation out from under her, no right to expect some profession of love from him.

And yet… She had to gasp in a breath to keep from crying. Squeezing her eyes shut, she tried to mask the emotions from her face.

She couldn't meet his gaze when he leaned down to kiss her. "Will you stay?" he asked, his mouth at the corner of hers.

"How long?" Somehow she kept her voice steady. Forever! she screamed inside herself.

"Can we take it a day at a time?"

She nodded, not trusting herself to speak. Then she pulled away from him, moved to sit at the edge of the bed. "I'd better go." She gathered up her skirt, panties and bra, remembered the shell top was downstairs.

"Are you okay?"

"I'd better go," she said again, dressing as best as she could before hurrying from the room.

She paused long enough in the living room to throw on her top, then raced from the house. I'm okay, I'm okay.

Maybe if she said the words enough times, she'd believe them.

Chapter Thirteen

Andrea did what she could to avoid Tom the rest of Sunday. She drove into Marbleville for a lunch she barely touched, then saw a movie at the Marbleville Cineplex. She wandered around the tiny regional mall after the movie, then had dinner at a nearby family restaurant. She managed to make it into her apartment without seeing either Tom or Jessie and spent the rest of her evening sewing crooked stitches into a patchwork quilt square.

Monday morning, Andrea slipped into the house and was grateful to see only Jessie at the breakfast table. A quick glance out the kitchen window told her Tom was busy working the colt in the round pen.

Jessie helped her make pancake batter, then carefully poured out a double J on the griddle. Once Jessie's hot-cakes were done, Andrea poured herself three conventional circles, then turned to the little girl as she waited for them to cook.

"I don't know if your dad told you," Andrea said as casually as she could. Jessie looked up, expectant. "I'm going to be staying past the end of the school year."

Jessie's eyes widened with a cautious joy. "How long?"

The question was a painful echo of what she'd asked Tom two nights ago. Forcing a smile, she flipped her pancakes, then poured a glass of milk for Jessie. "I'm not sure. Maybe through summer."

After giving Jessie her milk, she scooped the pancakes from the griddle and onto a plate. Stepping around the table to her place opposite Jessie, she sat down to her own breakfast.

As she drizzled her hotcakes with maple syrup, she berated herself for the thousandth time over her monumental mistake Saturday night. She'd wanted Tom so much, she hadn't thought past the first kiss, the first intimate touch. Like an idiot, she'd never considered how she'd feel after a night of passion so intense her whole world had exploded and remade itself into something foreign and strange.

She wasn't even sure what she wanted from her new world, what her place was in it. She only knew she needed something more, something intangible, yet as real as the table under her hands, the fork she gripped in her fingers.

Or as real as the little girl opposite her who'd stopped eating her J-shaped pancakes and now stared at her. "How come?"

Andrea could have stalled by pretending she didn't understand the question. But that would have taken more energy than simply answering. "Your dad thought it might be good for you if I stayed a little longer."

That was true enough, but Jessie's furrowed brow told Andrea the little girl wasn't buying it. "But I don't need a teacher this summer. And I'm going back to regular school for next year."

"You don't want me to stay?"

"Yes! Yes, I do." Her gaze falling to her plate, Jessie poked her fork at her pancakes. "I just wish—" the fork burrowed into the pancake as Jessie's cheeks flamed "—just wish you and Dad…" She lifted her head, eyes fierce. "How come you can't get married?"

Jessie's fervent plea just about knocked the air out of Andrea. Not because she didn't suspect it had been weighing on Jessie's mind, but because suddenly, the ready answers didn't seem to apply.

Could it be that somewhere deep inside her, she asked herself that very same question?

No. Marriage and commitment involved roots and a home and staying in one place forever. As she'd reminded herself over and over again, she wasn't equipped for constancy. She felt this ache inside her because she'd made the mistake of letting herself get too close, too involved—with Tom, with Jessie, with Beth and Nina. With Hart Valley itself. That might make it harder to walk away at the end of summer, but walk away she would, just as soon as the urge to wander overwhelmed the longing to stay.

Jessie's attention was still fixed squarely on Andrea. She had to come up with some kind of honest answer. "Your dad and I…we're just friends."

"You don't like him enough?"

"I like him a lot," Andrea said. "But I don't love him."

Why did the words sound so rote? It was as if she was repeating a line from a play rather than expressing what was truly in her heart.

But she didn't harbor love for Tom in her heart—surely not. Their night of lovemaking had shaken her, confused her, made her unsure of what she felt. But she didn't love him.

Even though the thought of leaving him, of leaving Jessie and Hart Valley nearly cleaved her heart in two.

"You don't like me enough?"

The quietly spoken question drove a dagger even deeper into Andrea's chest. She locked her gaze with Jessie's, wanting to be certain the little girl understood. "I like you more than enough, Jessie. I love you."

Tears glittered in Jessie's eyes. "Then why do you have to leave at all?"

"Because…" She shook her head, struggling to find the right words. "Because I do." Because I always have. Because I never stay. The excuse sounded lame and cowardly.

Jessie's expression turned mulish and she bent her head to her plate again. She cut up the two Js with her fork, then added syrup to the lake already flooding her pancakes. "Never mind," she muttered as she stuffed bites into her mouth.

"Jessie…"

She scowled at Andrea, her cheeks stuffed with pancakes. When she'd forked up the last piece, she guzzled half her milk then put her dishes on the counter next to the sink. She stomped from the kitchen, pushing past her father as he entered.

Andrea rose to her feet, unwilling to face him seated. He stared at her, heat in his blue gaze. She wanted to forget that heat, wanted to forget everything that had happened Saturday night. If she could forget, maybe her trembling would stop, the sensations jetting along her nerves would fade.

"What's she mad about now?"

"Nothing," Andrea said. "Everything." She left it at that.

He headed for the sink just as she did and they nearly collided. When she would have stepped away, his hand wrapped around her arm.

"Andy." Her name on his lips set a shivering off inside her. "We should talk."

Chin up, she met his gaze. "Should we?"

Irritation flickered in his eyes. "You know damn well we should. Saturday night—"

"Don't. Please." She didn't know what she was begging for, just that he had to stop talking. "Can't we just leave it be?"

"How can we—" He bit off the words. "You have me turned in a hundred different directions. I don't know what… I don't know how…"

She pressed her fingertips to his lips, then snatched them away when she realized how good they felt there. "Give me a little time. Then we can talk about it if you want."

His look was as dark as Jessie's had been. He grabbed a glass from the cupboard, filled it with water from the tap, gulped it down. He stomped from the room just as his daughter had.

She would have laughed if she didn't feel so desolate. Her shoulders sagging, she turned her attention to the breakfast dishes. She didn't have much time before the school day started.

As she and Jessie slogged through their day, Andrea felt as if they were back to square zero. Jessie was willful and stubborn, questioning Andrea's every request, intentionally botching every assignment. When Jessie flat-out refused to practice her cursive by transcribing a poem she'd written about her pony, Trixie, the week before, Andrea decided she wasn't willing to fight that battle. Instead, she ran Jessie through her times tables up to twelve, then they broke for lunch a bit early.

She and Jessie had already finished eating and were back in the living room when Tom came in for lunch. In the midst of wrangling with Jessie over a social studies report due by the end of the year, Andrea spared Tom a quick glance then nearly couldn't look away. He'd pulled off his T-shirt and slung it over his shoulder. Sweat beaded on his face, sheened the musculature of his chest.

She'd forced her attention back to Jessie and their latest argument. Jessie had nearly completed her report, but suddenly had balked over writing a table of contents and bibliography.

Nearly to the kitchen, Tom had paused and barked out, "Jessie!" loud enough that the truculent little girl fell silent. Her expression surly, Jessie had stalked off to the computer to type in the requested material. Tom had moved on without giving Andrea time to thank him for his intervention.

Dismissed to finish the day reading, Jessie was upstairs in her room, no doubt listing all the reasons she hated her teacher. Andrea neatened up the schoolbooks and papers on the coffee table, then sagged onto the sofa, her throat tight. She wished she could crawl into a hole somewhere and hide from the bewildering emotions rattling around inside her.

A sudden longing to talk to her mother overwhelmed

her. They hadn't had much time for heart-to-heart chats while she was growing up. Her mother was usually too preoccupied with keeping food on the table and a roof over their heads. Andrea had learned early on to handle her own problems, not because her mother wouldn't care, but because Andrea didn't want to burden her mother with what she could deal with herself.

Which made the urgency to pour out her troubles to her mother all the more baffling. As she pushed herself to her feet, Andrea tried to ignore her heart's pleading for comfort. But this time the need to spill everything out to her mother, to talk things over with her was irresistible.

Resolved, she hurried to her apartment where she'd left her cell phone. The phone was hers and her mother's one concession to staying connected. They might change addresses several times a year, but they could always reach each other by cell phone.

Settled on her bed, Andrea dialed her mother's number, then tried to frame the message she would leave if her mother didn't answer. Four rings later, she was listening for the click that would forward her to voice mail when she heard her mother's breathless ''Hello?''

Helpless to stop them, Andrea had to blink away tears that welled at the first sound of her mother's voice. ''Hi, Mom.''

''Andrea?''

She cleared her throat, swallowed her tears. ''How are you?''

''Fine,'' she said with enthusiasm. ''Really fine.''

''Where are you now?'' The question was a ritual, asked early in their infrequent conversations.

''Still in Modesto,'' her mother told her.

Andrea tried to absorb that surprising bit of news.

"You were in Modesto back in December." They'd managed to spend Christmas together.

"Yes." Excitement bubbled in her voice. "I've been here since September."

Eight months. Her mother had stayed in one place for eight months. "What have you…? How have you…?"

Andrea heard her mother's slow intake of breath. "I've met someone." Another breath, then her mother's shocking confession came out in a rush. "Honey, I'm getting married."

Andrea couldn't speak. She could barely breathe.

"Jeff and I met early this year. I'd gone down to the post office to see about getting my mail forwarded…."

Listening with only half an ear, Andrea tried to grasp the enormity of her mother's announcement. If her mother could commit to marriage, if her mother could choose to set down roots…

"Honey, I know I should have told you sooner. But first, it was all so new between Jeff and me, then when he asked me to marry him, I needed time to get used to the idea."

Andrea struggled to keep tears at bay. "Mom…"

Somehow her mother sensed Andrea's turmoil. "Sweetheart, what is it?"

Andrea could barely gasp out the words. "I'm so mixed up."

With her mother's full attention, Andrea poured everything out—meeting Tom and Jessie, losing her heart to the wounded little girl as she battled her attraction for Tom. The feeling of homecoming she'd felt the moment she'd driven down Hart Valley's Main Street.

"I feel as if I belong here," Andrea confessed, as much to herself as to her mother. "For the first time I feel part of someplace. And yet…"

"And yet?" her mother prompted.

"We're not made for settling down, are we, Mom? You and I...we get bored and we move on."

There was a long silence, the cell phone static crackling faintly in Andrea's ear. Then her mother spoke and the words seemed dragged from her. "There's something I have to tell you, Andrea. About your father."

The unexpected mention of a man she scarcely remembered baffled her. "My father died when I was two."

"He didn't," her mother said quietly.

Andrea's mind reeled at that revelation. Then her mother told her the rest—that her father had abused her mother throughout their short marriage, that the day he hit Andrea, her mother had had enough. She'd escaped that night while he slept.

"He came after us," her mother told her, her voice quavering. "The first time he found us, I called the police, but he charmed them into thinking it was a misunderstanding. After that, I couldn't take the chance. We kept moving, one step ahead of him."

Everything Andrea believed about herself tumbled like dominoes inside her. Her love of a rootless life, the wanderlust she'd convinced herself she relished.

"Where is he now?" Andrea asked, at once desperate for and fearful of her mother's answer.

"He died two years ago. I would have told you..."

She left the rest unsaid. Two years ago, Andrea was embroiled in the aftermath of her disastrous relationship with Richard. Her mother was one of the few people outside the Benton School District and Benton police department to know all the details of Andrea's harrowing experience.

"Give yourself some time, honey. I know it will work out."

Was it really that simple? Then why did she ache so much inside? "I don't know what I want from him. I know I care for him, and I love Jessie. But everything else is all muddled."

"Andy, please—don't let the past rule you."

As Andrea tried to absorb that advice, she heard a man's voice in the background. "In a minute, love," her mother called back in response. "Sweetie, I've got to go. When can you come down to meet Jeff?"

"I have to figure things out here. I'll call you."

Andrea hung up, then set the cell phone aside. Her foundation had been rattled loose, but somehow it seemed to be settling back down, even stronger. Her mother's revelations stunned her, but at the same time wiped the slate of her life clean, gave her the chance to rewrite it any way she liked.

In that moment she felt powerful, exhilarated. Her forward path wasn't the least bit clear, but within that insubstantial future, her choices were unlimited.

She could choose Tom and Jessie. She could stay here at the Double J with them, forever or for as long as they wanted her to. She could make a home for herself in Hart Valley, set down roots, become a part of this community.

What if I love him? The question shook her to the core, then close on its heels came another. What if he doesn't love me?

The pain of that possibility slashed deeply. She couldn't think about it right now. She pushed herself up from the bed, needing a distraction from her turbulent thoughts.

In her tiny front room, she settled in the easy chair

and picked up the quilt square she'd started Sunday. She was bound and determined to finish the quilt by the end of school. Until today, she'd intended it as a goodbye gift for Jessie. But if she stayed...

Later. She could decide that later. For now she would focus on the needle moving in and out of the fabric, the pattern made by the dashed lines of thread. The work soothed her and eased her mind.

His shoulders aching from fixing fence, Tom swung his leg over Sonuvagun's back and dropped to the ground. The yard, striped with late afternoon shadows, was empty, but movement on the front porch drew his gaze. Sprawled out on the porch swing, Jessie stared off across the pasture. From this distance, there was no telling what his daughter's mood might be. As edgy as he felt, he wasn't sure he could deal with a cranky, ornery nine-year-old.

Loosening the cinch strap on the gelding's saddle, Tom quickly untacked his horse, then led him to the pasture gate. Sonuvagun trotted off to a bare spot in the grass, then lowered himself to roll. Huffing with pleasure, the gelding rolled from one side to the other, then regained his feet and shook a cloud of dust from his bay coat. He ambled off toward the mares, ready to claim his own patch of grass.

Tom took his time returning the saddle and bridle to the tack room, then checked the stalls to see if they'd been mucked out. The stalls were tidy, filled with a thick layer of fresh straw, ready for the horses when he brought them in to feed. Jessie had done a good job.

Out of excuses to delay confronting his daughter, Tom stepped back into the yard and headed for the porch. Jessie didn't notice him at first, her attention focused on Andrea's apartment. Tom couldn't resist looking that way himself and was rewarded with a glimpse of Andrea as she pulled the curtains shut against the glare of the late afternoon sun.

That brief sighting was all it took for his body to respond. He'd been battling his arousal all day long, a damned inconvenience in the saddle, to say the least. But now that his fantasies of Andrea had been intensified by reality, he felt helpless to keep his body in check.

He climbed the porch steps and leaned against the railing facing his daughter. She gave him only a sidelong glance at first, then sat up, drawing her knees to her chest and wrapping her arms around them. She met his gaze now, her expression sorrowful.

"I think Andrea hates me."

He discarded his first impulse to say, "Of course she doesn't," and moved to sit beside Jessie. With a push of his feet, he set the swing in motion. "What makes you say that?"

Her shoulders heaved and dropped with a sigh. "'Cause I argue and I won't do my work and I'm a pain in the...neck."

Tom suppressed a smile at his daughter's last-minute censorship. "Probably Andrea isn't too thrilled when you argue, but I bet she likes you anyway."

Jessie gave him a dubious look. "How do you know?"

"I just do, pumpkin." He smoothed back dark blond hair that had fallen in Jessie's eyes. "She likes you a whole bunch."

At the sound of Andrea's door opening, both he and Jessie turned expectantly toward the apartment. A glance at his daughter revealed an adoration that caught him by surprise. Jessie had grown even closer to Andrea than he'd suspected. All the more reason for her to stay, to give his daughter a much-needed champion.

That Andrea's presence threw his own world into turmoil, that he could barely think straight after their wild night together was not the issue. His daughter's happiness took precedence over his feelings. If a continued physical relationship with him would make it too awkward for Andrea, he would keep his hands off her.

Andrea descended the stairs and crossed the yard, hesitating only slightly when she caught sight of them on the porch. She smiled as she approached, and an air of serenity seemed to follow in her wake.

"Hey, Jess," she said softly as she stepped up on the porch. "How's it going?"

For a moment, Jessie just stared, then she jumped to her feet and flung herself at Andrea. Jessie's small arms flew around Andrea's waist and she gave her teacher a ferocious hug.

"I'm sorry," Jessie muttered, her cheek pressed against Andrea's T-shirt.

Andrea stroked Jessie's head. "You just had a bad day. No biggie."

On his feet, Tom gave his daughter's head a rub. "Told you, sweetheart." His fingers tangled with Andrea's, sending sensation jolting up his arm.

She lifted her gaze to his, her smile tremulous. "Can we talk later?"

He nodded, fighting the urge to cradle her face with his hands, to press his lips against hers. "I have a great idea, Jessie. What do you say we all go into town for pizza?"

Jessie let go of Andrea, grinning. "Can I have any kind I want?"

Tom laughed, suddenly feeling as if he could move mountains. "Within reason. No sardines this time, okay?"

Jessie made a face. "Yuck. I'll go get my quarters for the video games."

She raced into the house, slamming the screen door. Tom gave in to temptation and cupped his hand against Andrea's face. He was gratified when she didn't pull back, instead resting her hand against his.

He traced his thumb along the line of her brow. "You wanted to talk?"

"Later." She turned her face, pressed a kiss into his palm. "When we have more time."

With that tantalizing promise to look forward to, he backed away just as Jessie exploded onto the porch again. "Let's go!" she shouted before clattering down the steps toward the truck.

As he and Andrea followed more slowly, he placed a surreptitious hand against the small of her back. His body prickled with heat on the drive into Hart Valley, with Andrea so near. At the pizza joint, he could barely keep his mind on Jessie's rapid-fire chatter, could barely taste the pepperoni and pineapple pie Jessie ordered. Although he wasn't certain his evening would end with Andrea in his arms, he sensed they were moving in that direction and he thought he would jump from his skin in anticipation.

By the time they jounced along the gravel drive leading to the house, dusk had fallen and the horses were waiting impatiently at the pasture fence for their evening feed. As he pulled into the yard, it took him a moment to register the gray BMW parked beside the round pen. Stopping the truck behind the sedan, he saw a figure in silhouette rising from the porch swing.

It wasn't until she'd stepped down into the yard that Tom realized who the woman was. Jessie was ahead of him; she'd already scrambled from the truck and dashed across the yard.

"Mom!" she screamed as she threw her arms around the woman with the same enthusiasm as when she'd hugged Andrea.

A question in her eyes, Andrea put her hand on his arm. Daggers in the pit of his stomach, it took him a moment to answer.

"It's Lori," he said with a dark sense of dread. "My ex-wife."

Chapter Fourteen

With her first glimpse of Lori standing there, lit by the glow from the porch light, Andrea understood how Tom had fallen in love with her. Tall and willowy, blond hair pale as moonlight, she had a figure straight from the pages of a fashion magazine. Even the most secure woman would feel thick-waisted and flat-chested compared to Lori, that her eyes were dull next to those deep golden ones, that her skin was blemished beside Lori's perfection.

Andrea glanced over at Tom, registered the cold light in his eyes, the hard lines of his face. If she'd had any fears at all that he still harbored feelings for his ex-wife, that quick look instantly dispelled them.

His gaze fixed on Lori, Tom opened the door of the truck, dropped down to the gravel, shut the door again. His every move seemed deliberate and careful, as if to contain a barely-held-in-check explosiveness.

Andrea slipped from her side of the truck, shutting the door Jessie had left open. She rounded the pickup and followed Tom across the yard to where Lori and Jessie waited.

Lori's gaze flicked from Tom to Andrea, strafing Andrea with a dismissive once-over before returning her attention to Tom. An immediate dislike bubbled up inside Andrea, but she quashed it. This was Jessie's mother and the least she could do was remain neutral.

But when Jessie squeezed her mother tighter, her burn-scarred arm brushing Lori's, the blatant distaste in Lori's face hit Andrea like a punch in the gut. Thank God Jessie couldn't see her mother's reaction. How could a mother respond to her daughter with anything but love? As exasperating as Jessie could be, as frustrating and sometimes heartbreaking, Andrea was completely besotted by her—bad temper, lightning mood changes and all. She hadn't given Jessie's scar a second thought after the first week, except to remind her to protect it in the hot sun.

Lori peeled her daughter's arms from around her waist, giving Andrea a look of pure malice. "So this is Jessie's teacher."

Tom took a step toward Lori. "What are you doing here?"

Jessie grabbed her mother's hand. "She came to see me, didn't you, Mom?"

Lori smiled down at her daughter, little more than a baring of teeth. "I'd love to see your room, Jessie. Go upstairs and make sure it's all clean for me. I'll be up in a minute."

Jessie dashed off like a rocket. Lori's surreptitious rubbing of her arm where Jessie's scar had touched her turned Andrea's stomach. Her hand tightened into a fist, itching to plant itself in Lori's pretty face. With an effort, she swallowed her ire and opened her hand again.

Another step and Tom loomed over his ex-wife, his shoulders taut with tension. "What are you doing here, Lori? And no bull about visiting Jessie."

Head tipped up, Lori looked down her dainty nose at Andrea. "I don't think we should discuss this in front of her."

"Anything you say to me, you can say to Andrea." He said the words with cool neutrality.

She flicked her fingers dismissively toward Andrea. "She might not like what I have to say."

If Lori had hoped to drag a response from Tom with her pronouncement, she was surely disappointed. Tom's silence stretched, tangled with the faint breeze gusting through the yard.

Lori's mouth tightened with irritation. "Can we at least go indoors? The damn mosquitoes are eating me alive."

A moment's hesitation, then Tom gestured toward the house. He held open the screen door for his ex-wife, then followed Andrea inside. They'd left one lamp on in the living room; now Tom switched on two more lamps and the overhead, as if he felt he could defend against Lori best in a well-lit room.

The bright lights gave a different twist to Lori's beauty. Lines around her mouth, smudges shadowing her eyes, a hardness in her face aged her even though Andrea suspected Lori wasn't much older than she. When Lori moved past Andrea, pacing restlessly around the room, Andrea registered what she'd missed outside—the reek of alcohol on Lori's breath, a bleariness in her eyes.

"Say what you have to say," Tom spat out, "then get the hell out."

His blunt rudeness stunned Andrea. She pressed her hand to the small of his back, stroked him, hoping to soothe him. His rock hard muscles didn't yield to her touch. When he shrugged off her hand and edged away, uneasiness roiled within her.

Lori turned to face them, arms crossed over her middle. "Quite a cozy little picture here. Pretty young teacher, big strong rancher living under the same roof."

"She lives in the foreman's apartment." His blue eyes burned into Lori. "You haven't been here in months. How the hell do you know about Andrea at all?"

Andrea didn't like Lori's smug, predatory smile. "I've kept in touch. Nina's always been a good friend."

For a moment, Andrea felt a twinge of betrayal that Nina might have passed on information to Lori. But Nina had been hurting, too much in pain over losing her dream to think clearly. No doubt Lori had preyed on that weakness.

"How do you think it looks to everyone in town, the two of you alone out here?" She smoothed her moonlight hair back from her face. "What kind of message are you sending our daughter?"

His hands gripped tight he took in a breath, shoulders heaving. "What kind of message did you send her four years ago with the foreman?"

Color stained Lori's pale cheeks, and for a moment she seemed shamed into silence. Then her eyes narrowed on Andrea. "I don't like it. I don't like her being here."

"Mom!" Jessie's cry turned them all toward the stairs. "My room's all clean!"

"Coming, sweetheart," Lori called back, then returned her focus to Tom. "I let you have full custody—"

"You damn well didn't want—" Tom cut off the shouted words, lowered his voice. "You never wanted custody."

"Maybe things are different now," Lori said. "You bring this woman in to teach our daughter and God knows what her background is."

"I checked her background. I've seen her work with Jessie. She's done ten times more for her than any public school teacher."

Lori's gaze raked Andrea from head to toe. "And I can just imagine what she's done for you."

Tom's body shook with suppressed rage. "You have no damn right—"

"I think it's time I took custody. I think it's time Jessie lived with me."

A gasp drew their attention to Jessie standing at the foot of the stairs, her eyes wide with fear. "Daddy, I don't want to leave."

Tom's jaw worked. "No one's making you leave, sweetheart."

But Jessie stepped into the room, tears brimming in her eyes. "Mommy, I don't want to live someplace else."

For the first time, empathy softened Lori's features. She went down on one knee and brushed the hair back from her daughter's face. "Daddy and I are just talking. Go back upstairs. I'll be right up."

Too savvy a child to completely believe her mother, Jessie nevertheless turned and walked slowly back upstairs. Lori waited for the sound of Jessie's door shutting. "Maybe we can work out an agreement."

"Jessie stays here. There's nothing more to work out."

The fleeting kindness Lori had shown her daughter vanished. "Mama and Daddy wouldn't think so. If I tell them how worried I am about Jessie, they might just sue for custody."

"No." Andrea could barely squeeze out the word. "Tom—"

Tom spared Andrea a quick glance before narrowing his gaze on Lori. "What do you want?"

Lori's mouth curved in a mean smile. "I need money."

There was no mistaking the disgust in Tom's face at his ex-wife's request. "What about the trust fund?"

Lori looked away. "Temporarily unavailable. I just need a few thousand to tide me over."

Andrea had learned enough about Tom's operation to know he had nowhere near that much ready cash. She thought about her own small savings account, resolved to offer every penny of it to Tom.

But he shook his head at Lori, said flatly, "No."

Tom's refusal didn't faze his ex-wife. "Then I'll be talking to Mama and Daddy." She let the threat hang there as she headed toward the front door, her promise to Jessie forgotten.

Alone with Tom, Andrea waited in the charged quiet of the room for him to speak, to at least turn toward her again. But he kept his back to her, his head bowed down, hands fisted at his sides.

"Tom—"

"Not now."

"But, I—"

"Not now. We'll talk later."

There was anger in his tone, a coldness that gave her

turbulent emotions another twist. Because she didn't know what else to do, because she couldn't have stopped herself if her life depended on it, Andrea reached for him, put her hand on his arm. Without speaking, she waited for him to accept her touch or pull away.

Then his arms enfolded her, brought her close to him. As if in the aftermath of a disaster, his body shook as she held him tightly.

"I can't lose her, Andy," he murmured into her hair. "Could she get custody?"

"I don't know. Maybe with her parents' help."

She tipped her head back to look up at him. "Maybe I should leave."

"No."

"I could go into town, stay at the inn."

"I won't have her running our lives like that." He lowered his head and brushed a kiss on her brow. "You'll stay here."

When Jessie's footsteps, uncharacteristically slow, sounded on the stairs, he didn't set Andrea away from him. He turned toward his daughter, holding out his arm for her. She threw herself at them, flinging her arms around them both.

"Don't make me leave, Daddy, please."

"No way, Jess." His voice rumbled against Andrea's ear. "You're staying right here."

With every fiber of her being, Andrea prayed he would be able to keep his vow.

Andrea fully expected Jessie to act out in response to her mother's abrupt reappearance her life. But Jessie's behavior the week following Lori's visit both surprised and worried Andrea. Rather than lashing out with her trademark belligerence, Jessie was in turns clingy and sorrowful. When she should have been reading her California history book or practicing her cursive, she stared off into space, her brown eyes achingly sad.

After turning to her for comfort that night, Tom had lapsed into silence, the closeness they'd shared forgotten. Sometimes she'd catch him watching her across the dinner table or in the yard, his gaze so hot it was a palpable thing, stroking along her nerves. Even so, he kept his distance, remote and unapproachable. With Jessie around, there were few opportunities for intimacy, but although the very air seemed charged with remembered sensation, he remained well out of touching range.

It didn't help that after dropping her bombshell, Lori took a powder. There was no way of knowing if she'd sobered up the next morning and gone back home or if she was just waiting Tom out. Either way, the wreckage she'd left behind her kept them all on edge.

Friday morning, when Tom came in while she was washing up from breakfast, Andrea decided it was time to confront the issue. She'd gotten Jessie started on her math out in the living room and for the moment, they'd be uninterrupted.

He seemed intent on avoiding her as usual, draining his glass of water, then starting back out of the kitchen.

"Tom." He looked back at her. She shut off the faucet, wiped her hands dry. "Can we talk?"

He didn't want to, seemed ready to continue to shoulder his massive burden alone. "Yeah," he said finally. "Sure."

Andrea leaned back against the sink. "Do you think she's gone?"

Arms crossed over his chest, he propped one shoulder against the refrigerator. "Maybe. Probably not."

"I talked to Nina." The café owner had been tearfully apologetic. "She hasn't seen her since that Monday."

"She could be at her parents'. They have a place up in Tahoe, on the North Shore."

"She has to know how much this is hurting Jessie."

A glance toward the living room, then he pitched his voice low. "When we split, Lori never even asked for visitation. She said a kid would cramp her style." He let out a long sigh. "But somewhere in her heart of hearts, the guilt is eating her up. It kills me that I wasn't there for Jessie. But Lori was only a few feet away, could have prevented the accident...."

Andrea's own guilt over what had happened with Richard two years ago seemed trivial compared to Lori's. "Then why would she do this?"

"She always drank too much. But she went even crazier after the accident, went through money like it was water." His face set, he shook his head. "Her parents must have shut off the trust fund."

This was her chance to make her proposition. "About that... You know I have a little bit put aside in savings—"

"No."

"But since I'm staying, it's not as if I need it."

"No," he said flatly.

"But I just want to—"

"Drop it, Andy. You're damn well not giving your savings to Lori." He glared at her. "And not another word about leaving, either."

He stared her down for a moment, then pushed off

from the fridge and closed the distance between them. He wrapped his arms around her.

"We'll work it out. She's probably just bluffing, trying to see what she can get from me. She may not even be back."

Despite his assurances, Andrea couldn't shake her uneasiness. "I don't want to be the cause of Lori taking Jessie away."

"You won't be." His hand moved along her back in a soothing stroke. "You've got a squeaky clean reputation. How could Lori possibly use you as ammunition?"

Something lurched in the pit of her stomach. Her past wasn't nearly as blemish-free as Tom thought. Files had been sealed and she'd done her best to cover her tracks, but what if Lori somehow dug out the ugly truth of what had happened with Richard?

Should she confess it all now to Tom, warn him just in case? But she'd promised confidentiality to the school district, to the kids who'd gone through it with her. She'd agreed to keep quiet about the details of that horrifying car ride, but not for her own benefit. It had been for those two terrified little girls in the back seat of Richard's sedan.

She couldn't betray that confidence. Even as guilt nibbled at her that she was keeping the shadows of her past from Tom, she had to keep her word.

Yet as she stood in the circle of his arms, the black cloud that Lori had brought with her left Andrea shivering with a sense of impending doom.

As the last of the school year unwound, it seemed that maybe Tom had been right. Lori hadn't so much as shown her face in town, let alone returned to the ranch. Whether she'd had a change of heart or simply decided the effort of battling for Jessie wasn't worth the trouble, Andrea wasn't sure. She only knew she was grateful for Lori's conspicuous absence.

It took a few days, but Jessie finally seemed to regain her equilibrium. The night she mouthed off to Andrea and refused to dry the dinner dishes, Andrea silently cheered. When Andrea insisted Jessie perform the chore, the little girl grumbled loudly, but at the same time seemed relieved that Andrea was still there, telling her what to do.

After their talk, Tom seemed to have dropped the barriers between them and took every opportunity to touch her, to kiss her. Jessie's eagle eye didn't miss much, so he'd wait until Jessie was out of the room, then steal the breath from Andrea's lungs with a kiss that burned her clear to her toes.

They hadn't made love since the night of the silent auction. At times Andrea thought she would go mad with wanting him, would incinerate to ashes from the heat of his gaze. When he caught her alone in the kitchen, ran his hand up under her T-shirt to caress her breast while his mouth claimed hers, she was certain she would explode if he didn't take her to his bed.

Tom was ready to do exactly that, but Andrea held back. Her feelings for him seemed to shift and change every day, growing stronger, more complex. She felt she was rushing toward one certainty, an admission she could only hold back for so long. Knowing that nothing stood between her and a commitment to Tom, the enormity of her emotions made her want to tread very carefully.

She had no idea if his feelings for her were moving in the same direction as hers for him. Despite his passion for her, the constant thread of attraction between them, she couldn't quite parse out the enigma that was Tom. If she told him what was in her heart and he didn't share those feelings, she didn't know if she could bear it. And she didn't want Jessie to even suspect there was something going on between Andrea and her father if it wasn't going anywhere.

The last day of school promised to be a hot one from the moment the sun peeked over the Sierras. Jessie had wolfed down her breakfast in record time then raced up to her room to brush her hair and teeth, excited about the last day picnic sponsored by the school. Since Tom was busy working the colt while the morning was still relatively cool, Andrea was driving Jessie over to the Hart Valley Community Park in the pickup.

At first, Principal Beeber had vetoed Jessie's attendance at the last day picnic, but Tom had refused to let the hard-edged woman deny Jessie that simple pleasure. He'd gone toe-to-toe with the principal, worn her down, then presented Andrea as his ace in the hole to vouch for Jessie's excellent scholastic progress. That and the mention of Sabrina's mom, a member of the Hart Valley School Board, was enough to tip the scales in favor of Jessie's petition.

Andrea screwed the lid on a sport bottle full of water and ice, then grabbed the sunscreen as Jessie came clattering down the stairs. As the nine-year-old wriggled with impatience, Andrea put a generous amount of sunscreen on her face, neck and ears. She was wearing a lightweight long-sleeved shirt only because Andrea had insisted she protect her burned arm. She seemed to have lost nearly all of her shyness about exposing her scar.

Jessie made a face as Andrea put a last smear of

sunscreen on her nose. "You know I have to take the shirt off to swim in the pool."

"Just put it back on when you get out."

Jessie scrunched her nose and puffed out a sigh. Sabrina's mom had taken the day off to volunteer at the picnic and could be counted on to make sure Jessie wore her shirt. Andrea had intended to volunteer as well until last night at dinner when Tom made it clear she should return to the ranch after taking Jessie into town.

Of course, she knew why, that he wanted to be alone with her about as desperately as she did him. Yet even as her body trembled in anticipation of this chance for intimacy, something inside her warned caution. Their passion would strip her heart bare, might tear a confession from her before she was ready to reveal it.

As she circled the pickup in the yard, Jessie bouncing with excitement, they passed the round pen where Tom worked the colt. He put up his hand to wave and Andrea could almost feel that hand on her cheek, his palm warming her skin. Her heart beat faster, the rapid staccato fluttering in her ears.

Beside her on the seat, Jessie laughed with unconstrained joy. "This is going to be the best day."

A last glance in the rearview mirror at Tom, and Andrea set aside her misgivings as she silently, fervently agreed.

The moment Andrea had driven off, Tom realized it would be useless to try and work the colt just then. Knowing she'd be back soon without Jessie, that they'd have hours alone before he had to pick Jessie up again, Tom could think of nothing but the smell of her hair, the feel and taste of her mouth. The colt would sense his distraction in an instant and run roughshod right over him.

So he led the colt back to the tie posts, brushed the sweat stains from his bright sorrel coat and returned him to his paddock. Then he headed inside to shower, wanting to get the smell of horse off him before Andrea returned.

Lori's sudden intrusion in their lives had momentarily derailed the relationship that had been growing between him and Andrea. Worry over what his ex-wife might do had overwhelmed him, made it hard to think of anything but how to protect Jessie.

Since his body didn't need to think, could only feel, it still clamored for Andrea's touch, her soft kisses. Even as his stomach clenched with anxiety, images of Andrea filled his mind—the way her sighs of pleasure felt against his ear, how she trembled as he stroked the length of her body, her slick heat as he slipped inside her.

His cool shower didn't do a thing to clear his mind. As he dried his hair in front of the bathroom mirror, he gave his reflection a wry smile. He might as well let himself fantasize—he'd be experiencing the real thing soon enough.

The phone rang just as he was pulling on his jeans. He grabbed the phone from the nightstand, concerned it might be Andrea, that there was a problem. The last voice he expected at the other end of the line was his ex-wife's.

He didn't bother with pleasantries. ''What do you want?''

''I wanted to let you know, I had a couple of Daddy's men do a little digging on that teacher of yours.''

Alarm prickled up his spine, but he kept his tone neutral. "So?"

"Two years ago Andrea Larson quit teaching."

"She wanted to travel. She told me that."

"She had to quit," Lori said, triumph in her tone. "If she didn't, they were going to fire her."

Chapter Fifteen

The moment Andrea stepped into the living room, she knew something had gone terribly wrong. Tom sat on the sofa, dressed in only a pair of jeans, elbows on knees, his head down. Fear trilled up her spine that somehow something had happened to Jessie in the short time since she'd left her. Then he raised his head, his blue gaze on her, his implacable expression revealing nothing.

"Lori called," he said quietly.

Relief spilled through her that Jessie was okay. "What did she—"

"When you quit teaching two years ago—they were ready to fire you, weren't they?"

She should have been prepared for the question. How could she have hoped to hide from her past forever? "Yes."

He swallowed, disappointment sharp in his face.

"And you had to agree you wouldn't take a teaching position for two years." This time it wasn't so much a query as a statement.

"Only in that district," Andrea confirmed. "But I decided it would be better if I didn't teach at all during that time."

He nodded, digesting this. "You kept it from me." Still that quiet, nonaccusatory tone.

Andrea would have preferred it if he'd shouted, raged at her subterfuge. Anything that would get past the barrier he'd raised against her. "You wanted to know if I'm a credentialed teacher. I am. The rest—"

He surged to his feet. "It's a pretty damn important thing, don't you think? That you had to quit."

"I should have told you." She put her hand on his arm. "I never should have kept that from you."

He shrugged her hand away. "Damn straight."

A knot hardened in her chest. "I'm so sorry."

"Why did you leave?"

"I can't tell you." She crossed her arms around her middle and met his hard gaze. "There was a confidentiality agreement, and others were involved." Reaching out for him again, she pressed her fingers to his cheek, prayed he wouldn't pull away. "Please believe me, Tom…I've never hurt a child, never would."

A long, excruciating silence, then he raised his hand, covered hers. He shut his eyes and let out a long breath. "I know you wouldn't."

He opened his arms to her then and drew her close. "Forgive me, please," she whispered. "For not telling you."

He stroked her hair, tucking her more securely under his chin. "Whether you had or not, it would still have been ammunition for Lori."

She pressed her cheek against his chest. "But at least you would have been prepared."

She felt him nod. "The rest of it—the part you can't tell me…could Lori—"

"They sealed the records. That was part of the agreement. Not for me, but for the students involved." Her heart still ached when she remembered the terrified faces of those two little girls in the back seat, clutching each other for comfort.

The tension in him eased a bit and he pressed his lips to the top of her head. "This wasn't how I intended to spend our time alone today."

She smiled, feeling his body's response to her. "There's time yet."

Tipping her head back, he cradled her face in his hands. "Then come upstairs with me." He lowered his mouth to hers, and his kiss sent her mind spinning.

With an effort, she pulled herself away. "I have to say one thing, Tom."

His thumbs grazing her temple, he looked down at her, his expression serious. "What, sweetheart?"

Her throat tightened at the endearment. "When they asked me to leave…" She took in a hitching breath. "I deserved it. I was responsible. It was an appropriate punishment."

"And you're past that now."

At the acceptance in that brief statement, emotion flooded her and she had to bury her face in his chest to keep him from seeing her tears. But then the feel of her mouth against the sleek bare skin of his chest sent desire jolting through her.

He seemed impossibly hot against her mouth, unbearably sensual. She drew her lips across the taut musculature, then the tip of her tongue. A groan rumbled through him as his heartbeat thundered in her ear. When she scraped her teeth lightly across his nipple, his body shook.

"Upstairs," he gasped as he bent to lift her in his arms.

She felt light-headed and dizzy with sensation as he carried her to his room, the world spinning around her. He set her on the bed, then shucked his jeans before stretching out beside her.

"You're wearing entirely too much." He hooked one finger under the strap of her tank top, tugged it over her shoulder. His mouth followed the path of his finger, trailing moist kisses along her skin.

She couldn't lie still, the intimate promise in his kisses making her restless. When she reached for the button on her shorts, he nudged her hand away and opened it himself. In moments he'd slipped the shorts down and tossed them away, then did the same with her panties.

While he reached into the nightstand drawer for a condom, she pulled off her tank top and bra, then welcomed him back into her arms. When he would have continued with his teasing kisses, she took the imperative, wrapping her legs around him in a blatant request. He accepted her invitation, pushing inside her, filling her with sweet fulfillment.

He thrust slowly, keeping his hot gaze on her face, watching her every response. She touched him everywhere she could reach—the powerful muscles of his shoulders and back, his narrow waist, his thrusting hips. All the while, sensations spiraled higher within her, centering white-hot between her legs, a taut unmatchable pleasure.

Just as climax overwhelmed her, she saw the look of

triumph in his face, the glitter of arousal in his eyes. Then the world spun out of control, her only anchor the man in her arms. When he threw his head back and groaned, overtaken by his own passion, she climaxed again, carried in the wake of his release.

He kissed her lightly on her mouth, her cheek, her brow. Shifting from her arms, he went into the bathroom to clean up, then returned to the bed. Settled beside her again, he spooned her against his body, his heat, the feel of his skin soothing her.

"Andrea," he whispered in her ear.

Contentment acted as a soporific, and she could barely keep her eyes open. "Yes?" The word came out on a sigh.

"Don't leave me."

At first she thought he meant don't leave him just then, that he wanted her to stay in his arms, in his bed. Then she realized he was asking her to stay at the ranch, in his and Jessie's lives.

It was as if his plea had placed her on a razor's edge, balanced in a perfect equilibrium that nevertheless could be swayed one way or the other with nothing more than a nod or shake of the head. She could choose to move on as she had for most of her life, continue on down the road. Or she could stay.

But she couldn't remain on the razor's edge anymore. She had to make a choice. Stay or go.

When her heart gave her the answer, she went tumbling from the edge, but not down. As if joy had gathered her up and pulled her directly to Heaven, she flew higher, straight into love. A love that had been growing inside her from the moment she first caught a glimpse of that rough cowboy on Main Street.

She laughed, her happiness noisy and exuberant.

Twisting in his arms to tell him, her heart melted when she discovered he'd fallen asleep. She laughed again, more softly. "I'm not going anywhere." She put every bit of her love into the promise, even though he couldn't hear her.

Pressing a kiss to his lips, she eased herself back down, snuggled against him. There would be plenty of time later to tell him.

Soothed by the sound of his breathing, she drifted off to sleep.

Tom woke with a start, his eyes going quickly to the bedside clock. He saw with relief there was still plenty of time to pick up Jessie, even a few spare minutes to revel in the wonder of Andrea in his arms. Their passion had been so quick, spiced by the days of abstinence, he hadn't lasted nearly as long as he'd wanted. But she wasn't going anywhere; they had time for more interludes like this.

He carefully eased his arm out from under Andrea's head, then waited to see if she would wake. She murmured in her sleep, then turned onto her side, a faint smile curving her lips. It was all he could do to not start all over with her, to touch her, bring her to the edge of paradise again. Instead, he tugged the quilt from the other side of the bed and spread it over her. One of these days they'd actually get under the covers.

Another glance at the clock and he dressed quickly and shoved his feet into boots. One last lingering look at Andrea that nearly led him back to the bed again, then he hurried down the stairs and out to the truck. Andrea had moved the seat forward to suit her smaller frame and he had to readjust it. The simple act was another reminder of her, warm and slumbering upstairs.

As he drove away, his head cleared as he forced his focus on navigating the narrow road. Lori's revelation still nagged at him, and he couldn't help but wonder what had forced Andrea to quit teaching. But beyond that, it dug at him that she'd concealed the truth, that she hadn't been honest with him.

He couldn't compare Andrea's holding back that bit of her past to Lori's wrenching betrayal. His ex-wife's affair with the foreman coupled with her desertion of him and Jessie after the accident had been agonizing to him and catastrophic for Jessie. Andrea's lack of openness about her history didn't throw his and Jessie's lives in disarray as Lori's betrayal had.

Even still, he realized as he turned onto Hart Valley Road, that little bit of dishonesty tore at his gut. It wasn't rational to feel the way he did. The pain was fed by old memories, by a four-year-old tragedy.

Suddenly, it hit him hard—his fears stretched much farther back than four years ago. A clear memory of his mother surfaced in his mind. He was seven years old and she was saying goodbye before his dad took her to the hospital. "Be a good boy," she'd said, "I'll see you later."

Except she didn't see him later. She went into septic shock on the operating table during a routine surgery. What she'd thought was the truth turned into a lie when she never came home.

Unexpected tears pricked at his eyes. Here he was, thirty-four years old and still missing his mother. Still afraid a woman would promise to stay, then would desert him.

I'm not going anywhere.

Had Andrea really said that? The half-heard vow lingered in his subconscious, and his heart was so full he thought it would burst. Recognition exploded within him and in that moment it was crystal clear—Andrea wouldn't leave him because he damn well wouldn't let her. He was in love with her, completely, utterly, totally besotted. Next to what he felt for Andrea, his feelings for Lori had been a lie from the start, a pale imitation of love.

As he passed the town limits sign for Hart Valley, he knew exactly what he had to do. The instant he got back to the ranch, the moment he returned to Andrea's side, he'd ask her to marry him. The three of them would make a family. They'd put all their old ghosts to rest. Maybe later they'd add one or two babies, sisters or brothers for Jessie.

Turning toward the community park, Tom grinned broadly, his heart featherlight. Andrea in his life forever. What a gift, what a glorious, incredible gift.

*

The phone's bleat jolted Andrea awake. Her heart hammering in her chest, she groped for the receiver, grabbed it from the nightstand. "Hello?"

A moment's hesitation, then she heard Lori's soft slur. "It's you."

Andrea checked the clock, realized Tom was probably on his way to pick up Jessie. "Tom's not here. Can I take a message?"

"No. It's you I wanted to talk to anyway."

Shoving herself up in the bed, Andrea clung to the quilt, disquiet rippling inside her. "What do you want?"

"I found out the rest. I know everything now."

Andrea's hand trembled. "You couldn't…the files were sealed."

"That almost stopped me. I thought I'd have to give

up.'' She laughed. ''But then Daddy's men found the principal you worked for then.''

Mrs. Pfeiffer. There had been no love lost between them even before the incident with Richard. When Mrs. Pfeiffer caught flak from the district because she hadn't somehow prevented a situation no one could have foreseen, the principal's dislike of Andrea had transformed into outright hatred.

''She told me all about Richard,'' Lori drawled.

Andrea wanted to clap her hands over her ears, slam the phone back in its cradle. She didn't need Lori to tell her what had happened. That horrible day had hung over her life for two long years, had haunted her dreams. When Lori began to relay every detail of what she'd learned, Andrea just let the memories roll over her.

She'd felt uneasy that first moment Richard had stepped into her classroom. His hair, usually precisely combed, was mussed and one side of his white dress shirt had come untucked. His gaze had roved the room almost wildly, locking onto her when he spotted her.

It must be the problems with his job, she'd thought at the time. Things hadn't been going well. He was constantly complaining the head of sales had it in for him. The man was an SOB and Richard couldn't do anything right for him.

If he hadn't looked so frantic, Andrea would have told him it wasn't the best day to visit. She was in the middle of organizing her second graders into groups for a field trip to a local dairy. A half-dozen parents waited in the back of the room for the students assigned to their cars and the students' restlessness was quickly turning into out-and-out misbehavior.

When she'd realized she was short car space for two

of her students, she was ready to throw up her hands and cancel the field trip. School policy didn't permit teachers to transport their own students and she couldn't let anyone travel without a seat belt. Unless another parent showed up, she was sunk.

When Richard offered to drive, something inside her, some instinct wanted to say no. But with the racket growing and the students running amok, she ignored her intuition and gratefully accepted his offer.

She knew she should take him to the office, have him fill out the appropriate forms. But Mrs. Pfeiffer would have made a stink about handling that detail at the last minute and might have canceled the field trip out of spite.

So Andrea had buckled Jenny Arverson and Ayesha Mills securely in the back seat of Richard's sedan. Best friends, the girls had chattered up a storm, counting red cars, reading street signs, making up stories. Distracted by their nonstop conversation, Andrea hadn't noticed Richard's distraction at first. But when he started mumbling under his breath, all the wrongness she'd sensed suddenly became crystal clear.

Without warning, he diverted his sedan from the caravan of cars headed for the dairy and pulled onto the nearest freeway. When one of the girls asked where they were going, he screamed at her to shut up. Then he stomped on the accelerator and tore up the freeway.

She didn't know where he'd hidden the gun—in his pants pocket, under the seat. All she knew was suddenly it was in his hand and he had a look of deadly intent in his eyes.

"I'm going to kill him," he'd said, his calm tone spearing her with terror.

Andrea could barely form the question. "Who, Richard?"

"My boss. I'm going to blow that bastard's head off."

While the girls sobbed in the back seat, Richard raved about his supervisor, the way he'd fired him, had never given him a chance to prove himself. Andrea tried to soothe him, calm him, even as she desperately sought an escape.

Endless miles later, they passed a sheriff's deputy who had stopped to help a motorist. Richard's erratic driving captured his attention and when he caught up with Richard, he saw the gun and radioed for help. It took four patrol cars and every ounce of persuasiveness in Andrea to finally convince Richard to set down the gun and pull the car over.

The ordeal had only lasted a few hours, and no one had been hurt. But Jenny and Ayesha would never be the same. Andrea had tried to stay in touch afterward, even after she'd quit. But the two little girls' parents refused to talk to her beyond letting her know they were suffering, their lives were torn by fears and nightmares....

Lori finished her diatribe and her tone turned even nastier. "I won't have a woman like you teaching my daughter."

"I'm a good teacher," Andrea said.

"That's not what Mrs. Pfeiffer says." Lori fell silent a moment and Andrea heard the clink of a bottle against a glass. "She says you were in on it with Richard. That the two of you planned to kidnap the girls, hold them for ransom. You only turned him in when you got caught."

The chill that coursed through Andrea set off a trembling in her hands. She had to clutch the receiver to keep from dropping it. "That's not true," she whispered.

"Even if it isn't, it's more than enough to convince my parents to remove Jessie from Tom's custody."

Her throat constricted, Andrea could barely speak. "Please...." She swallowed, tried again. "He loves her so much. Please don't take her."

"Don't you think I love her?" Lori's voice broke, and she took a hitching breath. Then the meanness returned. "I don't want you there. I don't want you around my daughter."

"What do you want?" Andrea asked, although she knew.

"Leave," Lori spat out. "Today. Now. Get out of their lives."

If her heart knotted any tighter in her chest, Andrea was sure she'd die of the pain. "If I leave—"

"I'll keep what I've learned to myself. I'll let Jessie stay with her father."

Andrea squeezed her eyes shut, tried to keep the tears from spilling down her cheeks. "Then I'll leave. I'll be gone within the hour."

She was only dimly aware of Lori hanging up the phone, scarcely noticed her own hand dropping the receiver back on the cradle. For a moment she felt frozen, then she forced herself to move, spurred herself to quickly dress, then hurry over to the foreman's apartment.

Still used to traveling light she had little to pack and finished the job in minutes. As she carried her suitcase through the tiny living room, she saw the quilt she'd finally completed for Jessie draped over the back of the sofa. She'd intended to wrap it, then give it to her later today. But she hadn't time for that now.

Once she'd loaded her few things into the car, she took the quilt up to Jessie's room and laid it carefully on the bed. She'd wanted to write the perfect goodbye note, words that would somehow make up for the fact that she was deserting Jessie exactly the way her mother had. But all the platitudes and assurances in the world wouldn't make a lick of difference to Jessie. So she simply wrote, *I had to go. Please believe I love you with all my heart,* and hoped the little girl would someday understand.

There was no way to convey to Tom everything she felt in a note. She was tempted to leave without any good-bye at all, but her cowardice shamed her. So she scribbled out, *I'm sorry. I couldn't stay,* and set it on his pillow. One last quick stop in his office, then she locked up and hurried to her car.

She feared she'd pass Tom and Jessie coming back home on the small county road leading to the Double J. But she made it past the Hart Valley turnoff and onto Interstate 80 toward Reno without encountering Tom's pickup truck. She should have felt relieved that she'd successfully escaped, but she felt only grief and regret and a painful longing for what might have been.

By the time Tom made the turn onto the long gravel drive leading to the ranch, he thought he would go mad with impatience. The quick drive into town to pick up Jessie had turned into a much longer delay. First, he'd gotten roped into helping tidy up the area of the park where they'd held the picnic. With tables to tote back to their usual locations and a prodigious amount of trash to carry to the Dumpster, the teachers were grateful for the muscle power of another dad. He figured if Sabrina's dad could take time from his vet practice to help out, he could spare an hour or so.

Then two friends of Jessie's had needed rides home and since they were pretty much on the way to the ranch, Jessie had volunteered him. He didn't mind giving them a lift, was glad his daughter's friendships were branching out beyond Sabrina. But even the short detours taken to deliver the two girls to their homes added to the duration before he could see Andy again.

As the ranch house came into sight, his heart was hammering a million miles a minute, and his hands shook. He knew he had a silly grin on his face and that Jessie no doubt suspected something was up. When he glanced over at her, she smiled in return, her avid curiosity evident.

"Where's Andy?" Jessie asked as she turned back to the yard.

He quickly scanned the empty space, searching for Andrea's car. Pulling the truck up next to the round pen, he climbed out and walked past the barn to see if she'd moved her car there. But Andrea's car was truly gone.

Tom turned one last time, certain he'd somehow missed seeing the four-door compact. "She must have gone into town."

Jessie looked worried now. "Then why didn't we pass her?"

"We could have missed her while we were taking your friends home."

"Yeah, I guess."

Dread scraped in the pit of his stomach as he headed for the porch. The front door was locked and he had to fumble in his pocket for the little used key. When he stepped inside with Jessie on his heels, the house felt empty, abandoned.

"Where is she, Daddy?"

The thread of tears in his daughter's voice about broke his heart. "I'll check the kitchen for a note."

He'd barely had time to register that Andrea hadn't written anything on the kitchen message board when he heard Jessie's mournful cry from upstairs. "Daddy!"

He raced up the stairs to her room, saw her standing there with a quilt clutched in her arms and a note crumpled in her hand. Tears streamed down her cheeks. "She's gone, Daddy," she sobbed.

He read the note, then with a sick feeling headed for his own room. She'd neatened the bedcovers that they'd rumpled with their lovemaking. A square of paper, just like Jessie's, sat on his pillow.

I couldn't stay. The inscription was written neatly, the letters in Andrea's flowing cursive script. The same precise lettering she'd taught Jessie these last several weeks.

If it was possible to die of a broken heart, he would have perished on the spot. As it was, his legs lost their strength and he sank onto the edge of the bed, the note balled in his hand just as Jessie's had been.

She came into his room, dragging the quilt, her eyes red, her nose running. He held out his arms to her and she flung herself at him, her slender body quaking with tears.

He knew that somehow they'd get past this, just as they'd gotten past their grief at Lori's abandonment. But in that moment, the hurt seemed insurmountable. In that moment, it took everything in him to stay strong for Jessie.

Which was exactly what he had to do. He had plenty

of time to wallow in self-pity, to surrender to the pain. He could wait until he was alone. He'd done it when Lori left; he could do it with Andrea.

Except with Andrea, the pain was a thousand times worse. And he wasn't sure if he'd ever get over it.

Chapter Sixteen

At the dinner table that night, Jessie stared stolidly at her plate, her chicken leg untouched, the pile of peas mixed into her uneaten mashed potatoes. She hadn't taken so much as a sip of her milk. She insisted she'd eaten too much at the picnic and wasn't hungry, but Tom knew better.

Her red-rimmed eyes strayed constantly to that empty third chair, Andrea's place at the table. The slightest sound of the wind through the trees had her on her feet, certain it was a car approaching the house. The third time she leaped up and raced to the kitchen window, he felt ripped straight to his soul.

"You don't have to eat if you don't want to," he told her as she returned to the table, feet dragging, eyes downcast.

She sat down, shoved the plate away from her. Jessie's grief loomed a hundred times larger than when

Lori left. Four years ago, Jessie's physical pain had consumed her, driven everything else from her young mind. She'd barely been aware of him by her bed, let alone that most of the time her mother wasn't there.

But she had nothing to distract her from the loss of Andrea. Even worse, she'd gone from the giddy joy of her day at the picnic to unrelenting sadness in the time it took to read Andrea's note. Tom wondered if his daughter would ever be happy again.

The ringing of the phone startled him, started his heart pounding in his chest. As he rose to grab the kitchen extension, his gaze met Jessie's and he saw the flutter of hope in her face. He tried to thrust aside that same sensation struggling to life inside him, but he couldn't quite kill it.

He could barely squeeze out a hello, then sagged against the counter when the caller spoke. Not Andrea. He shook his head at Jessie, unwilling to leave her hanging.

"Who is this?" he asked.

"It's Helen," the woman said softly. "Lori's mother."

That she had to identify herself brought home to Tom how his ex-wife's desertion had completely cut Jessie off from her mother's side of the family. He'd always assumed that had been their choice.

Still, there was nothing to be gained from being rude to her. "How are you, Helen?"

"I'm calling about Lori." Her voice shook as she spoke. "I'm afraid she's done something terrible."

The story spilled out of her. How Lori had dug out the details of Andrea's past, how she'd threatened to expose her. That she'd demanded Andrea leave or she'd have her parents remove Jessie from his custody.

"She was drunk, Tom. She didn't mean it."

"Lori never means it," he said bitterly.

"She didn't leave, did she? Jessie's teacher?"

"She's gone." The agony washed over him again. "I don't know where."

A long silence, then Helen murmured, "I'm so sorry."

He scarcely heard the rest of what Helen said, her assurances that they would never take Jessie from him, that they would try to persuade Lori to enter a rehab clinic. He muttered a goodbye at the appropriate time, then hung up the phone.

Jessie rubbed at her eyes, wiping away new tears. He pulled out Andrea's chair, and although it felt wrong that he should sit there instead of her, he lowered himself into it.

Taking Jessie's hand, he waited for her to look up at him. "We'll get through this, sweetheart. I promise."

She didn't believe a word of it. "Can I go to bed now?"

It was barely eight o'clock. But it had been a difficult day and she had to be exhausted. "Sure, sweetheart."

She scooted back her chair, then trudged from the kitchen, shoulders drooping. Her footsteps were quiet going up the stairs.

He dropped his face in his hands and dragged in a breath. There was a certain relief in knowing Andrea hadn't abandoned them after all, that she'd only tried to do what she thought was best for him and Jessie. But didn't she know he would have fought tooth and nail not only for his daughter, but for her? She didn't have to sacrifice herself.

I'll track her down. I'll find her. He pushed to his feet, hurried to his office. Yanking open the desk drawer where he stuffed papers to be filed, he dug through the mess searching for the resume she'd given him with her contact information. When he couldn't find the paperwork in that drawer, he went through all the others, then through the filing cabinet.

But her resume was gone. She must have taken it. She'd severed the only link he had to her, obliterated his only chance of finding her.

He sank into his desk chair, overwhelmed by the loss. Andrea's absence left behind an enormous emptiness, a darkness that clouded his mind. He knew he had to keep going for Jessie's sake, but in that moment, he just needed to grieve.

It was dark by the time he pushed to his feet and headed for the stairs. He went through his evening routine by rote, stumbled to the bed feeling half-alive. When he pulled back the covers and caught a trace of Andrea's scent, his knees nearly buckled. He laid his head on her pillow, drew in her fragrance as he struggled to sleep.

It was hours before he finally drifted off. He woke briefly near dawn when a horse's whinny reached into his fitful dreams. The brilliant morning light cutting through his unshaded bedroom window jolted him fully awake.

Something about the stillness of the house sent alarm rushing through him. Quickly tugging on a pair of jeans, he hurried down the hall toward Jessie's room, slapped open her door.

Her bed was neatly made. Her dresser drawers hung open, the contents rumpled. The backpack she always hung on the back of the door was missing.

''Jessie!'' he shouted, then listened to the silence. He

went to her window, opened it, looked frantically around the yard. *"Jessie!"*

She didn't answer.

The sun barely topping the pine covered mountains to her left, Andrea punched down on her car's accelerator as far as it would go. Reno was a good hour behind her, but she still had at least forty-five minutes of driving between her and the Double J. Her desperation to get back to Tom and Jessie after realizing what an idiot she'd been kept her lead foot down and her hands tight on the wheel.

Sleepless hours in a cheap Reno motel room had thankfully brought her to her senses. She loved Tom with all her heart, she loved Jessie as she would her own flesh and blood. How could she have deserted them both without so much as a fight? She knew the truth about what had happened and she knew Tom would believe her. Somehow the two of them would make sure Jessie stayed where she belonged.

She glanced at the car clock yet again, wishing she could somehow teleport herself to the ranch. Tom had to be awake by now. Would Jessie sleep in on her first day of summer vacation? Or was she too heartbroken over Andrea's departure to enjoy that luxury?

Guilt tugged at Andrea and she had to swipe away tears. Just focus on driving, she told herself. Get yourself home. The rest will work itself out.

Home. The word resonated inside her, spurring her on down the road.

Tom looked up from tightening the cinch on Sonuvagun's saddle when Andrea pulled up beside them in the ranch yard. A million emotions roiled inside her as she climbed from the car and tried to interpret what she saw in his face. Was he angry? Would he tell her she didn't belong there? Would he insist that she leave?

But all her doubts were washed away when he ran toward her and pulled her into his arms. "Thank God, thank God," he murmured into her hair as he held her close.

"I'm sorry," she whispered. "So sorry I left. I want to explain—"

He held her away from him, his expression serious. "We'll have to talk as we ride. Jessie's gone, Trixie with her. I was just heading out to look for her."

Without another word, Andrea rushed to the barn, led out Sweetpea. She had the mare tacked up in record time and despite her worry over Jessie, she felt proud that she could do the task so easily. It made her even more a part of the ranch, of Tom's and Jessie's lives.

Once they'd both mounted and cut through the pasture, Andrea asked, "Where do we look?"

"She has some favorite places she likes to ride. The meadow. Over by Dry Creek."

Andrea bit her lip, unease eating at her. "What about the old mine?"

His blue eyes darkened with worry. "Let's try there first."

They loped off, as fast as they could go while still keeping the horses safe in the uneven footing. When they finally drew near enough to spy the tumble of boulders, Andrea caught a glimpse of Trixie, riderless, trotting back and forth along the cliff edge beside the mine.

The pony was lathered with sweat, her eyes rolling with fear. Tom jumped from Sonuvagun's back and grabbed the little mare's reins, then led her and the gelding to Andrea. Andrea tied the two horses beside Sweet-pea to a nearby tree then hurried back to Tom.

"Jessie!" Tom bellowed into the mine.

"Daddy?" The faint response came not from the mine, but down in the ravine.

"Do you see her?" Tom asked.

"No," Andrea said, then caught a glimpse of something moving. "Yes! Behind that scrub pine."

He took a step down the cliff, but the shower of rocks he set loose stopped him. "Jessie, are you okay?"

"I'm stuck," she said tearfully. "Trixie spooked and I fell."

"Jessie!" Andrea called down. "I'm going to climb down and get you." To Tom, she said, "I'm lighter. A little less chance I'll set off a rock fall."

He nodded. "Let me get some rope from Sonuva-gun's saddle."

He tied the rope securely to her waist, then fed it out as she picked her way down the hillside. Each time her feet sent loose rocks down the cliff, she paused, then sought firmer footing. It seemed to take forever to reach Jessie.

The little girl looked up at her, worship in her brown gaze. "You came back."

"Of course I did," Andrea said, her throat tight. "And I won't be leaving again. Ever."

Extricating the little girl from a tangle of manzanita and scrub pine, she lifted Jessie in her arms. Struggling to her feet, she let Tom's strength pull her back up the hill. Twice she slipped, her feet going out from under her, but she never lost her confidence that Tom would get both her and Jessie to safety.

When they finally reached the top, Tom pulled first Jessie, then Andrea into his arms. He held her so close,

Andrea could barely breathe. She clutched him just as tight, letting the last of her fears ebb away.

"She came back, Daddy," Jessie whispered from between them. "And she says she's staying."

Tom looked down at Andrea, his expression fierce. "Damn right she is."

Andrea took Tom's face in her hands, wanting to be sure he felt the strength and conviction of what she had to say to him. "I love you, Tom."

A moment's hesitation as he absorbed what she'd said, then he replied fervently, "I love you, too."

He pulled her head into his chest, and she could hear his heart thundering against her ear. As a quiet joy filled Andrea, she murmured, "Let's go home."

They returned to the horses and mounted up. Jessie rode with them for the first part of the journey back, her scare forgotten, her one-sided conversation flowing fast and furious. Then the little girl asked to ride on ahead and she and the pony loped off, their near tragedy a thing of the past.

Tom rode close alongside Andrea, his leg brushing hers, their fingers linked. Several times throughout the ride he looked over at her, as if he wanted to assure himself she was still beside him.

Back at the ranch, they untacked the horses quickly, then headed inside. The urgency to be alone with Tom overwhelmed Andrea and she thought she'd go crazy if they had to wait until Jessie's bedtime. But thankfully, the morning's adventures took their toll on Jessie's energy and she went up to her room for a nap without even being asked.

Finally in the privacy of Tom's room, Andrea wanted everything at once—to kiss Tom, to hold him, to profess her love and hear him echo that promise back to her.

In the end, they held each other, her heart beating against his, the pleasure of being in one another's arms a healing balm for every hurt, for every moment of pain.

He brushed his lips against her forehead. "I would have found you. Somehow."

Her throat tightened at the awesome power of that vow. "I know."

Drawing back, he fixed her gaze with his. "Don't you ever leave me again."

She shook her head. "I won't. I'm here for good."

He nodded, then his gaze grew even more intense. "You're going to marry me." She heard only the slightest waver in his demand.

"Yes," she answered and nearly smiled at the relief in his expression. "There's nothing in the world I want more than to be your wife. To make the Double J my home."

He kissed her then, a kiss of possession, of fervent love. This was her place, in Tom's arms, this was her forever home. She could let her roots grow here as deep as her love for Tom and Jessie Jarret.

She chose Tom. She chose love.

She was home.

Epilogue

He never should have let Beth talk him into wearing a tux.

Tom squirmed in the ruffled shirt, the bow tie pinching him, the cummerbund like a too-tight cinch around his middle. Out in the crowded pews of the Hart Valley Methodist Church, his sister smiled up at him, as if she recognized and relished his discomfort.

Up at the altar with Reverend Pennington, Tom would have slipped a finger under his collar to loosen it, but with nearly all of Hart Valley watching him, he didn't dare. Besides, he wanted everything to be perfect for Andrea, even if the late summer heat killed him.

Then the organist launched into the processional music and Tom's heart slammed into overdrive. He wondered how he'd ever put the ring on Andrea's fingers with his hands shaking and his knees quivering like a newborn foal's.

He took a big gulp of air as Nina's son Nate marched down the aisle with the rings tied to a satin pillow. The pint-sized three-year-old grinned from ear to ear, then when he reached Nina's seat, shouted, "Look, Mama! I got the rings." A murmur of laughter rippled through the audience as the boy ran the last several feet down the aisle to Tom's side.

The crowd quieted again as Jessie entered. Tom's heart squeezed tight as he caught his first glimpse of his daughter, beautiful in pale-blue satin, her arms bared by the short puffed sleeves of her dress. For once, her hair was pulled back neatly, and her eyes shone with pride. Tom swallowed against a lump in his throat, then had to choke back a laugh when Jessie's feet peeked out from under the hem of her long dress. She wore her old scuffed sneakers; comfort had won out over style.

After Jessie joined him at the altar, the organ music swelled. Tom thought the tension might shoot him straight through the roof. Andrea had kept with tradition, refusing to let him see her dress before the wedding. He'd tried to picture how she'd look, to imagine how she could be any more beautiful today than she always was to him.

But nothing he'd tried to conjure up even came close to the vision that stepped into the aisle before him. His jaw dropped and he didn't feel a bit foolish doing it. More than one man in the room looked as stunned as he felt. The simple dress of creamy satin and delicate lace, and the woman who wore it, seemed like something from a fantasy.

His fantasy.

He smiled at Andrea's mother, Phyllis, as she escorted Andrea down the aisle. Newly married herself, Phyllis wore her knee-length ivory wedding dress as she walked with her daughter. Andrea's mother gave her husband, Jeff, a quick squeeze on the shoulder as she passed him, then handed her daughter over to Tom, sure serenity in her face.

Tom turned toward Andrea, taking her hands. The bouquet of white gardenias gave off a sweet fragrance and it was hard to resist lifting her veil and kissing her right there. Instead, he drank her in, from head to toe, then didn't know whether to laugh or cry when he saw scuffed sneakers on Andrea's feet too. She shrugged and smiled and his love for her seemed to grow large enough to fill the universe.

He leaned close to her ear. "I'm the luckiest man in the world," he whispered. The glow in her eyes told him everything he needed to know—that she loved him too, that she always would.

Then they turned to Reverend Pennington, to speak the words that would join their lives forever.

*   *   *   *   *

eHARLEQUIN.com

For **FREE online reading,** visit
www.eHarlequin.com now and enjoy:

Online Reads
Read **Daily** and **Weekly** chapters from
our Internet-exclusive stories by your
favorite authors.

Red-Hot Reads
Turn up the heat with one of our more
sensual online stories!

Interactive Novels
Cast your vote to help decide how these
stories unfold...then stay tuned!

Quick Reads
For shorter romantic reads, try our
collection of Poems, Toasts, & More!

Online Read Library
Miss one of our online reads?
Come here to catch up!

Reading Groups
Discuss, share and rave with other
community members!

For great reading online,
visit www.eHarlequin.com today!

INTONL

If you enjoyed what you just read,
then we've got an offer you can't resist!

Take 2 bestselling love stories FREE!
Plus get a FREE surprise gift!

Clip this page and mail it to Silhouette Reader Service™

IN U.S.A.	IN CANADA
3010 Walden Ave.	P.O. Box 609
P.O. Box 1867	Fort Erie, Ontario
Buffalo, N.Y. 14240-1867	L2A 5X3

YES! Please send me 2 free Silhouette Special Edition® novels and my free surprise gift. After receiving them, if I don't wish to receive anymore, I can return the shipping statement marked cancel. If I don't cancel, I will receive 6 brand-new novels every month, before they're available in stores! In the U.S.A., bill me at the bargain price of $3.99 plus 25¢ shipping and handling per book and applicable sales tax, if any*. In Canada, bill me at the bargain price of $4.74 plus 25¢ shipping and handling per book and applicable taxes**. That's the complete price and a savings of at least 10% off the cover prices—what a great deal! I understand that accepting the 2 free books and gift places me under no obligation ever to buy any books. I can always return a shipment and cancel at any time. Even if I never buy another book from Silhouette, the 2 free books and gift are mine to keep forever.

235 SDN DNUR
335 SDN DNUS

Name _____ (PLEASE PRINT) _____

Address _____ Apt.# _____

City _____ State/Prov. _____ Zip/Postal Code _____

* Terms and prices subject to change without notice. Sales tax applicable in N.Y.
** Canadian residents will be charged applicable provincial taxes and GST.
  All orders subject to approval. Offer limited to one per household and not valid to current Silhouette Special Edition® subscribers.
® are registered trademarks of Harlequin Books S.A., used under license.

SPED02   ©1998 Harlequin Enterprises Limited

*Sometimes love lurks in the shadows
between dusk and dawn...*

WHEN DARKNESS FALLS

Dangerous strangers, irresistible temptation and soul-stealing
ecstasy—find them all in three new, spine-tingling tales

by *USA TODAY* bestselling author

Susan Krinard

award-winning author

Tanith Lee

and reader favorite

Evelyn Vaughn

Available October 2003

Only from Silhouette Books!

Visit Silhouette at www.eHarlequin.com   PSWDF

 *Silhouette*®

COMING NEXT MONTH

SPECIAL EDITION

#1573 A LITTLE BIT PREGNANT—Susan Mallery
Readers' Ring
Security expert Zane Rankin could have any woman he wanted…
and often did. Computer hacker and wallflower Nicki Beauman
had contented herself with being platonic with her sexy friend Zane.
Until one night of unbridled—and unexpected—passion changed
their relationship forever….

#1574 HER MONTANA MILLIONAIRE—Crystal Green
Montana Mavericks: The Kingsleys
Sunday driving through life was billionaire and single dad
Max Cantrell's way. Celebrity biographer Jinni Fairchild preferred
living in the fast lane. But when these two opposites collided, there
was nothing but sparks! Could they overcome the detours keeping
them apart?

#1575 PRINCE OF THE CITY—Nikki Benjamin
Manhattan Multiples
When the city's mayor threatened to sever funds for Eloise Vale's
nonprofit organization, she reacted like a mama bear protecting her
cubs. But mayor Bill Harper was her one-time love. Eloise would
fight for Manhattan Multiples, but could she resist the lure of her
sophisticated ex and protect herself from falling for her enemy?

#1576 MAN IN THE MIST—Annette Broadrick
Secret Sisters
Gregory Dumas was searching for a client's long-lost family—
he'd long ago given up looking for love. But in chaste beauty
Fiona MacDonald he found both. Would this wary P.I. give in
to the feelings Fiona evoked? Or run from the heartache he was
certain would follow…?

#1577 THE CHRISTMAS FEAST—Peggy Webb
Dependable had never described Jolie "Kat" Coltrane. But zany and
carefree Kat showed her family she was a responsible adult by
cooking Christmas dinner—with the help of one unlikely holiday
guest. Lancelot Estes, a hardened undercover agent, was charmed
by the artless Kat…and soon the two were cooking up more than
dinner!

#1578 A MOTHER'S REFLECTION—Elissa Ambrose
Drama teacher Rachel Hartwell's latest role would be her most
important yet: befriending her biological daughter. When Rachel
learned that the baby she'd given up for adoption years ago had lost
her adoptive mother, she vowed to become a part of her daughter's
life. But did that include falling in love with Adam Wessler—her
child's adoptive father?

SSECNM1003